SOMETHING TO
Dream ON

DIANE RINELLA

Copyright (C) 2015 Diane Rinella
Cover art copyright (C) 2015 Diane Rinella
Cover art and design by Heidi "Azurylipfe" Darras
http://azurylipfe.daportfolio.com/
Cover model Janna Prosvirina

ISBN: 0692359400
ISBN-978-0692359402

For Trishalana

"You have to give people
something to dream on."

~ Jimi Hendrix

Acknowledgements

Something to Dream On was not only inspired by my childhood experiences, but also by a recent event that happened to a friend. How a grown man can claim to be mature and then go online and harass a sweet woman because of the gifts God gave her is beyond my comprehension. Worse, it was done in code, much like a child would do, yet it could not have been more obvious at whom the joke was aimed. Within a few days, work on this book began. Thus, I'd like to acknowledge those who inspired this story: The victims who stand strong.

On a much happier note, thank you for allowing my words into your heart. Many of you are reading this because you enjoyed *Scary Modsters … and Creepy Freaks*, a story that is far more personal than anyone imagines. Maybe you dared to dive into controversy and read *Love's Forbidden Flower.* That story means the world to me but not nearly as much as the people that it brought into my world. I love each and every one of you.

A special thank you to my Modster Squad, a small but dedicated group who choose to tolerate me. Heaven help you! Seriously, your support means more than I can express.

To my beta readers, N. Stevenson Jennette III, Brian Preston, and Dione Marks. Thank you for not sugar coating it. You are gold!

The cover is the creation of Heidi "Azurylipfe" Darras, who can be found at http://azurylipfe.daportfolio.com/. She is also the artist for The Mystic Dreamer Tarot. If you are looking for an artist to create a custom piece, I could not recommend her more. Not only is she a dream to work with, she took a description of the painting mentioned in this book and brought it to life as if she had waved a magic wand.

Autumn Davis and Jessica Baker, thank you for taking a

chance on me when so few were willing. Most of all, thank you for your friendships. You probably have no clue why I am saying this, but you two gave me the confidence I needed to push forward and keep going. Seriously. For reals.

A special thank you to all of the bloggers who have supported me over the years. Bloggers bust their butts without personal gain and often without a word of thanks. Please know that all of the love you have shown this author is appreciated.

Being an author is incredibly hard work. Some days you can't help but wonder if it is worth the stress. That's when you cherish the ones who support you on a daily basis more than ever. Jennifer Theriot, I will be your proud partner in crime any time and in any place. I look forward to years of us starting our conversations with the words, "I just had a great idea." Those conversations always lead us down the craziest roads, and I am ready for more adventures. Darla Roybal, please don't ever stop stalking me! However, I would really appreciate it if you would stop breaking the branches in my tree. Your life would be much easier if you would just use the key I left you.

Last, and in no way least, my husband, Brian Preston, and our daughter, Trishalana Rinella Preston. Brian, how we constantly manage to love each other through all of our crazy projects bewilders me. Thank you for always understanding when I need the world to go away so I can let my creativity flow and embrace my madness. With you I can be a wife and mother while staying true to myself.

Sticks and stones may break my bones,

but your words can forever scar me.

Prologue

ONE YEAR BEFORE DESTINY
Tuesday, April 5

Lizetta

If a psychic yanks you by the arm, forces you into a seat, and states that you "arrived just in time"—all without even looking at you—should you panic? That just happened to me, and I am a little weirded out.

Griffin made this appointment so he could get advice on his stinky love life. Since I am just tagging along, the experience is now all kinds of freaky. Plus, the psychic looks like Angela Lansbury on *Murder, She Wrote* and calls herself The Amazing Zolta. This can't possibly go well.

Zolta clasps her hands together. The widening of her eyes complements the broadening of her smile. Does she always get this excited over roping people into readings? Just how much is this going to cost?

"Take five cards from anywhere in the deck. Place them before you on the table, any way you want." Her fingers dance above a red tablecloth, encouraging me to scatter the cards. Her liveliness reminds me of a Bugs Bunny cartoon.

Griffin and I exchange smiles. Part of me has always felt psychics are full of malarkey. However, I do believe that there is more to the universe than what we see. That is why I am so weirded out over Zolta's sense of urgency to get me in this chair and actually hope it is just a scam.

From the one-third mark, I cut the deck and grab a stack of cards off the top. I set three of them like the points of a triangle. That seems off, so I use the two left in my hand to turn it into an arrow. Griffin tilts his head. He's right; it still feels wrong. I slide the two cards on the side down to form a diamond with one card in the center.

"Why did you make the change?" Zolta asks.

"I don't know. Instinct, maybe?"

"Good, good, good." She studies the spread with raised brows.

The card at the top of the diamond is called The Star. A cluster of little stars, along with a blinding, yellow one, hover above a woman pouring water. It's a peaceful scene, and I know this interpretation is totally wrong, but I can't help but feel sorry for the poor woman who is being hit in the head and is seeing sparks.

On the sides of my diamond are two other women. One of them is upside down and has a bird on her wrist while the other sits on a throne. Am I the one with the bird? That would make sense since I'm a vet tech and live in a farmhouse where I am Mom to a pen of chickens, two dogs, and a pig. The one on the throne has a rabbit at her feet though.

A hand holding a coin dominates the bottom card, but I am more drawn to the garden in its background. It reminds me of that recurring dream.

Oh, no way.

In the center of it all, lightning strikes a building, causing people to plummet to their deaths. Once I absorb the power the card depicts, my stomach drops with the victims.

"Fascinating …" Zolta utters. She reminds me of how concerned my mother sounded when my scrawny brother announced he wanted to join the football team. Where did all of Zolta's excitement go? "Something is going to happen that will shake up your world. This Star," she taps on the top card, "it is a card of hope, but …" Her attention turns to The Tower. She raises a finger to her pursed lips and taps. "Sometimes glory can only come through loss. Some kind of battle is going to happen. These two women on the sides hold the key to the outcome. The reversed Nine of Pentacles shows someone who is lacking, while the Queen of Pentacles represents a person of true compassion." Her eyes meet mine, and I am certain that I look like a cartoon ghost—sheet white with black voids for eyes. Zolta pats my arm. Why do I sense she is offering comfort? "Fear not, dear girl. This Ace of Pentacles at the bottom is the best card in the deck."

The two women, the grass, and the star above—I know this picture all too well. "My dream," I utter.

Her curiosity sparks. "Dream? You've had a dream about this? Tell me about it."

"It ends with me flying into the stars."

"Hmm ..." Zolta muses. The tightening of her brow concerns me. "Grab another card and set it off to the side."

With that Tower wildly freaking me out, I pray for a better card. My nerves make me sloppy, and the top few cards in the deck fall aside. I go to the ones that stayed behind.

Ice creeps down my neck and into my arms when I see the word Death. I drop the card like it's about to bite. It lands next to The Tower, and my lungs forget how to work. I can't die! I'm only twenty-four. What will happen to my babies at home? My brother can't care for himself let alone a pen of chickens. What if they—

Zolta again pats my arm. The rapidness of her *thunks* shows she can't hide how uncomfortable she is. "Don't be scared. The Death card means change. While it can mean physical death, it rarely ever does."

She can say what she wants, but those Death and Tower cards are freaking the sugar out of me. Maybe it's a warning about my weight. The doctor did say that I should dump a ton. Unlike some people with true medical issues, this weight is all me. I need to stop making excuses.

Zolta sweeps up the cards in haste while avoiding eye contact. Does she not want me to ask questions, or is something turning her blood into a Slurpee, too? "Some type of ... *incident* is going to happen. Something will shake your world, like lightning has struck you in the head. In the end, it will bring you the ultimate joy."

The ultimate joy? Isn't that what they call Heaven? Unless someone changed the rules, you only get there by dying. "When will this happen?"

She scoffs. "The cards do not know any more than the universe does. Time only matters to us because we limit our minds so that our days here are all that exist."

That's it. I hear the exit calling. "Thank you for your time." I grab my purse and start to head out. My fluttering nerves turn both of my feet into left ones and my hip smacks into the table, causing a stack of cards to slide off and spill onto the ground. The card that falls dead into the middle of the heap has a giant wheel on it. It spins to the left so that it lands with the top numbers pointing down. My mind reels along with it.

Griffin rubs my shoulder. "It's okay, Baby Cakes. Catch your breath. Remember, she's saying you will get the prize." I shudder as he says it, and then grab a swift inhale. No wonder why I am dizzy. My freak out has stolen my ability to breathe. "Whatever happens, it's finally going to explain everything."

Griffin is right. My dream is going to come true, whatever the bejesus it means.

JENSEN

This bitch has lost it. Seriously, who the fuck does she think she is?

"Jensen, what has happened to you? You used to be such a wonderful person and now …" She sobs while mumbling something to herself. I guess it's to herself. Shit. I don't know. Women are weird. They only seem to be good for one thing, so why am I bothering with this one?

I take another swig from my friend, Mr. Jack Daniels.

The crazy woman drops her head into her hands and the waterworks come on stronger. It's a hell of a show. Let's see what happens when I chug.

They must be making this stuff weaker, because the three shots worth go down like water.

The bitch screams at me. Like she lets loose as if she wants fucking China to hear. Then she has the balls to try to steal my buddy. She pulls at the bottle, and I laugh at her feebleness. She yanks and fails to get it, so she yanks again, and again. I have to give her a little credit for effort.

Finally, I've had enough, so I let her have it; not the bottle, but a lesson in the form of a body check against the wall. "Baby, please stop," she begs.

She's right. I should back off and give the old broad a break. I step back and laugh before taking another swig. She actually has the nerve to go for the bottle again. Fine, if she wants it so badly, she can have it. I toss the thing at her. Actually, it's more of a calculated throw that is intended to scare her. Instead, I graze her enough for it to give a little bounce off of her temple. The thing reminds me of rubber, like I am in a cartoon. It's the funniest fucking thing in the world, and I can't stop laughing as she pulls her hand away from the spot I hit, checking for blood. It's too bad there isn't any. It would make a great pattern on the floor with the way she's shaking her head.

"Get out!" she yells, again like she wants to be heard on Mars. "Get out, and don't come back!"

Yeah, right. We've been through this before.

"Get out!" I'm shoved, hard, towards the door once, then twice. On the third time I'm done and rid myself of the control freak. I've got better places to be. "I mean it, Jensen. Don't come back!"

I wave her off and head to my car. Whatever. She'll be sweet as punch in the morning.

Dawn is cracking open as I return home. With my guitar strapped onto my back, I lug an amp up the walk and step on something soft. A T-shirt? Then I almost trip over a shoe. "The hell?"

The walkway is littered with clothes—*my* clothes! "That whore!" My feet hit the ground like thunder as I make for the door and fumble for the right key. I try to jam the thing into the lock, but I'm so fuming I have to try slamming it in three times before finding it won't turn.

"Son of a bitch!" I yank the key out and stare, then draw the thing closer to bring it into focus so I can be certain. Yeah, that's the right one. This time I brace on the door with my free hand and get the key in on the first shot. I try to turn it with so much force that my fingers hurt from the pressure when the lock refuses to budge.

"Shit!" I rattle the fuck out of the door. There is no way she'd have the balls to lock me out, so I start pounding. That's when I notice the note taped above the bell.

Jensen,
If you want your stuff, you can come for it on Thursday. Uncle Rob will be here to help you. Do not contact me again until you are clean for at least ninety days. I know you can do it. Until then, we are done.
Mom

The fuck!

The thing gets ripped down and then crumbled into a tight wad. How fucking dare she? My own mother! Moms are supposed to always have faith in you and thus put up with your shit. What kind of lame ass mom turns her back on her fucked-up kid? Doesn't she know she's the only real family that I have left?

The paper gets slammed down onto the porch. In a flash I'm driving off without looking back. Screw picking up my stuff on Thursday, and screw grabbing my stuff that she threw on the lawn like it's crap. I don't want to bother to even look at the mess she made because—

Because looking at it will be too much like looking at myself.

SIX MONTHS BEFORE DESTINY
Saturday, October 13

Lizetta

Griffin and I sit in our usual corner booth at Daddy Bear's Lair. I'm not a drinker, but I am a fan of the atmosphere—despite the fact that the music is always a little on the disco side. Then again, isn't there a law that states gay bars must play dance music; else their license to be fabulous is revoked?

It's still early, so even though I am tucked in the shadows, where I can see everyone who flashes in, the only things worth watching are the three male damsels on the dance floor. Griffin and I toast to the sparkling trio who are whooping it up and playing ride 'em cowboy without a care. People should live every moment like that.

Across the room, a group of college bro-types sit at a table. The way they shift in their seats while watching the boys dance clues me in that they are likely looky loos with no desire to "make friends." One of them catches my eye. His short, sandy hair and hazel eyes are attractive, but he's a little ... shall we say, military looking, for my taste. That's cool though. All that matters is a guy's heart, and I'll never find what I am looking for if I'm not open to whatever package it may come in.

He smiles and raises his shot glass to me. I return the gesture with my Coke. Just because he's not my type, is sitting in a gay bar, and for some reason that I can't place, creeps me out a bit, doesn't mean I shouldn't give expanding my horizons a shot—again. If he won't refuse this book by its cover, I owe him the same courtesy.

Shoot, I don't care if he has three eyes; I only care about his soul. My man of compassion has to be out there.

He takes a swig, sets down his glass, and heads over. A friend follows him while snickering. Now I'm really uncertain. The closer they get, the more I notice the staggers in their walks. "Hi," the flirty guy says. I return the greeting and smile. He is kind of cute, despite being wasted. Tipsy I can handle, but I really dislike being around anyone who is hardcore wasted.

He nods. "What's your name?"

"Lizetta."

"Hi, um, *Liz*. I'm Denny. This is Jerry."

Jerry steps forward so that he is now by my side. Once I get the up/down full body glance from him, I accept what the game is. It's proven when Jerry snickers. Even if I do stand a chance with Denny, Jerry's judgment will likely convince his friend that I am not worth it.

Jerry motions to Denny not to bother and says he wants to go for another drink elsewhere. Denny steps up to shake my hand. He takes a good look at my body before saying it was nice to meet me and then makes his way back to his friends.

My eyes close off the scene. You'd think I'd be used to this by now. You'd think it would no longer rape my self-esteem, yet it does. This is so unfair. I have so much to offer. There is so much inside me that I long to share. My shell may not be perfect, but is it really all that bad? Doesn't my heart matter? What about my soul?

The rap of Griffin's fingers on the table creates a roll of thunder. He's more tired of this happening to me than I am. Still, he sits in the shadows with the light barely catching the skin on top of his head and lets me handle it. He may not allow that for much longer though.

"Bye." I give a friendly wave while trying to hide that my ego has been stomped on and smeared like a spider.

"What did you expect?" Jerry says. "Fatties turn into hags because they can't get anything else."

Griffin slams his hands onto the table, commanding their attention. When he steps out of the booth, Denny and Jerry turn to face a monolith. It's like the scene in *2001: A Space Odyssey* where the apes worship a wall of onyx; only instead of caressing it in wonder, these monkeys freeze in fear. Griffin's voice sounds like God's vibrato is rippling through Heaven and he is challenging them to a smack down. "I believe you meant to say, 'It was a pleasure to have met you.'" Despite Griffin having muscles the size of machine-guns, that voice may be his scariest weapon.

I'm wished a nice day before the jerks grab their friends and flee the bar. Griffin sits, and his voice goes back to the way I am used to hearing it in casual situations—moderately flaming and laced with hospitality that makes you expect him to have a Southern accent. "You okay there, Honey Boo?"

I look Griffin in the eyes and tell him in no uncertain terms that I am fine. We both know I am full of it, but it is either that or do what I really want—give Denny a piece of my mind and then feel like an even bigger fool as I break down in front of him. I shouldn't have to get used to childish people who have issues with *my* body, but that is what it comes down to. I can tell myself that their opinions don't matter, but that doesn't stop incidents like these from happening. I don't know how many more times I can pick my shattered self-esteem off of the ground before I vow to never leave the house again.

I have got to do something about my appearance. Sadly, every diet in the book leads me down the same road—an instant loss of five pounds, then weeks and weeks of painfully adjusted eating that amounts to maybe another two pounds before I hit a wall and can't seem to lose another ounce. Then the initial five pops back on. How can I be motivated to exercise when I come home exhausted each day? If I could see progress, I could find motivation. But to have my body reject my efforts, time and again, leaving me as embarrassed over myself as Denny just did, makes me question the point of trying. Why not just surrender to the other gifts God gave me and enjoy my life?

Sometimes I try to accept that I am really not all that big, but then moments like these happen and …

What is it going to take for someone to see that I am worth loving? It's such a painful road that sometimes I am left to question my own value.

JENSEN

Larry chugs the last of his beer. The smacking down of his near-empty cup signals the end of the encore. The cold splatter that flies onto my face feels awesome. It's like a victory shower after a hard-played game where you scored every goal you took a shot at.

Even though the pressure is off, it'll take a long time for my adrenaline to dive. Nothing is better than playing, and nothing revs me up as much as being on stage—not even blow.

Laura's smoldering body is all over me before I even get a chance to shake off the sweat and beer. She gets a polite smile before I make it into the dressing room, grab my friend for the evening—Mr. Johnny Walker—and toss my ass onto the sofa. Two chugs later, we already have company to let us grace them.

Of course we have company. That's part of the deal. Free booze and the bar allows anything with tits and a lack of dignity backstage. I get paid, too. I should spend every weekend like this.

Oh, wait. I do.

Laura jumps on top of me and snags the bottle to quench her own thirst. I don't let her have much. Every other guy in the band is happy to give her what she wants. I take back what is mine while flashing her green eyes a smile that makes her want to drop her panties—not that she's wearing any under that microscopic skirt. In fact, it's rather obvious that she's not.

More of my friend refreshes me. When the bottle leaves

my lips, our company catches my eyes again. Two really hot babes in corsets and mini-skirts have their business in front of me. Next to them is a girl that I'd rather not look at. She leaves a lot to be desired. She also looks sweet.

I don't do sweet.

Sweet means trouble. I do easy girls, which is why Laura and I are *almost* a couple. When I do get attached, it's going to be with someone who commands respect.

I don't get attached, and I certainly don't do girls who look sweet, like that girl does.

Laura catches me ogling the two babes and tries to get my attention by going for my zipper. I smack her hand. "Not now. I'm busy." Yeah, I'm a prick, and it disgusts the hell out of me. I'm disgusted with myself for a lot of reasons, but I'm also another swig away from not caring about any of it—if that's possible.

It's not possible, but I'm a damn good liar.

My pseudo-girlfriend gets pissed and relinquishes her spot of honor on the sofa. The two hot girls slip in, one on each side. The gawky one just stands there, lightly swaying with nervous energy. I really do feel for her. It's not her fault God didn't bless her with the flawless skin and trim curves he gave these other women. I'm about to play the gentleman and ask her name when Larry starts chatting her up. He's got that look in his eyes. I chug again before turning to the babes next to me so that I don't have to witness whatever cruelty is about to happen. Larry's a way bigger prick than I am, even though that doesn't seem possible to me.

Guilt and stupidity can turn a person into a real bag of all that is unholy. Diversions help you hide from how much you can't stand yourself. Not being able to stand yourself shelters you from what turned you into a scumbag. It's a vicious spiral that keeps sucking me down. I should care about that.

If I let myself think, I find I care about a lot of things.

Thinking kills joy, so I down a little more of my friend.

My eyes are all over what is next to me, and my hands are

about to go for gold when Laura catches my attention. It's her standard game. She tries to divert me away from whatever competition she has so she can claim victory for the night. In her eyes, the fact that she usually wins the battle makes her my girl.

It's convenient to let her think that way.

Laura stands behind the homely girl with the zitty face and braces. She's already flipped her head upside down and scrubbed her hands through her long, sandy locks to make them appear frizzy. Now she starts making like she has buckteeth and chomping like a horse. I lie to myself that my cringe isn't because she is rude. Laura is really pretty, but now she looks like a donkey that has been kicked in the jaw. She then balloons out her face and gut. It's ridiculous, because the girl she mocks may be a little chubby, but she's hardly the whale Laura makes her out to be. It makes me lose my shit to the point where laughing hurts.

The poor girl catches on and hurt blankets her face. Her friends stop giving me their attention and, rightfully, bail on all of us while tossing expletives and half-empty bottles of beer. One nearly misses my skull and smacks the wall, spraying beer all over my head. Still, I can't stop laughing.

More girls come in, and as much as they look like a gourmet buffet of willing, I pretend not to notice. The second I walked off that stage, I had already gotten what I came for, so I let my girl, who is so not my girl, drag me back home.

THREE MONTHS BEFORE DESTINY
Saturday, January 2

Lizetta

My purse strap wraps over my shoulder as I head off for lunch. I'm almost in the lobby when the receptionist says to Griffin, "I can't believe the owners had the audacity to abandon that poor dog. Imagine hearing that your friend has a tumor and needs to be put down soon, then asking for the cremation bill and leaving. Now Rufus is spending his last moments alone in a cage."

No. Not Rufus. We've all known he was getting up in years, but ...

I head to the back where the scraggly angel sits in a cage with his chin to the ground. His sorrow brings water to my eyes. How could anyone abandon such a sweet creature?

Griffin steps up and puts his hand on my shoulder. "Poor Rufus. You are never going to believe—"

"I heard. How long?"

"Dr. Leopold returns in an hour and a half. Imagine having to sit there like that while—"

I can't, and I won't.

Without a word, I dash off for a leash and then hook the darling, black and white Shih Tzu up.

"Crazy Bloomers, what do you think you're doing?"

How can Griffin be so clueless? We've known each other far too long for him not to figure this one out.

Finally, he tosses up his hands and shows me he gets it. "You just return before the good doctor does. I've no idea how I would cover for this antic."

"Griffin, today is a special day for Rufus. Do you really think I care what anyone else thinks? I'll be back in an hour."

Not far away is a park with a man-made lake. Rufus's tail wildly wags, and his eyes grow round in hope when we approach it. His spirit soars the moment he is free of his leash, and he flashes off with new vigor. A few yards in, he slows to a fast walk and then down to a normal pace. Though his breathing is a little labored, his smile screams, "This is the best!"

You are right Rufus; this is the best. This is how we are supposed to live every moment.

He returns with a stick, and we spend the next half-hour standing by the water's edge and playing fetch. He's so excited that I have to wonder how long it has been since anyone did this with him. Some people think that just because a dog's glory days are over, that the thrill of being alive is gone. As Rufus finds enough energy to run across the park so he can play Frisbee with a couple of kids, he proves the naysayers wrong.

The time drifts away like a whispered prayer. Tears form as I put Rufus on his leash. Why must we die? Death frightens me, yet not a drop of depression is anywhere near Rufus. Being abandoned was his concern before, not what lies next. "You are so beautiful, Rufus. No matter where you go or what you do, always know that."

His paw goes to my knee, as if saying, "Don't cry. My last dream just came true."

We head back, and he walks tall and proud while I bawl my eyes out. As soon as my hand hits the door, Griffin dashes up and takes the leash. "Doc came back early. She wants to see you in her office, *immediately*."

My insides should be cringing, but if Rufus does not know fear, than neither will I. That hour with him will stay with me a lifetime.

I carefully shut the door to Dr. Leopold's office behind me. She barely peers over her shoulder while pulling a file from her cabinet. "It is a huge violation of company policy to remove an animal from the premises without my permission."

Company policy? Her priorities are wrong. Does business really matter over life? Pets are selfless creatures, and it is our duty as humans, to be selfless in return and support all creatures that need us. How can I make her see what she already should?

She turns, and the glow of a proud mama lights her tear-streaked face. "What you did was so selfless. When I first heard, I was angry. Then I realized what you did was exactly the reason why I became a vet. You gave Rufus dignity. If there is anything we all deserve, it's dignity, especially in our final moments." Her arms wrap around me, and I'm in tears all over again. "You want to be there when he leaves us?"

"Of course I do."

As the doctor puts him to sleep, I cradle Rufus in my arms and sing lullabies. He drifts off, and I give him two kisses—one from me, the other from his owner—because Rufus is worthy, even if she isn't. Everyone deserves dignity, and everyone deserves a second chance at life.

JENSEN

Ah crap, my head hurts!

Where am I, and why am I wadded up like crumpled paper? Every molecule is throbbing.

My eyes open, and the brightness coming through the door makes me slam them shut. Am I on the floor of a bathroom?

Oh. Yeah. The motel …

I peer through my lids again and look up at a showerhead. My foot slips, and my head slams back on to the rim of a bathtub when I try to stand. It wasn't just a hangover that caused that fall. What did I slip on?

I look down at puddles of red. Shit!

There are streaks and globs of yellow mixed in. Ketchup

and mustard? I'm naked and decorated like a giant hot dog. Where are my clothes?

On the third try, I'm able to stand without slipping like a dork in a comedy show and rinse off. Where are the towels? What kind of crappy motel has no towels?

My room is nowhere near the semi-clean way I left it. Red and yellow stained sheets cover a lump. Instead of finding Laura, three naked guys are in there—also coated up like hotdogs and looking like they had a raunchy time. My stomach twists and nearly spews. Holy shit in hell, what the fuck happened? Last I remember, I was drinking and ...

My arm looks like someone attacked it. That's no scratch mark, and this isn't my room.

I grab the nearest set of clothes, which is some other guy's shirt and boxers, and head out. The thought of wearing some guy's dirty shorts is vile, but not nearly as bad as the reason why I may be naked. I fight down the contents of my stomach again. That life is fine for someone else, but I've got zero interest in any man's swingy parts other than my own.

After I spend about five minutes pounding on the door of what I am pretty sure is my own room, Larry answers. He looks worse than I do, and I woke looking like I'd been run over by a gay condiment truck. Larry moans something unintelligible and crawls back into *my* bed with some girl. Instantly he's out, snoring his way to dreamland.

My brain slows as I pan the room. All I notice is carnage, bodies, and my clothes. That means I went across the hall without them, and then got covered in goo, just like those guys in the bed. Oh God, did I ...

I can't do this anymore.

With my guitar in hand, I make for the door but stop when I trip on Laura. She's so pale that if I didn't see her chest moving, I'd swear she was dead. I drop to my knees and try to wake her. Nothing happens. It's cruel to leave her like this, especially since I'm the only one around here who actually gives a shit about her.

Eventually she groans. How much did she have? She started drinking long before I did. In fact, when she brought me the rig …

Fuck! I promised I'd never cross over so far as to let anyone jab a needle into me. Laura knew that! Last night she pulled out that rig, tied me off, tapped my vein, and then introduced me to the other side. I was already so far gone from the booze that I danced on in without a care.

Why am I living like this? Because it's easy? Because I don't want to be a lone wolf? I've always told myself I was here for the music, but I'm also here because I want a family. I had one. Nearly all of it died before I emotionally beat the last member standing and she threw me out. Everyone in this room has been a placeholder. Larry fills in for my brother. The band takes on the role of friends. The girl in my arms is only a pseudo girlfriend because I want someone to love me, and she does.

My heart breaks for her as I place her head back on the ground with a kiss. *Goodbye, Laura. Please forgive me for being yet another person to hurt you, but we are both on our own now.*

Screw my clothes. Putting them on would give me time to talk myself out of bailing. Without pondering any more of the hell that may have occurred, I drive to Larry's house— my home since Mom kicked me out—grab my stuff, and leave behind a trail of destruction.

Life isn't about obtaining the ideal of perfection; it is about embracing the perfection that is in front of you.

1

DESTINY ARRIVES
Monday, April 4

Lizetta

"Ouch! Son of a beetle!"

My jerk isn't fast enough, and the fangs of the vicious creature graze my hand. I can't blame her. I certainly don't want anyone sticking a thermometer up my caboose either. During one last attempt, Poopsie the poodle (whom I think of as Poojo) nips at me again. I set down the thermometer so that her mom can calm her, but before I step away, the vampiric thing—I mean, the sweet angel—bites me. It's the icing on the cake as my previous patient scratched my arm to the point of needing bandages.

Outside of the exam room, I gather the remaining pieces of my sanity. Griffin, my partner in lab-tech crime, comes to the rescue. Our friendship started in 4-H Club when a scrawny kid plopped down next to me while I stared at a pig. "You look depressed," he said. His tone showed he felt as outcast as I did.

"Some stupid girl at my school made fun of me, again, while I was eating lunch. She said that I felt at home among the cows and pigs because I am fat like one."

Griffin snickered. "If we are only here because we are like the animals, then this branch will soon fold because all of the animals are gay."

21

It took awhile for that to sink in. Griffin's paused expression told he felt he took a risk in sharing what he had to get off his chest. It made no difference to me. "Great, I hereby dub you my best friend, so I can get your cast offs."

He smiled and nudged me. "What's the evil bitch's name?"

"Laura Muler."

He was so amused that he actually slapped his leg while laughing. "Seriously? You need to forgive her."

I didn't get where he was going with that.

"Lady Parts, her name has mule in it, which is perfect because she is an ass." With that comment he sealed the deal on obtaining the title of Best Friend for Life. Nearly a dozen years, several cases of black eye liner (He goes through it faster than I do.), and countless tales of men who wronged us later, this now buffed-out, bald, Goth, black Will keeps my lily-white Grace in check.

Griffin cleans my wound as I get a good look in the mirror. My only clean scrubs this morning were ones in an unflattering shade of slate blue, making my skin look grey. My eyes usually gleam while I am at work, yet now they are dim. Worse, my golden locks droop out of my ponytail the way Mom's used to at the end of a long day when we kids had been "helping" around the house. I look like someone dragged me through spit.

Griffin finishes bandaging my arm and kisses it. "You need a bath!"

"Gee, thanks. I've often wondered why I have nothing in my life other than a TV set, a gay bestie, and animals. Now I'm scratching one of those off the list."

"Yeah, you're just jealous of how fabulous I am."

"You're about as fabulous as a wolf in a cat pen." Oh, that was a terrible attempt to keep up with him.

Griffin flicks a hand at me. "Ooh, you must be tired, because that comeback stunk!"

The screech of tires coming from outside makes my eyes cringe shut. Instinct sends me racing out the door. About a half a block down the street, a car speeds off. From behind, another driver jumps out and runs toward the side of the road with swift movements that imply urgency. I start dodging through traffic towards what appears to be an injured Shiloh Shepard.

JENSEN

No, not again. This can't be happening. How can anyone be so cruel as to hit a creature and then drive off without a care? Have people no compassion? I've never been a saint but ...

My knees go to the ground as I stare down at the poor dog that whimpers a plea for help. Thank God we have been spared the horror of blood. She is curled in the gutter like she is cowering from the cruelness of the world. I don't blame her in the least. Dirt covers the side of her face that rests in the gutter. How do I help? I know nothing about animals.

Please, God, I can't handle watching another being die. You have been guiding me for months into doing the right things. Don't stop now. This dog needs a doctor.

Yes, a doctor. If I can get her to a vet ...

I stand to go back to my car for my cell phone and catch sight of a woman in scrubs running toward me. Behind her is a sign reading "Good Samaritan Animal Clinic."

Thank you!

I need to get the dog out of the street and in to one of those exam rooms.

With a swoop, she is in my arms. "Hold on, girl. Help is on the way." We head toward the clinic as the blond-haired woman puts her hands out to stop traffic.

Lizetta

Before I can tell him not to move the dog, he is already racing it towards Good Samaritan. "Try not to move her too much. She may have injuries you can't see." His eyes hit my scrubs, and he nods. "And be calm. Animals pick up on fear."

The beautiful creature whimpers as the man twists his way through the doors. I call out to Griffin to get Dr. Leopold, to which I get a reply that she is at lunch. Great, I'm on my own. I can barely see the guy around that huge dog. How is he managing to carry it so effortlessly? The thing seems like it's my size, and that's kind of saying something.

"The car in front of me suddenly slammed on his brakes, then sped off," the guy says, sounding defensive. "The jerk must have hit her."

He sets the dog on the table, and I wrap her in a blanket to ward off shock. "I'll never understand how people can be so cruel. It was really wonderful of you to stop and help her."

"Of course. What type of person wouldn't?" His voice cracks from emotion enough to tell me there is something deeper than the obvious behind his words. The power of it draws my attention away from the patient. I want to say that I am sorry for whatever experience he is recalling, but how he keeps his eyes cast to the ground tells me he'd rather not talk about it. He rattles his head, clearing the memory, and then nods to the dog as she whimpers. "She okay?"

"I've no idea." My soothing voice becomes aimed at her, helping her turn calm. "It's okay, sweetie. I promise to take really good care of you." You're not supposed to scare a dog by looking it in the eyes, yet this one draws mine into her's. Her eyes droop in a plea that reminds me of Rufus in his cage.

Thankfully, her vitals check out as healthy. "She's definitely still feeling the scare, but there doesn't seem to be any immediate danger." The poor girl. Her teeth are rotting, and her coat is brittle and coarse while her skin is greasy and flaky. She is hurting from more than the accident. I grab the FRID scanner and search for a microchip. I get exactly what I expect. "No ID whatsoever. Have you seen this dog before?"

Finally, I look up to the man. My words may have glided out, but now the blood pumping through my veins is stammering. A rush of adrenaline may have aided him in carrying the dog, but he's not exactly out of shape. His tight, black T-shirt reveals he's probably got a gym membership that he actually uses. He is tall with features that are dark; short, nearly onyx, hair, skin that has a permanent tan, and eyes so chocolate-brown that they make me want to dive in and slurp.

Is he Indian? Like American Indian? I've no point of reference other than the ones I've seen on TV.

Despite the fact that the rest of his skin is smooth and glowing, he has just enough stubble to look like I've woken up to him after a wild night of naked party games. And God, those cheek bones! They give him an air of strength that no amount of muscle could.

Doggone it. I'm stooping, and my scrubs are covered in cat fur and dog slobber. I brush at them as if it will help.

Oh, noodles! I never fixed my hair. Why did this guy appear when my one model-worthy feature looks like a rat invaded a bird's nest? Combing it with my fingers is useless, but I try anyway. God, I feel twelve years old and in the presence of a live issue of *Tiger Beat*.

"No," he says.

No to what?

Oh, yeah. I had asked if he had seen the dog before. An embarrassed giggle slips out. Criminy. Now I feel even lamer.

"I live just up the road," he continues. "This is the first I've seen her."

The dog looks up at the man who hasn't stopped petting her and whimpers a request to ease her pain. My mind and heart go back to the beautiful creature—the dog, that is. "I need to get her x-rayed. Why don't you take a seat in the lobby while you wait?"

"But she's not my dog."

"Really? Because with the way she keeps nuzzling against you, nobody's told her that." I give him a shy smile. I also fight another giggle. "Congratulations, you're the proud father of a beautiful girl."

JENSEN

It's okay.

The dog is okay. I am okay.

If I tell myself that enough, I'll no longer feel the need to head for the nearest bar. Sure, seeing that dog on the side of the road set me back emotionally, but that doesn't give me the excuse to blow months of sobriety. I tell myself it is all so easy—just decide to quit, let the universe guide you, give up all vices and crutches so it's a lifestyle change—but every day has challenges of its own. Nearly facing death, again, is topping the list right now.

Thank God that dog didn't die. Hospitals freak me out—even pet ones. At least I didn't exactly see Dad die, but last I saw him, he was so close to going that … Man, blood disease is creepy. The thought that it could just hit so hard and without warning …

Granddad's passing wasn't much better.

The way my leg bounces reminds me of a drummer in search of a beat. This room smells of antiseptic, and the sand-colored walls feel sterile, as if made of white-painted concrete. The aluminum framing on the windows reminds me of an institution. It can't be that bad in here. It must be my state of mind. However, the fact that this chair could use a cushion is not making anything easier.

A magazine. That's what I need.

In the corner sits a table with a few tabloids on it. Something cheesy, like *Star*, will help. I can't think about watching things die. Not after seeing Eddie …

I know too many dead people, and trying to avoid thinking about it right now is making me scatterbrained. Seeing that dog reminded me of what happened to Eddie. Someday I need to face those memories, but I can't trust that I can do it now and not slip. That is what is making me so edgy. It's not just the memories of Eddie; it's knowing where that incident led and fearing this one will take me back down that path.

Okay, find something new to ruminate on, like school or work.

The bell over the front door tinkles, and a Benji-like mutt strolls in. Did that girl say I was a proud father? If you save an animal, does that mean it is yours? That dog is huge. Do I even have space for her? Putting me in charge of another life sounds like a horrible idea. Then again, I've grown a lot, and having another reason to stay on the right track is never a bad thing.

Since I walked away from drugs, it's been pretty clear that everything in my life has happened for a reason. Being at the scene of that accident may not have been an exception. If that is the case though, why did that poor dog have to suffer for my attention to be grabbed? Maybe it was so I would feel I owed her. Now I really feel horrible for the poor thing.

The handle on the door to the exam area rattles and then stops, like someone started to open it and got distracted. I hope it's that woman with good news.

Lizetta

I head out to the lobby, anxious to talk to that guy again and give him the good news, but stop just short of entering it to touch up my hair. Sadly, it does little to improve how disastrous I look. Lame scrubs. They are the most unattractive things in the world, but at least they hide some of my padding. The curves on my personal road that I want this guy to drive his hands up may be glorious, but all the speed bumps that come with them make me crazy.

Oh, who am I kidding? Even I don't believe what I am telling myself. This is a disaster. Also, the news regarding the dog is pretty odd. I'm not even sure if I should give it to him straight.

The moment I enter the lobby, the man who needs to father my children pops up from his seat. I'm kind of surprised he stayed. Don't most guys bail when a girl tells them fatherhood is looming?

"Is she okay?" he asks.

His eyes are big and hopeful, yet a twinge of fear coats them. He reminds me of a little boy on Christmas morning that has just seen Santa but fears he wasn't good enough to rake in the presents. God, that look is just adorable. "She's fine, sort of. Her leg is slightly fractured, but it looks to be a few days old. Honestly, we don't think she was hit, at least not today."

His head tilts with curiosity, and his brows narrow in thought, yet he barely takes a moment to ponder before spitting out, "So it's like she was tired of hurting and just decided to hang out on the side of the road to see where life would take her?"

What a weird question, but yeah, now that I think of it, it's kind of like he was supposed to find her. "What are you going to name her?" Now I'm certain that he needs to adopt her. If he says he can't keep her, I'll take her, but how can he not?

"Well," he looks at my nametag, "Liz, maybe—"

"Lizetta."

"Lizetta? That's lovely. Why does your tag say Liz?"

"It's easier at work." Frankly, I'm not crazy about whacking off part of my name, but I've gotten used to it.

"It reminds me of Etta James, the singer. Do you think Etta is a good name for her?"

Who is Etta James? I halt just short of asking to spare looking like a fool. "I think it's sweet. What is your name?"

Wait. Is he naming her after me? Aw!

"Jensen."

"Nice to meet you, Jensen." He's still a little wide-eyed and racy despite hearing Etta will be fine. I touch a hand to his arm to comfort him. A surge of electricity hits me. Sadly, Jensen seems unaffected. "If you can't do it, I'll take her. I promise she won't wind up in a shelter." Oh, that was just lame. This dog clearly trusts him, and Jensen not taking her will ruin the plan that's slowly forming in my head. "However, if you do take her, we'll cover the follow-up visits." That statement may cost me dearly when Dr. Leopold finds out.

He scratches his temple.

Come on, Jensen, don't let us down.

"It's just that, I don't know the first thing about animals. I've never had a pet before."

Seriously? How could anyone grow up without animals? That would be such a drag.

His whole body pauses, except for his eyes that flick back and forth as if searching for an answer. Though I am holding my breath, I can't help but fight a smile. He seems to be concerned about doing the right thing. It's so sweet.

With a swift toss back of his feathery hair, I get a dead look in the eyes. "Yeah, I'd love to take her. I feel something greater than I am is telling me to, so I'll accept that. It will be good for us both."

Another weird answer.

My mind flashes back to that appointment Griffin and I had with the psychic about a year ago. On the way home, Griffin told me, "You can't fight the universe, Shortnin' Bread. It's going to take you where it wants you to go, so you might as well work with it." It took months for me to stop being freaked out after hearing that. Now it's flashing back into my brain with this man's words. Oh, that's just creep—

"Lizetta?"

Huh? Oh, yeah. He is taking the dog. "You take her home and get her settled. In a few hours, I'll drop off all the supplies you will need. I'll also give you my cell phone number. If you need anything, all you have to do is call."

He smiles in agreement, and, oh sweet baby goodness, my heart is trying to race through my veins and out my toes.

Maybe the universe has sent Etta to pave the path to our futures.

Nah. This guy could never see anything in me.

Could he?

JENSEN

A then G, no C. Son of a— Ugh!

Writing music was once as simple as breathing. All I needed to do was go for a walk and start humming. Halfway through I would race home to write it all down. It would just need a little tweaking and whala, brilliance! Now it's like I've forgotten how to progress chords. That song should be working. Maybe my hearing is jacked.

Was it the drugs? Nah, I wrote just fine before I started getting wasted. Didn't I?

I try it again, and the dog howls. Her pain isn't just from the injury. My serenade is probably making her ears bleed.

The guitar gets ditched for both of our sakes. I sit and share a blanket with Etta so we can watch the game on TV. "You a hockey fan?" She gives me a blank stare. "Don't worry. You will be. No one is allowed in this place unless they are hockey fans." I lean in to whisper, "But if they are Kings fans, I am counting on you to nibble off their knee caps."

Etta gets a good rub behind the ears. Having another responsibility really is a good thing. Shoot, anything to keep me on the straight and narrow is a good thing. It's only been a couple of hours, and I'm already used to her. I just wish that I knew more about dogs. How much do you feed them? How often do you take them to the vet? Did Etta come potty trained? I need to jump online tonight.

The sound of a car pulling up comes from outside. That must be Lizetta. Shoot, I should have cleaned this place more. She is going to think I can't take care of myself, let alone Etta. I pop up and head to the kitchen for a towel and start dusting.

My crazy plan is deviously brilliant! Truthfully, I may have stuck Jensen with a dog he isn't ready for. However, I never would have tried to sway him if I wasn't certain he could provide for her.

Then again, his little-boy look could deceivingly mean he is an expert serial killer and I am screwed.

I sneak a peek into the rearview mirror. Why don't I keep a makeup kit in my desk? That changes tomorrow! I want to scrub off my face and start over. At least now my hair is presentable. Thankfully, I had a soft pink blouse and a decent pair of jeans at work, so I am no longer in those hideous, spit, blood, and fur-covered scrubs.

A couple of pinches to my cheeks to bring out a natural glow do nothing. Why do magazines give useless makeup tips and imply everyone can look perfect with a little lip gloss and a smidgen of mascara? Can that possibly work for anyone?

Yeah, it can. It always worked for Laura, my arch nemesis who mocked me for my eating habits. "Fat-etta, eaten' sloppy burgers with chedda." What a horrible person.

I smooth my blouse and check to see that the buttons are all fastened and I am covered. As I run my hand over my stomach, the memory of Laura's taunting amplifies. Who am I kidding? I'm a fool for getting my hopes up.

Gah! This stops now! I swear, once she gets in my head, it's like I've stepped into quicksand.

The stairs of Jensen's duplex are nearly defeating, thanks to me bringing two, overfilled, paper grocery bags. The weight in one shifts, and I am barely able to twist and stop cans from toppling onto the hood of the car in the driveway below. It's the one I saw while helping Jensen—a nineteen seventy Dodge Challenger that is in the most unfortunate color of bile green combined with urine yellow that has been diluted with muddy water. That poor thing looks so sick that I feel as bad for it as I would an ill uncle.

Behind the door, Etta barks. Aw, she sounds happy! Jensen answers before I can knock and darts to grab a ripping bag. "Did you rob a pet food store? You didn't have to do this." He takes the second bag and invites me in.

"I was serious about helping. You should be set for a while." Etta hangs out on the floor. Her jumbled blanket makes me suspect she's had company while watching the Sharks game on TV.

He's a hockey fan? Oh dear God, yes!
Lord, please don't let him be a Kings fan.

I join Etta, and she nuzzles against me like she did to Jensen in the clinic. "How are you both holding up?"

A beat-up copy of *Beowulf*, a couple of textbooks, and a stack of CDs sit on the coffee table. *Beowulf?* That book is way over my head. Why couldn't he have a copy of *Steppenwolf?* Then I could make a joke about the band.

Would he get that? My family would never accept him if he didn't.

My eyes flash back to the CDs and catch an Aerosmith logo. Whew! If it was Bach, we'd be doomed.

"We're good," he says.

We sure are.

Oh, he was talking about him and Etta.

In the corner of the sparse room sits a practice amp. Just beyond that is a nook of a kitchen. Inside it sits a six-string electric guitar along with a Marshall half stack. I've heard that many musicians are cold-hearted and bad news for women, but they aren't all sex-starved pigs who only bang models and keep notches in their bedposts, right?

Jensen joins us on the blanket, and Etta sticks her head between us. "Aw, that is so sweet. I just love this girl. I'm so glad to hear you say it is going well."

JENSEN

"You know, I always wanted a dog. There may have been a reason why I never made this place too much my own. Now she can help me fill it."

"That is such a sweet answer, but I can't help but still feel a smidgen guilty. I didn't mean to pressure you."

I can feel my eyes deepen in warmth. "You didn't pressure me. If anything, you reminded me of what I want out of life." It feels so good to be honest, but man, I sound like a chick. Am I okay with that? There are so many changes for me to digest. It would probably be easier if I could get past worrying about how I come off to people. I am a good, responsible person now. I can do this. This dog thing, it's totally going to work out.

"That is such a sweet thing to say. You two are going to be great together."

"I hope you are right."

"I'm certain of it." Lizetta checks out the room again. I should have cleaned more. She doesn't seem to be judging though. She's probably looking around because that is what you do when you enter someplace new, but what if she thinks my place isn't good enough for Etta? You need to childproof a home, but do you need to dog proof it? Why didn't I think of this before she got here? Maybe I should ask her.

My lips start to move, and then I realize my question is foolish. What do I expect, that I am supposed to put plastic plugs in the outlets so Etta doesn't zap her paw? That's ridiculous!

It is ridiculous, right?

What kind of guy gets this nervous over taking care of a dog? The Man Club is going to yank away my balls and cancel my membership.

I should say something. Now would be the prime time to

ask questions about caring for Etta.

This man gives some of the sweetest, most amazing answers. It makes me feel like he should be easy to get to know. However, he seems a little apprehensive when it comes to conversation. Do I make him uncomfortable? Honestly, he seems distracted. He does have textbooks on the coffee table. I'm probably interrupting his studies. I don't want to be rude and overstay my welcome.

Since my hopes for an offer of a glass of water, a soda, or a drawer to put my belongings go unanswered, I stand and grab my purse. "Well, call if you need anything. I'll see you in two weeks for that follow-up appointment."

"Uh, yeah. Okay." He says it like he is surprised that I am leaving, and then a look of realization crosses his face. "I'm sorry. I've been a terrible host. Truthfully, I have too many things on my mind, and I'm worried about giving Etta all that she needs. I didn't mean to come off as ungrateful for what you have done."

"It's fine, Jensen, but are you really okay? Do you need me to take her? I can give her a good home."

His answer jumps out quickly. "No, we will be fine. I am absolutely certain of it."

I smile. "I am too."

Just short of reaching the door, a glimpse at a photo locks my feet in place and nearly takes the breath out of me. A boy and a woman stand next to a painting that makes me dizzy with disbelief. Patches of trees and flowers sit among the desert. Midnight blue embraces the earth. Stars fill the sky, yet a cluster of them dominates the center. They remind me of The Star Tarot card. "Wow! Where was this taken?"

"My mom's old house. My brother took the photo about fifteen years ago, not long after she finished the painting. That's her and me next to it. Eddie tried to get as much detail as possible."

"Seriously? She painted that? Did she copy it from something?" This painting is a perfect match for my dream—the same dream the psychic saw in the cards— except I've never seen it from this angle before. The patches look more like paths. Is it that I am freaked out, or is there something in this painting that makes my eyes drift left?

"No. Why?"

"Maybe I've seen it before, like in a gallery or something."

"I doubt it. Are you much of an art lover?"

"No, it just seems familiar." Part of me wants to share the craziness of how, but can I tell him it matches both a recurring dream and a Tarot reading without sounding nuts? A lot of people roll their eyes at even the notion of Tarot cards and psychics. Also, the only person who knows about that dream is Griffin. It's always felt too personal to share.

But there must be some reason that Jensen has this painting. Is he the thing that shakes up my world?

No, that Tower sounded more like an event than a person. Besides, Jensen seems too sweet to cause me problems. If he were dangerous, Etta wouldn't have warmed up to him.

I've got to find out what this all means. Unfortunately, Jensen has given absolutely no indication that he would ever be interested in seeing me outside of Etta's appointments. How could I change that?

I leave with a simple good night and a determined resolve. I may have to get creative, but I will find a way to draw this man into my life!

2

Wednesday, April 19

Self-confidence is everything—or so they say. When it comes to my job, I have it in abundance; however, when it comes to men ...

I tell myself I am pretty, which deep down I think I am, but I don't feel attractive. When you don't feel attractive, you often see yourself as ugly. When you have spent years hearing you are ugly and that no man would ever want you, it is hard to believe elsewise.

Today is Etta's two-week follow-up appointment, so I spend the morning fidgeting with pens, my ID tag, my nails—anything to keep my hands busy. I need to give Jensen the right impression. At least my scrubs are pretty pink ones that complement the green in my eyes and bring out the rose tones in my skin—and they are clean. Even if I'm having a bad day, these scrubs make me look like I'm little Miss Sunshine.

Dr. Leopold calls me into an exam room. What exactly do I say to Jensen? I can't turn into a giggling mess again.

The doctor keeps asking me to take care of just one more thing before I head off. Doesn't she know I have important work ahead? Sure, I've had two weeks to figure out my words, but I'm still clueless.

Each tick from the clock adds another flutter to my nerves. Rats! Etta's appointment is now. I have to be the one to see her. If I miss Jensen today, I'm hosed for a few more weeks.

Five minutes after the scheduled appointment time, I manage to break free and dash to the lobby with hope of being greeted by Etta. The room is empty.

Griffin slips up and gives me a hip bump. "Saved him for you. Sugar Booger's in room two."

"Sweet!" I shoot him a quick smile of thanks before hightailing it back. Just shy of turning the knob, I halt in my tracks. I'm still without a plan. Why does the dating game play so easily for some?

No time for wallowing. I will not let this guy know that he has control over my emotions. I will not turn into a giggling fool.

My words come out before I even finish turning the knob. "Hi! How's everyone feeling?" Etta is already on the table and playing keep away with Jensen and a squeaky toy I gave them. Jensen certainly looks happy—not at all like the guy who was freaking out over never having a dog before.

Etta sees me and tries to stand. Jensen and I both race to ask her to sit. She obeys, and then pants happily with her tail wagging to her right, over the edge of the table.

"We're great, though I think Etta's going a little stir crazy. I borrowed my neighbor's wagon the other day and took her out for some fresh air. All the kids came out to pet her. Etta's going to be the hit of the block once she's active."

The thought of this gorgeous man pulling a huge dog in a little, red wagon warms my heart. No matter how many kitten pictures I see on Facebook this year, nothing is going to compare to that image.

"Of course she'll be a hit!" I go about my routine, which includes the ever-embarrassing taking of Etta's temperature in a rather private place. Etta's a trooper, but Jensen's eyes stare widely as I lift her tail and insert the thermometer. His demure squirm makes me giggle. So much for not letting him know that he has an effect on me. "Well, she seems great."

"So, things are going well? I'm taking good enough care of her?"

Wow. That's too sweet. "You are taking excellent care of her. I never would have suggested you adopt her if I didn't know you would." Jensen turns his head towards Etta. His sigh of relief is actually visible. He's just so lovable. "Well, the doctor will be with you in a moment."

His brow scrunches. "Yeah, okay. Thanks." I hope that doesn't sound like I am brushing them off, but I want to save myself from further embarrassment.

Etta laps at my face when I bend over to pet her. I giggle, and Jensen follows along.

A guy just giggled? That's so freaking cute that I am not even angry with myself for slipping. Dating games suck!

I wish them a nice day and leave. Part of me kicks myself for not having more nerve, and part of me is proud as a queen bee for not turning into a drooling fool.

JENSEN

The door closes and ...

Wow. Was that really the same girl? I've spent two weeks thinking about how to impress her with how well I am taking care of Etta, and then she walks in looking like that. I've been telling myself that I couldn't get her off of my mind because I was seeking approval—that I needed to know I was doing all the right things—but she just made my nervous system hum like an ungrounded mic.

She also put me in my place. I mean, she was so generous with Etta that I thought she might like me at least enough to chat. Maybe she is just a thoughtful person, which makes me all the more fascinated.

I shrug at Etta. "Some chick magnet you're turning out to be." She whimpers and sets her head on the table. I massage her cheek with my thumb. Damn, how I have come to adore this sweet girl. "Sorry, honey. You know I didn't mean it. You gotta get used to me though, because if I can't banter with a woman, even a canine one ..." I kiss her head and cuddle it into my shoulder. "You know I love you, right?"

A warm tongue licks slobber onto my face, and I laugh.

"Hey, Etta. Did I really giggle?" I look to the door that the girl I am now realizing I have spent two weeks pining for closed on me. "What is it about her?"

Lizetta

This situation has made me feel awkward, giddy, hopeful, and disappointed all at once. What did I expect? That Jensen would drop everything to run over to kiss me?

I need to learn more about him and that painting. If it were a reprint, I could totally justify that I'd seen it before. But his mom painted it? She must have copied it from something.

Maybe if I continue to play it cool, it won't seem fangirly if I talk to him at the next appointment. I don't want to come off as an idolizing dork. I only want a real chance.

Would trying to start an actual conversation be so bad?

"Hey, can someone get the door please?" Jensen yells from around the corner.

The paperwork I hold is dropped on my desk when I dash for the door. So much for playing it cool. Jensen turns around and his smile almost makes my hand forget how to turn a knob. Lord, I want to run my fingers through his silky hair and yank him down so he can smother me like gravy on mashed potatoes. "Everything okay?" The words choke their way out. Embarrassing!

"So far, so good. Etta's amazing."

An adoring "Aw!" slips out of me. My embarrassment makes me giggle. Seriously, I have to get a grip on the giggling. "She's sweet. I just adore her."

A familiar tinkle of tags coming from behind the reception area grabs my attention. Oh, no. Not Socrates. Not now.

A hound that is as lovable as a cartoon mutt tromps and slobbers his way out of the exam area and drags his mom toward my desk. The dear thing always wants to say hello.

The only problem is, he often gets a little too personal. This is not the most ideal time to run into him.

Socrates comes out and puts his paws on Jensen's legs so he can sniff Etta while his owner heads to the counter. Jensen smiles down at him, but his attention quickly returns to me. "I'm going to drop Etta off at home and head back to work. Tonight we are going on another wagon walk. You would have the most beautiful smile if you saw how happy she gets."

Socrates shoves his nose deeper into my crotch. Is he trying to bore his way inside? This is totally embarrassing and a dead giveaway that I am fully enamored! "I've got to get back to work. Call if Etta needs anything."

"Yeah, okay." Jensen shrugs to Etta. She gets droopy-eyed, and her ears flatten as I hold the door open and Jensen carries her out. As soon as they are out of earshot, Griffin tromps over, smacks me on the arm, and shows no mercy. "What the hell is wrong with you? I thought you liked that guy?"

"Majorly!"

His words whip out like he wants to slap me with them. "Really? Then why did you blow him off when he was asking you to join them for that walk?"

"Yeah, right! Why would he ask me?"

Lord, I must be in trouble something fierce because his hands just flew around and smacked on his hips. "Please, girl! Why wouldn't he like you?" Griffin points a finger at me and continues to shoot out finger after finger to add a dose of sass to each point. "You're fun to be around. You hooked him up with a friend he obviously loves. And you are totally beautiful, which he was subtly trying to point out."

"He was?"

"Yes! He mentioned how beautiful your smile would be while you were walking together. *Think about it.*"

My face warms in hope, but Griffin is like a girlfriend, and girlfriends are supposed to tell you you're beautiful and be encouraging. It's what we do.

"I dare you to go get that man. This pretending you are not interested is going to bite you in your pasty ass. Go for the kill!" Griffin flicks his hand at me as he heads off to tend to a patient. I don't know what in the Sam Hill just happened, but I may need to rethink my strategy.

I spend the afternoon pondering my choices; show up on Jensen's doorstep like an obvious stalker, hide in the neighbor's bushes and then pretend to just happen to be in the area like a crazed stalker, or look up his number and call like a sane person.

On the sixth digit, I stop. He didn't actually get around to inviting me, so am I crashing his walk? This is weird.

No wussing out! Just go the half-chicken route and send a text.

"Hi. It's Lizetta. I can't stop smiling over the thought of Etta in that wagon. Mind if I join you on that walk tonight?"

How long is considered non-obsessive to wait for a reply? A minute? Ten minutes? Three days? My stupid lack of self-esteem tells me to pack it up and go home. My shoulder dips at the weight of my purse just as my phone buzzes. *"Sure! Head on over."*

Seriously? Not only was the response positive, it was fast—and he did it with an exclamation mark! Maybe Griffin was right.

Hold up there, Lizetta. You're about to walk a dog, not get wined and dined. Keep those expectations realistic.

Oh, screw you, brain! Is it so wrong to allow a little hope for once? I swear, once one person damages your self-esteem, it's a slippery slope to Stupidville.

Without giving it another thought, I head out.

Although the distance between work and Jensen's apartment isn't great, the difference in the environment is vast. It doesn't take long to go from modern shopping centers and tall office buildings to dry hills and outdated strip malls. A quick trek up a hill later, and I'm on a long stretch of road that may not have been paved since the automobile was created. This town is strange. On this end it is practically desert, then you shoot through a mini-Metropolis and land in the lush canyon where I live. Though it is not far from San Francisco, Fremont is like a mirage in the middle of nowhere.

JENSEN

This ... This is ... Okay, this is just weird.

I'm in a lawn chair, staring at Etta in a little red wagon that barely fits her, and waiting for a girl that makes feedback run through my nerves. "Seriously, Etta, what is it about her? You know she's not my type, right?"

I swear Etta is cocking an eyebrow and asking me to elaborate.

"Well, she's pretty and all, and her eyes dance with life, and wow, that hair. And that giggle! But ... Okay, I don't want to sound like an ass, but every other girl that has caught my eye has been, well ... has been a little more on the athletic side."

That's a flat out lie. They have been skinny, regardless of how they got that way. Honestly, I don't know how I would feel about those few extra pounds if I were handling them, but Lizetta is a gorgeous girl who makes my heart flap like a dying fish.

Etta shrugs. Like I swear she freakin' shrugs as if to say, "So? They have also all been tarts." Sometimes living with Etta is like living with my mother.

My head slams back into the chair. My poor mother. When will I face myself enough to talk to her? The only requirement to return to her life was to hit that ninety-day sobriety mark. I've accomplished that and so much more. Still, I was such a monster. She raised me better than to be a heartless screw-up who basically abused her.

But I have faced that aspect of my life. I've looked in a mirror and called myself out on being an abuser of both substances and people. I've called myself a heartless womanizer. I've listed the names of everyone I hurt and why, all while looking at my reflection. Still I can't call my own mother—the woman who would forgive me faster and deeper than I could ever forgive myself.

And there lies the problem—forgiving myself.

A car pulls up, and my heart races in anticipation of seeing Lizetta. When she steps out of the car, I stand to greet her and my knees weaken.

Lizetta

Thankfully, my pipe dream of seeing Jensen outside of his appointment persuaded me to bring a change of clothes. This time I arrive in a denim skirt and a pink, capped-sleeved blouse that is a step above a T-shirt. I also touched up my hair—not too much, just enough to make it look like I took it out of the ponytail and shook it into waves, like in a shampoo commercial. Adding a makeup kit to my purse paid off as well.

When she sees me, Etta struggles to sit. Her tail starts wagging heavily to her right. Her bark warms my heart like I'm Mom coming home to her sweet baby. It is so darling.

Jensen's smile seems uncertain as he grabs the wagon and heads towards me. Since I can't pull it together enough to talk to the guy, I came prepared with an icebreaker. I probably should have written notes on my wrist, too. "Hi. We just got a bunch of samples of ridiculously expensive dog food. I brought you some."

"Wow, really? That was nice. I figured while we were out I would take you to dinner as a thank you for persuading me to adopt Etta. You hungry?"

Whoa! Really? Dinner? Am I crazy for thinking this is kind of like a date? Yes, I'm hungry. I'm always hungry. The name Lizetta must be synonymous with famished.

I nod to his inquiry and he motions us to head off. "Everyone's eating dinner now, so the kids will be out when we get back. You like burgers?"

Another ridiculous question. I practically live at the

burger joint down the road. "Yeah, Burger Hut sounds great."

"I have something better in mind. Have you ever eaten at Bert's?"

That place is awesome! Before it was a gourmet burger joint, it was an old-time diner. It still has the vintage decor. Since the area around it never really developed, it reminds me of a time capsule on a deserted road. It's also totally overpriced because they use organic, grain-fed beef and nothing is ever frozen. Unfortunately, it's also a couple of miles away. I choke back my fear of the trek ahead. "Sounds great."

Thankfully, I have the foresight to ask Jensen about that equipment in his kitchen. He briefly mentions leaving a band due to immense drama, and then segues into a rambling speech about his love of classic rock. That's great because my breath is a little shallow, and I don't want Jensen to realize how out of shape I am. Shoot, *I* don't want to realize how out of shape I am. Just to be sure I don't start huffing, I occasionally stop to point out distractions, such as a patch of flowers that catches my eye, along with a rabbit that runs across the road. None of these really warrant a stop, but taking an occasional break is all I need to hide that I wish he would walk a little slower. However, when we arrive at the restaurant, I'm all too ready to guzzle back down the calories I just burned in the form of a Coke.

"I can't bring Etta in, so I'll go order for us and we can eat outside. What would you like?"

A jumbo burger, gargantuan fries, and two of the largest Cokes they have. While they are at it, can a massage be tacked on? Preferably by Jensen, while naked.

Part of me feels I should answer like a stereotypical girl on a date and order a salad, but I'm starving and the fine aroma of one hundred percent Grade A Chuck is wafting past. Besides, when you have a back that looks like a stack of mushrooms, why deny the obvious? "A cheeseburger sounds great, please. American cheese." Before I can spit out the rest, I'm asked if I want fries. My overwhelming hunger and exhaustion must have kicked in, because right now, even thinking about having a tiny bit of pretense disappears without my consent. "Of course I want fries. Who in their right mind wouldn't?"

Jensen's smile makes me goo up a little. "I totally agree. I've been trying to wean myself off of them, but it's nearly impossible. How about I get us an order to split?"

"You know, there are a lot of things that I'm willing to share with a man. My fries are not one of them." I force it to sound like I'm teasing, but I'm totally serious.

Jensen laughs. "Nope, I will find ways to divert your attention so that I can steal them. I will not be bullied into eating an entire bucket of fries alone. Now, how about splitting a shake? Those things are huge."

"Are you saying you have no self-control?" I love the thought of Jensen without self-control!

"Only when it comes to fries."

Dang. "Did you just bring me here so you could pawn off half your food so you won't feel guilty for eating it?" Where has this level of comfort and confidence come from? "Do I even have a choice in the matter? It sounds as if I say I want my own order, you'll just buy one and steal half anyway. I get it. The shake is a diversion. If I'm concerned about you nabbing the shake, I can't keep my eyes on the fries. You're sneaky!"

He bats his lashes and fakes a demure blush. "Who? Me?"

Oh, that's so damn cute! But I won't let it take me out of the game. "Yes, you! Quit the mock innocence. I see what's really going on here."

As he makes for the door, he points at me. "You're awesome."

I about die on the spot over how incredible that gesture made me feel. Still, what just happened? Did I really let down my defenses and banter with a super hot guy? I turn to Etta for an explanation. She's unfazed. To her this all makes perfect sense.

When Jensen returns, the banter again flies. Then the food arrives, and the sight of it makes me salivate. Jensen was right about the mammoth amount of fries. I'm a little bummed that I get my own mini-shake though. I was hoping for one of those big metal jugs with two straws so we could sip while staring into each other's eyes. Then again, if I got that close to Jensen, I'd jump across the table and plant one square on his lips.

Yum … Tasting a shake off of Jensen's lips … Yeah, let's share this shake. I know just how I want to slurp it!

Maybe I should stick to the plastic cup it came in—for today at least.

Unlike how I was on the walk over, I'm now confident enough to start a real conversation. "So, it's time you confessed." I set my shake on the table for emphasis.

"To what?" He leans back in his seat, relaxed and unaffected by my tone.

"The name of your car."

With a swoop to grab his shake, he snickers. "What makes you think I named my car?"

"Every gearhead names his car, whether he admits it or not. My stepdad is constantly fixing up cars and selling them. The sixty-five Barracuda was Isabelle. His sixty-seven Mustang was Jacqueline. The sixty-six Corvette was, of course, Yvette. I gave him grief for years about how unimaginative that was. So, what name did you give a nineteen seventy Challenger?"

His eyebrows cock in surprise at my knowledge of the model of his car. "The Beast." He dips a fry into some ketchup and pops it into his mouth. He seems rather satisfied with his answer, but I'm pretty sure he's fibbing.

"Nah, that name is better suited for a poodle. What did you really name her?"

He keeps me in suspense by taking another sip of his shake, possibly while floundering for a creative retort. "Bertha."

"Bertha?" That name always makes me think of a robust woman that you wouldn't dare piss off. "Good call." I tip my shake to him in salute.

"Okay," he says while dusting off his hands. "Let's talk about something real. Have you found the perfect career or is this a stepping stone?"

This is kind of a rough one for me because I've had to accept some things about my life that I didn't want to. "I'm there. I originally wanted to become a vet, and while my family was very willing to help, they aren't rich enough to pay for eight years of school. Plus, science baffles me, so my grades were lacking. I'm happy though. You?"

"I'm assistant managing a small warehouse while taking night classes. It's a long road, but I'm an English major because I had a rough time fighting a learning disability and one person changed my future." Hope fills his eyes, giving me a newfound appreciation for him. "I want to become a teacher and give that same gift to other kids."

"What about music?" I ask.

His lips press together. For some reason this seems to be a complex question. "That's important too, but finding balance is always hard. There is more for me, and searching for it hasn't worked, so I'm trying to let it come on its own."

I completely understand. Finding balance can be hard. I didn't just want to be a vet; I wanted to make a difference. Am I really making a difference now, or have I settled? Can't my dreams still come true, even with modification?

For weeks, Jensen was the guy who had me fighting back hormone rushes while I projected ideals onto him. Now those ideals are turning out to be true. He has solid goals.

Suddenly, my gut feels weighted, and I can't finish the last of my food. This never happens. Does Jensen tie me in knots that much, or can't I stomach how I have let myself down? "This is weird. Normally I would lick the plate clean." Oy! Did I say that aloud? How did I let that happen? I was so relaxed but ... Now, I am really disappointed in myself.

Jensen's eyes go to his lap, and his voice softens in a way that implies discomfort. "A person's weight doesn't matter to me. What matters is her heart and how well she takes care of herself."

I know I am over-sensitive about my body, but was that directed at my weight?

I look for an indication. Jensen's eyes slowly peer up. His soft features imply that he is sincere.

You'd think being bullied would have gotten me to do something about my body. Instead I slipped deeper into a Ho-Ho's aided rebellion. I peer down to make sure my blouse is fully buttoned and I am covered; yet I catch how his eyes suddenly widen.

"I'm sorry," he quickly adds. "That may have come out wrong. All I was trying to say is that you are a beautiful girl and should never lose sight of that."

Beautiful? Again he seems sincere. No one outside of my family or Griffin as ever referred to me as anything above cute.

"It's fine. I'm just a little surprised by how this conversation has flowed, since we barely know each other."

"Actually, we know each other better than we realize. Can't animals sense more about a person than humans can? When Etta saw you today, she didn't just wag her tail, she did it heavily to the right. She only does that with you. I looked it up and learned that it is a sign of deep happiness. Etta sees that your soul is beautiful, so it must be true. Sometimes you have to listen to voices other than your own."

Jensen gives what I can only refer to as a reflective glance to the road. This conversation has taken such an odd turn. First I see that painting in his home, and then the honesty today, and now there is a story in his eyes. There really is something more special here than just a good-looking man. I'm about to ask what is on his mind when his buzzing phone grabs his attention.

JENSEN

For years I haven't bothered to learn what any of the girls I've spent time with were really about because I didn't want to face that I wasn't dating girls of substance. I should play the gentleman and ignore my phone, but I'm embarrassed from getting a little too personal with my comments. It makes me feel the need for a diversion. The moment I look at the text, I regret it. *"It's been awhile. Waiting for me to come get you?"*

Laura's timing is always impeccable. I've come too far to open that Pandora's box again, no matter how tempting she constantly makes it. Still, I pinch my lip like a conflicted boy who doesn't want to try asparagus even though he has been told it will taste like ice cream.

"Jensen, are you okay?"

"Yeah. We, uh ... We should get going if we want to catch the kids while they are still playing."

The three of us begin our trek back. Inside my neighborhood we are flooded with kids that are dying to pet Etta. The three of us being together feels natural. When we reach Lizetta's car, she thanks me for a fantastic time. I couldn't agree more. "I had a feeling we would get along. I never expected it to be so easy though."

My butt vibrates. The perfect timing tells me who is making my phone buzz. *"Just for making me wait, I'm going elsewhere tonight. If you are lucky, I'll give you a chance some other time."*

If I am lucky, the earth will abruptly halt and Laura and her friends will be the only ones to fly off of the planet.

Etta places a paw on Lizetta's hip. I don't want Lizetta to leave either. "Goodbye, sweetie," Lizetta says. "I'm sure I'll see you again at your next appointment."

Why am I blowing it by reading a text from someone who tried to bury me in the ground with her and still lives in a world that almost cost me everything? This stops now. "Um ... Actually, I was hoping I could see you sooner. Are you free Saturday night?"

"Sort of. I have tickets to the Shark's game. My stepdad and I usually go, but he can't make it. Wanna join me?"

She's a hockey fan? Yes!

Wait. She's a pretty hockey fan with an adorable giggle. She knows about cars, I can be honest with her, and she can keep up with my banter. I am so screwed.

And I love it!

Laura

I try to drown out the crappiest music ever made by burying my head under a pillow. Sending Jensen a text was a preemptive strike, because with how shitty that new guitarist sounds, it won't be long until my pissed-up brother staggers in, sits on my chest, and goads me into doing it anyway.

Dammit, Jensen! You left, knowing I needed you. You were the only person who I ever thought gave a crap about me, then you packed up and left in the middle of the night without a word. I woke to a deserted motel room, an empty garage, and a shattered heart. The real mystery is why this surprises me.

My head peeks out just enough to be sure that my bedroom door is locked. The last thing I need is to be expected to make an unwanted visitor happy. Why couldn't those jerks have left instead of the one person I trusted?

"Ya hear that, Jensen?" I scream. No one will hear me above the racket outside. Even if they did, they wouldn't care if I were being murdered. "I trusted you, you stupid ass!"

I throw the pillow so hard that it smacks the lamp right off of the nightstand. The bulb breaks, and the room goes dark. "Fucking shit!" Screw it! It's better this way. If any of those guys do get in here, I don't want to have to look at him. At least the bottle of tequila didn't knock over, not that there's much left to spill.

Tequila … I miss Jensen and our tequila nights.

The rest of the bottle gets downed, and I bury my head back under the pillow while praying for the mercy of passing out.

Where did everything about me go wrong, and why can't I wise up enough to fix it? Can't there be a way to right my wrongs like Jensen did? Or am I destined to live the life of a drunk, bitchy, blow-up doll?

3

Saturday, April 22

JENSEN

Houses like this still exist around here? I knew this was an old part of town, and that Lizetta said she lived in a farmhouse, but this is nothing like what I expected.

Bertha's V8 engine and dual exhaust command the attention of two guys in a barn at the end of the driveway of Lizetta's Victorian-era home. The two-story house has several peaked mini-roofs and a porch that wraps from the front all the way to the side. A huge lot sits behind it where dogs run freely and chickens are penned. Just a few blocks from here, the biker scene is alive and well among antique stores, a decades-old head shop, and a refurbished train station.

A robust guy of about sixty, with tied-back, salt and pepper hair and some serious scruff, comes out to greet me. If he were wearing something more intimidating than coveralls, I'd think that wrench in his hand might have my name on it. Then again, he's got one of the toothiest smiles I've seen. "Now that's a wicked engine! Nice wheels!"

I like this guy already.

Even though it looks perfectly clean, the guy wipes his hand on his leg before extending it. "Nice to meet you, Jensen. I'm Paul, Lizzie's second dad." That's got a great sound to it. It's so much better than stepdad.

A thinner (some would say gawky), male version of Lizetta comes out and introduces himself as Jimmy, Lizetta's little brother. He can't be younger by much.

"Good to meet you." What is that weird snorting sound? Do I hear a pig? Forget what I am hearing, it's the taillights on the car in the barn that are screaming at me. "Oh, I have got the check out this fifty-seven beauty." My combat boots hightail it to the Larkspur Blue jewel. "Where did you get such pristine trim?" For each of its three years, Chevy refined the Bel Air body style, tweaking it into perfection. Though the Bel Airs have their differences, what it really comes down to is how the sharper fins and side trim's flare make the fifty-seven the sexiest. The two bikes sitting in the corner, a Harley and an ancient Indian, aren't bad either. That Indian is sixty, if it's a day.

"My brother owns an electroplating shop up in Red Bluff," Paul says. "They specialize in auto parts."

"Man, you sure got the right model. The other two years can't compare to the tail of the fifty-seven. The grill is better too. The grill on the fifty-six looks like it ate something bad."

Paul smacks his hand on my shoulder. "You're all right, kid. If you keep up like this, I'll let Lizzie keep you." Then he leans in and whispers his joke. "Remember those words. The part about me letting her is important, but not as important as her thinking she's doing the dictating. Women like to think they are gracing us with their presence. You know what? They are. Remember that and you'll be fine." My shoulder then gets a squeeze to punctuate the life-lesson. I'm uncertain as to if I now feel like I have a dad again or a new best friend. All I know is this is someone I can appreciate. He's just that warm and welcoming, much like the family I was once a part of.

The Bel Air isn't the only thing in the barn that draws me toward it. In the corner, next to a sofa that looks like a pack of cats tried to drag a fish out of it, is a drum kit and a couple of Fender amps. What really grabs me are an old Stratocaster and a Gretsch White Falcon, known as "The Dream Guitar". This one may be a little beat, but its gold trim and pick guard make up for the scratches. Seriously, the baby makes my heart go all a flutter like a twelve-year-old girl at a Beiber concert. "Whose Falcon?"

"Mine," Jimmy and Paul answer in stereo. "Give her a shot," comes out of Paul as Jimmy's "Don't touch her!" overlays him. "Nah, go for it," Jimmy says with a chuckle. "Lizetta said you play. You any good?"

Am I any good? Well, I am no Steve Howe, but I hope Eddie Van Halen wouldn't embarrass me too much. I pick up the Falcon. Paul and Jimmy cross their arms and the pressure is on. I give her a whirl with a complex riff I wrote before I almost burned my brain out.

Paul and Jimmy give a synchronized pause, glance to each other, and then shrug. Jimmy chimes in, "Yeah, he's way better than we are."

"Yeah, we suck." Paul hangs his head in mock shame. "You playing with anyone now?"

That phrasing was odd. Maybe I am paranoid from drug damage, but the pang in my gut screams that I've been outed. I watch my words, just in case. "No, I'm between bands. I'm trying to live a drama-free life."

"Jim, why don't you see what is keeping that sister of yours?"

Why do I feel that was more his exit cue than a suggestion? It makes my lungs freeze up. If Paul knows about me, I may be screwed. I don't want to lose Lizetta before I even get her. She's a nice woman who seems respectable. My past may not make me worthy, but Lord knows I am trying to be. I've learned my lesson, and I'm ready to prove it.

Paul watches Jimmy dash to the house. Meanwhile, I try not to turn blue from holding my breath.

"You used to play in the clubs around here, didn't you?"

Shit. Paul's a biker and we played all the bars, clubs, and rallies from San Jose to Sacramento. That riff may have been familiar and tipped him off. "Yeah."

He gives me the biker stance, the one with the crossed arms and firmly planted legs. Worse, I get a sideways glance that practically growls not to fuck with him. "You suddenly disappeared from the scene. What made you quit? And I'm not talking about the band."

Crap! I'm an idiot, but I'm not stupid enough to play dumb. "I woke up in a tub wearing only condiments and remembering nothing." I leave out the part about the naked guys in bed together. I just can't consider what that may mean; even though there was no indication that anything had happened. I would have been sore, or crusty, or something, right?

Right, God?

As much as I want this conversation to end, Paul's scrutinizing eyes scream that he is not going to let me off easily. I lean against the Bel Air and voluntarily spill the rest of my guts while hoping that the more honest I am with him, the more slack he will cut me. Plus, there is an alarm going off in my head. It's not a warning klaxon; it's more of a nudge telling me that we have something in common. Someone who doesn't understand that a person can right his wrongs would have tossed me out already. "You would have thought that the time I was in the back seat when a friend hit a pole and died would have done it, or when I almost ran over a kid on a bike, but no. It came down to it being all about me. It just goes to show all the more how pathetic I was and, by extension, still am."

Paul holds the tough-guy pose. "How long ago did you stop?"

I look at him dead on. "I hit the ninety-day mark just over two weeks ago, the day before I met Lizetta, so not long at all."

"Yeah, that's about what the whites of your eyes say. I take it Lizzie doesn't know."

Geez, even now he can see the damage. Of course he can. He doesn't have to say any more for me to know we are birds of a feather. I'm catching a hint of gravel in his voice, so he's a former smoker. I'm betting he's kicked several addictions. If anyone is going to get me, it's him. "No. I can't bring myself to admit it to her, but I'm determined to live right, so soon I'll have to. It's just nice that she's getting to know the real me before she learns of the demon that I once was."

Paul seems to get the full picture. Still, he won't give me a clue as to whether or not my ass is getting booted out to Bertha for a lonely ride home. "What triggered it?"

Now that is an odd question. A reasonable one, but an odd one. "Stupidity and thinking that was the way musicians live. I was on the verge of getting help when I saw my brother get hit by a car and die. He had just gotten clean. Instead of that being a wake up call, I let it send an excuse that living clean is pointless, because you just die anyway. Part of me wanted to die so I would never have to worry about watching someone suffer again."

Paul sets his hand on my shoulder. On the rise of my eyes to meet his, I catch rivers of scars on his arms. The track marks are just about faded to nothing, but I sure see them. "Been there. Done that," he says. "You got a sponsor?"

Here is where I am going to lose the battle. This will sound crazy to him, but I keep my eyes on his anyway. "As stupid as this may sound to some, I've found my best success on my own. For some reason, whenever I get around people, even those with the best intentions, I make excuses. When there is no one to face other than me, I'm stronger. There is also the fact that I lost every good friend I had when I became an addict. The ones I made after that wanted me to stay wasted, so I'm going it alone. I don't want to risk trusting the wrong people and failing."

"Well, you're doing a pretty good job at talking to me now."

My eyes stay locked, and I don't even blink when I say, "Maybe it's because you understand that banishing the scum in your life and then getting and staying sober for yourself is one thing. Once you start meeting good people, it's even more crucial that you don't fall from grace. Second chances are important, but I'm not so sure that people deserve a third."

Paul sucks in his lips, and I can sense the pondering. I may have overstepped, because how many chances did he need? His nod is subtle, but it drives home the point before his words do. "If you need help, you call me. You and I, we're cool, but if you fuck up, even if my little girl is nowhere around when it happens, you will wish I only ripped your balls off. Got it?"

I make certain to not let the eye contact waver. "Loud and clear."

"Don't take too long. You make sure she knows before she gets attached, and you certainly don't make any moves until she's got the full story. Agreed?"

"Most definitely." Shit, my voice didn't crack, did it? It felt like it cracked that time.

He double pats my back. It seems to be his signature thing. From the neck of the Stratocaster, he grabs a pick, writes on it, and then hands it to me. His eyes square in on mine again, and I nod in acknowledgement of being given my ninety-day sobriety chip. As soon as I do, he heads back to the car like the case is closed and we can move on, but I'm not ready. "Hey, Paul. Thank you. I needed someone to know and to not have him treat me like scum. It helps."

"I get that, too. Any time, kid."

Lizetta comes out wearing a Sharks jersey, and as much as Paul says we are cool, I also feel she has saved the day because I am so done with my past and don't want to think about it for another second. The sparkle in Lizetta's smile reminds me that she is one of the many reasons why I am staying clean. I have missed out on so much.

"Hey, Paul," she says. "You'd better hurry. Mom's standing in front of her jewelry box, so she's almost ready."

"That's my cue! Funny how it takes men about as much time to shower, shave, and throw on a suit as it does women to pick out jewelry. Have fun kids! Catch a puck for me."

The bed feels unusually comfortable as I slip in. It's much like I imagine a cloud in heaven would feel.

Tonight I had a date with a guy who opened doors for me, carried my jacket, watched hockey with me, shared garlic fries with me (even if he did fib and say it was only so we could share garlic breath), and who gave me the sweetest kiss goodnight after walking me to my door. It was one of the most perfect evenings I could imagine.

With a sigh of bliss, I drift off to sleep …

I'm walking through a valley. Beneath me are patches of green among a desert of sand and dry grass.

My bare feet trudge through the heat. Each step sizzles as I seek patch after patch of cool grass and pieces of shade. Every time a breeze brushes the hair from my face, I long to stop and enjoy the peace, yet my feet keep moving.

In the distance, a rainbow sprouts from a field of grass and wild flowers. I run toward it, stop in the middle of the field, spread my arms, and then twirl in the glory of comfort and light. My eyes close off the world so I can savor the cool air as it whiffs up my nose, bringing in the scent of flowers. I smile, reveling in the glory of life.

Suddenly I tense. I know what comes next, but this is all in my mind, so logically, I can control it. I just have to stay locked on the bliss.

My body loses all weight as it floats heavenward. No! This can't be happening!

I try to return to Earth. As my will deepens, my body descends. The grass below tickles the tips of my toes. I can do this! I can stay!

A force yanks me upward and into the heavens. My eyes open to find I'm among a cluster of stars. On the ground below, a figure races into the field where I just stood. She throws open her hands, twirls, and falls to the ground, spreading her arms like the wings of an angel, as if claiming the land as her own. A sense of injustice fills my heart. I want what is mine, yet a sense of peace keeps me tethered to the stars.

JENSEN

My cell phone feels like a brick weighing down my hand, but it's not as heavy as the burden I've been carrying. Mom told me to wait ninety days. That mark has long passed. Tonight I was given a sobriety chip to show for it.

I bounce my leg wildly to release tension. Etta's head rests on my other leg, while her eyes gaze intently on my hands. It only takes pressing one more button to take the first step in correcting the last of my horrible wrongs. I'm a heart-felt apology away from putting our relationship on the mend, yet I can't bring myself to place the call.

What if Mom comes unglued? What if she doesn't believe me? Could I handle it? Would I slide backward?

That's ridiculous. Mom gave me chance after chance because she knew I could recover. She even said it in the note when she kicked me out. Her other son recovered, and she accepted him. No problems, no questions.

And then he died anyway, which is why I turned into such a disaster.

Calling Mom always seems like it should be such an easy thing, but once I start thinking about it, so many little things pop into my head that I want a drink to calm my nerves. Then I couldn't call her because I wouldn't be sober anymore. Instead I would be back on the road to self-destruction.

Etta nuzzles my leg, grabbing my attention. She then nods to the coffee table. She's right. If I am that worried about blowing it, I shouldn't take the risk. I need to cut myself some slack and follow the path that I know will keep me clean.

The phone is exchanged for my latest reading assignment. I'm sorry, Mom, but I can't do this yet. I can't face how much I let you down. You, the woman who raised two boys on her own while working two, and sometimes three jobs. The woman who let me stay with her because I kept promising to clean up. You held on to faith in me until I pushed you too far. I need to find the right words to apologize for that, but I don't think they exist.

Not only did I lose a father, a grandfather, and then a brother, I watched you lose your husband, your dad, and your first son. Then I forced you to lose me. What words start that apology?

Maybe if I stop thinking about it, someday the words will come.

4

Monday, May 8

JENSEN

Ambushed.

The moment I get home from work and step inside my apartment there is company on my tail—company with sweet breath that tickles my ear and reminds my body that it is male. "There you are. I missed you." Usually when Laura does this, it's a seductive whisper. Now she sounds like the Grim Reaper who has come to stake claim.

I sigh. "We've been through this already."

I knew by the tone of the text she sent this morning that she'd soon pop in for a romp. It ain't gonna happen, which is why I responded with a firm, "No, we are done."

Laura strolls her way into my apartment as if I have rolled out the red carpet. Etta immediately comes to attention. Why can't I shove Laura out the door like an intelligent person would? There is a difference between being a gentleman and being a doormat. I don't mind becoming a bit of a wuss when it comes to Lizetta, but with this girl? No way.

"You mean the same game you and I have played for the last year? Every time you stop taking my calls it's only to build the tension. I don't mind you toying with me, but this go around lasting two months is pretty ridiculous."

I never should have slept with her after I bailed out. The brain inside my dick that overrules my sanity needs to be lobotomized. It took forever for her to give me a break after that. It finally seemed to be working, too. The last time Laura called was the same day her brother, Larry, tried to get me to come back to the band, again. Coincidence? Probably not. A few hours later I reached my ninetieth day of sobriety. With the exception of the text I got when Lizetta and I were on our first date two weeks ago, I took the few weeks of quiet that followed as congratulations from God for making it. It's been insanity ever since.

Hey, God. Thanks for nothing.

Laura also makes me bitchy as hell.

"It's not a game, Laura." I was always serious when I said no. It's just that she can be rather persuasive in changing my mind.

She leans back on the sofa with one boot resting on it. Combat boots? What happened to heels? Given what she had started experimenting with when I left, this is a bad sign. Her skirt exposes the fact that she's not wearing any underwear. I hate when she does that.

Actually, I wouldn't exactly call it hate.

Why does everything with this woman have to be so challenging? Can't she just be normal?

No, with the hell she has been through I suppose this is normal enough. I can't think about it, or I'll want to help her. She turns my compassion around and makes me defenseless. She doesn't want sobriety; she wants love. She wants someone to swoop her up in a grand gesture of devotion. I can't give her that. I won't risk my sobriety for her, no matter how much she is hurting my heart.

Etta snarls at Laura, reminding me that I'm not supposed to feel for the woman. The spitefulness Laura brings out in me nearly has me hoping that Etta's raised ears and tail mean she will turn vicious. I don't want Laura harmed, but she's exasperating. My head feels like it is going to explode, so I rest it against the wall and point to the door. "Laura. Please."

She slides down farther, thus sending her skirt up, just in case I missed the obvious. To ensure that her message is sent she tugs down her tank top. It's not a display of modesty like it is with Lizetta, but more an act of exposure since the neckline stretches down past where her bra *should* be. Sweet Lord. She may not have any class, but memories of those boobs come rushing back. How I'd love to—

Man, I know Lizetta and I have only had a few dates, but even if Laura weren't such a skank, I couldn't go there. I'm just trying to do something right in my life. It seems to be working, because not long ago I would already have been down to business.

I toss my keys on the coffee table—despite knowing I should keep them at the ready to use as a weapon. I'm not getting my ass, or any other part of my body, near that sofa, so I squat beside her. Laura may have serious issues, but that doesn't mean she can't be reasonable and that I should not try to be decent to her.

"Look. That reply I sent was serious. We are done. Please respect that and wish me happiness, just like I wish you."

She stands like she is going to leave. Instead, she tromps up to Etta and looks down on her. "Where did *this* come from?"

Scratch what I thought about being a decent human. I've always known that Laura is more of a bitch than I want to admit. She's proving me right. "That's Etta. I adopted her."

She stares straight at Etta and snickers. "*You? You* adopted a dog?"

"Why are you so surprised?" *Etta, honey, if you rip her a new one, I promise not to think ill of you.*

"What's up with its leg?"

Etta growls. I'm with her.

"*Her* leg is fractured. I rescued her."

"Like, seriously? Why would you care about a dog?"

Wow. I've known Laura quite a while, but clearly we don't know each other at all. It's not like we have ever been masters of deep conversation, but I've heard her stories, time and time again, about all the bad things that happened and the marks left both on her body and her soul—stories that make my heart bleed. Has she never listened to me? Maybe I neglected to share what I want out of life, because I knew someday I'd have to leave her behind. "Yes, like seriously. A lot has changed. I need you to respect that." I open the door and step aside. I hate being a total dick, but if I don't, she'll keep ambushing me and eventually I'll cave. This girl is capable of taking me places I can't allow myself to go. The zipper between us is the only thing stopping her from making my head spin.

With a shrug, she heads out, and then slips in a quick kiss on the cheek. I feel like a prick as I start to close the door, but that feeling disappears when she spins around, grabs me, and slips her tongue into my mouth. God, this girl can kiss! Her hands grip my back and pull me in tightly against her tits, reminding me of a damsel clinging for rescue. My dick twitches in response as I remember the talent of that tongue when it's in other places. She goes for my zipper. "Come on, Jensen. Let me have another taste of that long, wide—"

The last of my compassion disappears. I resist the urge to shove her off of me with my hands by doing it with my voice. "If you want something long and wide, there's a produce stand down the street. Go grab yourself a cucumber. I said, no!"

The amount of force must have been good because her eyes have gone wide and are locked that way. Gauging from her bark and attempt at standing, Etta is taking it pretty seriously, too. "It isn't a game this time?" Laura asks.

"No, I'm serious. Please, go."

Laura gives a demure nod and finally leaves. I close the door and slide my ass down to the ground. Etta looks like she is asking what the hell that was all about, but something tells me she already knows. "Do you hate me now?" She nuzzles her face into mine. "Why are you being so nice? I've been a dick, and I fear my past may someday blow up in my face, and I'll lose Lizetta."

Etta's bark is a soft rumble that threatens if I pull any shit, she'll kick my ass.

"I won't. Believe me, I won't." Lizetta's smile crosses my mind's eye. I let out a happy sigh as my head slams back into the door. I am seriously smitten.

Laura

I brace myself for the sound of the door slamming. It'll be just like a kick to the head as yet another person tells me to go to hell.

Go to hell? *Hmph!* The joke's on all of you. The keys to the kingdom have been fused into my backbone.

The door shuts with a respectful click that turns my attitude solemn. I turn back to stare at the barrier. The fact that he was kind enough not to slam it deepens my hurt. Jensen really isn't like those other guys. He never was, though for a while he sure played the part well. I just wish the real him could see the real me. Shoot, *I* can't see the real me any more. How long has it been? A couple of decades?

I stare at my boots as I hit the bottom step. I hate wearing combat boots with a skirt and Jensen knows it. He's no idiot. Of course he's figured out I'm hiding track marks. I need to go back and tell him what else is going on—how I've become smelly cheese in my brother's sick game of cat and mouse. He will help me then. He has to.

I want to head up, but my feet flee to my car so I can hide from the truth. He doesn't want me. He abandoned me. The dirty bastard! Why am I not worthy?

Screw you, Jensen! This is me leaving something behind for once, even though we both know I'll be back—because I'm not strong enough to stay away—because you are my only friend.

What the hell am I going to tell Larry? How can I walk back into that house a washed up old bitch that can't turn a free trick? I need to stop off at the liquor store and load up. I'm gonna need something a lot more blissful to get me through this night, but at least that will get me started. Lord knows what I am going to have to do now to get what I really need.

5

JENSEN

Moby freaking Dick! Why did I choose to be an English major? Is helping kids worth having to read this book? Dare I even call it a book? This thing is like the world's most glorified paperweight. Never before have I rooted for mankind to lose. The only good thing to come out of this book is a Zeppelin song.

I dig out *Zeppelin II*, skip to the eighth track, and crank that baby. The drums hit, and all is right with the world. With my axe in hand, I wail along with Page. Sometimes I forget how good I am.

The drum solo kicks in, and I kill the Zeppelin in exchange for doing finger exercises. My foot starts tapping, and I'm basically jamming with myself, creating my own beat.

Ah! Finally, I'm able to get somewhere. I go to the song that I've been working on for the last few weeks. It flows along, but the moment I get to where I left off writing, I feel like I've jumped off a cliff and smacked into an ocean of boulders. I back up a few bars, give it another go, and manage to add on a few notes before stopping. "That sounds stupid."

Sounds stupid? How old am I? I haven't said something that I've written sounded stupid since I was twelve and about two months into learning how to play.

I give it a repeat and then jam on it a bit. The flow starts off heavenly before something smacks it down. What the hell is wrong with me?

My back goes to the floor, and I stare at the ceiling. Why

am I so stuck? I can't say it's never happened before—although it's pretty rare. In the past, I just called Larry and we worked it out.

We would also get wasted.

Maybe I'm just expecting everything to come too easily. Maybe I just need the right inspiration. I used to go for long walks and would come back with a song. That's probably all that's necessary.

With the intent of borrowing the neighbor's wagon to take out Etta, I head for the door. A glimpse of the picture of Mom and the painting she did stops me. I touch my hand to the glass, caressing where the photo of the painting lies underneath. The patches of dried grass remind me of how I once shriveled and withered. Slowly I am turning green again.

My eyes gaze upward, to the stars on the top. I want them to gaze to the image of Mom, but the thought of doing so brings pain to my brow.

The actual painting should be here, just like it hung in my room for years. I need to call Mom and make amends. Only a person who fears himself would hide from his own mom like this.

Inside the green field sits a little dot next to a tree that reminds me of the one I planted in memory of Granddad. That area was once barren. Since I planted that tree it has sprung to life. That is where I need to be.

I pet Etta. "I'm sorry, sweetie. I really need some me time."

With my guitar on my back, I head out for greener pastures. I can't still be this pissy when Lizetta gets here.

Lizetta

My toes press into the cool tile of the kitchen floor, raising my body so that my lips can get closer to Jensen's. Our eyes stare into each other's, and the sparkle they share coats me in happiness. A simple kiss leads to another, then another, then more gazing. Then I ruin it with a giggle, making Jensen laugh. Oh dear God, that was awesome! Can I do only this for the rest of my life?

This is how it's been since our first date at Bert's. For weeks we have fixed dinner at Jensen's on Wednesdays and had Saturday night adventures at movies and pinball arcades. He's already become a fixture at my house for Sunday night family dinner. It's barely been a month, and we've got a routine down.

You'd think with being so young we'd rebel against this sort of thing, but it's the life I've always wanted. As for Jensen, at the end of one date, he's already planning the next. From date to date he brings me the feeling of stability. It's still surprising, because with all the gear around here, it's hard to get the rock star—a gig here, a date there—image out of my head. I've yet to find notches in his bedpost though.

Actually, I've yet to make it into the bedroom much at all, which I'm fine with, for now. Becoming the occasional domestic couple is something that I am ready for with him, but revealing the physical aspects of my glory can take a little longer. Jensen doesn't seem to have a single hang-up with my body, and while that is comforting, I can't say that I share those feelings about my curves. It's unfair, because the hormone rushes he gives me make me want to spread him all over me like salted caramel on ice cream.

Jensen finishes tossing the salad while I grab some juice out of the fridge. The same four bottles of beer that have stared at me every time I've opened this door grab my attention. I know they are the same ones, because someone wrote a date on them in Sharpie. It's about five months ago—around the time Jensen quit the band. Celebratory beer left in memory? "Hey, what's the deal with the dates on the beer?"

When I turn back around, Jensen has paused his tossing.

JENSEN

Crap!

Then again, I'm surprised it's taken her this long to ask. Can I brush off the truth a little longer? How can I ever tell an angel of a woman, whose dad was an alcoholic, that I'm basically a recovering junkie who used to womanize, all so he could hide from reality? The thought of hurting her makes my heart ache. I want to do right by her though. Not telling her is probably worse.

Maybe I can ease into it by giving her the end of the story, then fill her in some other time on the terrible person I was that got me there. "That's the date I gave it up. I was tired of feeling like garbage all the time. Since then, I've been pretty cautious about what has gone into my body. If I see a daily reminder of how long it has been, I've less desire to ruin it by going back to my old habits."

"You don't drink at all?"

I need to tread lightly regarding the meaning of those relics. At first I thought I only had to quit drugs and hard alcohol, but on my first day of "sobriety" I had gone through nearly an entire case of beer when I decided it wasn't strong enough and almost made a call. Clearly everything had to stop. "Yep, not since the date on those bottles. I plan to let them stay in there until I die." The strength of that statement may have made it sound like I had a problem. Dammit. I did, but I don't want to freak her out.

"Not even a drop?"

"I'm just not all that interested in it now. The last time I even considered it was on Granddad's birthday. He was such a Cognac lover that I thought of toasting his memory." But that was paving a fool's path. "It seemed shallow, so instead I went to a spot I frequent and planted a tree in his honor. Every now and then I hang out there and think of him." There, a simple truth. We need to let this go now. I grab a piece of lettuce out of the bowl and feed it to her. "Enough dressing?"

She winks at me. "Not if you want to forget you are grazing like a rabbit, but it will do."

As much as it is a relief to hear the man in my life doesn't even touch beer anymore, there is something really odd about the situation. Something big must have prompted his lifestyle change. Who makes a display out of when he changed his eating if it wasn't for a life-altering reason? It's another puzzle piece in the picture that is my boyfriend, and it's one that makes me feel like my skin is too tight.

Life altering ... Like a Tower of destruction?

These random thoughts are disturbing.

I grab the chicken breasts from the oven and we plop ourselves on the floor in front of the coffee table to watch the hockey game. I long to dive into the food that looks so fantastic, yet I can't resist pausing to enter harassment mode. "You've ruined me forever." Jensen snickers. Without looking away from the game, he sees that I'm building up to something. "I can't even look at Burger Hut anymore. Truthfully, I walked there a few days after our date at Bert's. One bite of those processed fries after having just been reminded of how real potatoes taste almost made me gag."

"Good. The chemicals there will pickle you."

"Then again, having a salad with so much stuff that it is like eating a pizza is kind of crazy when actual pizza exists. Croutons, cheese, meat, olives—you've just disguised the ingredients under the lie of dressing instead of tomato sauce and crammed in a bunch of lettuce. You're a strange man with food rebellion issues."

He sucks his lips together. They complement his scrunching brow. I wait ...

And wait ...

He's got nothing, which is ridiculous because there's not

nearly enough stuff on here to make this anything like eating a pizza.

His attention goes back to the game. While he's wrapped up in the action on the ice, I put a cluster of my croutons onto my napkin, place tomato chunks on them, and then top it with cheese before slipping it in front of him. He raises an eyebrow to it. The best I get out of him is a slip of a smile, and then a kiss. "Cute." His eyes go back to the game.

He's letting me get away with that? It wasn't hysterical, but normally it would get a stronger reaction. "That's it. Next week I am making my infamous Chocolate Cherry Salad."

Nothing.

"It's a real thing."

Jensen fails to react. I don't even get a blink. I did say that out loud, right?

"Hey." I touch his arm. "You okay?"

His eyes go to my hand. "Yeah, I'm sorry. It's been a long day, and I had to deal with a lot of stuff."

A lump forms in my throat. He may not be lying, but I am pretty sure that he is hiding something. I fear pressing further, because it might be that he wants to breakup and doesn't know how to tell me. I should change the subject. We can talk about the—

No. If something is really wrong, I want to be here for him. "Anything you want to talk about? You can tell me anything. I promise."

Though his expression remains constant, my gut tells me he is running a gamut of emotions. Finally he puts down his fork and turns toward me. His eyes search into mine as he caresses my cheek, stalling out my heart. "It's fine, honey. I promise." He kisses me, and while his gentle touch conveys adoration, my comfort dissipates as he wraps his arms around me and the hug turns tight. I feel it might be one of desperation.

Something is not right here. It's so easy to surrender to him like this—to dare let myself think our relationship is one that can last. My gut tells me it's true, but the ugly voice of doubt chips away at the fulfillment I feel when I am with him. How do you continue to put your heart on the line when it tells you the situation is magic, yet your mind senses a red flag waving in the distance?

The kiss ends. Another quick one, along with a smile, follows it. A moment later we are back to watching the game, and Jensen returns to being the man I've dated for a month. Still, I can't shake what I know in my heart.

Whatever is on his mind does not bode well for us.

6

Thursday, May 18

Lizetta

Why have my calls for Rufus's mom to pick up his ashes gone unanswered? Not only was it horrible of her to dump him here to be euthanized, but now she has fully abandoned him. For months, my friend has sat in a walnut box on my desk. Can she not see that he was worthy of love? Maybe she's had a hard life filled with so much suffering that she had to turn away. I have to have faith in humanity and believe that there is a reason. Still, Rufus deserved better.

Griffin walks past my desk on his way to a file cabinet. He backsteps and stops, looking down at me looking at Rufus. The warmth of his hand on my shoulder is comforting. "I know. I have sympathy for him too."

"Today it is more like empathy."

Griffin and I know each other so well that I can see his pressed lips and downcast gaze in my mind, even though my sight remains on Rufus. "You finally ready to talk about it," he says, "or are you gonna tell me you are fine again? We both know you are not."

I close my eyes, not wanting to look at Rufus while wallowing over only having a taste of how he felt. "The distance in Jensen's voice last night has me concerned that he is discovering I may not be what he wants."

"Yeah, I figured His Studness had something to do with it." Griffin pulls up a chair and takes a seat next to me. His leaning in with clasped hands is his way of signaling that he is here to share the load. Frankly, I'm not sure how he can help, because the emotions flowing through me …

Well, I just can't seem to grip them.

"This is lame. Sure, Jensen was a little distant, but is that really a red flag, or am I stupidly insecure that I'll be abandoned like Rufus?"

"Has Jensen given you any indication that he doesn't want you?"

"No, and maybe that is the problem. I can tell something is wrong. God, am I being a total idiot? I really have nothing to go on other than my gut."

He takes my hands, and I can tell what's coming. Griffin knows that when I get confused, a little direction goes a long way. "Lizetta, have you considered that maybe you have nothing to do with whatever is wrong? It's a new relationship. He may not be ready to open up. Generally, when it comes to the needs of others, you are selfless, but that is not how you are acting now. You are assuming the problem is your fault instead of accepting that the best way to help Jensen might be to give him space and be there when he is ready. It's just like how I asked you this morning if you were okay, and you told me yes because you weren't ready to talk. Why is he different? Because your heart is on the line?"

He's got me. "Yeah, that's exactly why."

His grip tightens, lending me strength. "There is more though. Why do your eyes keep floating to Rufus?"

I didn't realize they were, but he is right. My eyes are dead on him right now, and I can't get the smile on his face when we played fetch out of my mind. It's like he is sending me a message from beyond that I can't get. "Rufus was such an amazing dog. The way he faced his final day with courage and grace was admirable. He allowed himself to see the beauty in his last moments and drank it up."

Griffin moves his face closer to mine, commanding my attention. "You need to ask yourself why you can't see the beauty in your life like Rufus did. For years, you have allowed others to make you blind."

I release one hand from Griffin's to pick up Rufus's box. Though my eyes are locked on it, all I see is the happiness that radiated when he was free to run again. "You are right.

Rufus knew on his dying day that he was no longer the graceful pup he once was; yet he didn't let that stop him from enjoying the moments that he had. When I took him off that leash—"

Griffin puts his hand on mine, halting my thoughts with his tone of assurance. His love for me makes my eyes well up. "Lest you forget, he had those moments because you gave them to him. You put your job on the line so he could be happy again. Now, would you trade that for anything?"

"Of course not," I choke out.

"Apple Butter, you are too wrapped up in what others have said. You deserve to see yourself as I see you."

I can't argue. "You are right. Absolutely right."

"Now, what are you going to do about it? And I don't mean about Jensen. I mean about taking care of you for once."

I look straight to Rufus's ashes. Although the words hitch in my throat, they come out with determination. "Rufus, you are coming home with me, because I love you for everything that you were and the joy you brought into the world. You deserve a real home and we deserve respect, both from ourselves and from others."

Griffin gives my hand a rattle of encouragement. "That's a start. Now get to the meat of it."

"There is beauty in me, and from now on, even if I don't see it, I won't doubt that it exists. It's just healthier that way."

"Amen, sister! Just remember, even if Jensen is a fool and bails out—"

"Don't worry, Griffin. I promise that this lesson will stay with me. You know, since Jensen has entered my life I have faced two things: I'm an unhealthy eater, and I have a golden heart. The first thing I am changing; the second I wouldn't dream of letting go—with or without him."

Griffin pulls me in to a tight embrace. "Now *that* is my Bestie Boo."

JENSEN

Why did I take a call from an unknown number? It may have been the stupidest thing I have ever done. No, scratch that. Acting on it was even more idiotic.

I get being frustrated over not being able to write, but to come to Larry's place, especially when I am so freaked out over telling Lizetta about my past, was just plain stupid. What could make me put everything on the line like this?

Being around these people also makes me bitchy as hell. That's one plus to coming here today—I now see what my former band mates do to me. It is no wonder why I lost all of my respectable friends.

I can't change my number in case Mom needs to reach me, so I've purposely given all of the old scum from my past a ring tone that sounds like an air raid siren. I don't even look before ignoring it. Larry must have gotten wise to that trick. I should have known better than to take a call from an unknown number, but what if it had been Mom or Lizetta needing help? Sometimes I think I look for excuses to return to Hell, though I'm really not sure why. This moment proves it.

Is it because being a junkie is easy? Is it how these people accept me, no matter what I say or do, as long as I am high? Is it that misery loves company?

Seriously, I need to figure this one out. I can't blow it off to a momentary lapse of reason or drug damage. There has to be something behind it.

I sit in Larry's living room on a shag carpet that may have once been green and bright orange. It was probably put in when the house was built in the sixties. Now it's faded and its colors are uglier than poor Bertha's. I feel lost here. I sit cross-legged and prop my axe onto the ground so it stands between my legs with the neck over my face. I start tapping on the sides of the body in an effort to release tension.

Is wanting to make a little music so wrong? What about missing the rush of being onstage? This is definitely one of those times when being true to myself is not easy. Should I simply accept that I need to either give up my passion or succumb to being an ass?

Larry exchanges his guitar for some Jack and then guzzles. As soon as I came through the door, Larry's three-day-old stench and greasy ponytail reminded me why I left the band. "Come on, bro. Let's get together and play," he said. "Just you and me writing killer stuff. What harm is that gonna do?"

Now I am noticing how Larry's words sounded like those of a pusher to a junkie.

Laura has yet to show her face, but a lethal smell coming from the kitchen tells me she's here. Among her talents, Laura can bake some pretty amazing cookies.

Larry takes another swig and tries to hand me the bottle. How many times do I have to tell the guy I don't want any? If I give in, I'll soon be drunk off my ass, back in the band, putting powder up my nose, and allowing his sister to yank down my pants. Again, there are things that are more important, so why am I here? Am I that desperate to make music, or is something else calling me?

"Hey," Larry says. "Do you remember where we left off on that song we were working on?"

"Yeah, I think so." I move the guitar into a playable position and go into it. Larry's smile builds. I expect whipping the tune out flawlessly to feel good, but the victory is lacking.

"Yeah," he says while nodding. "That's it."

At the point we last left off, I stop dead, and then try to pick up the pieces by adding on a few notes. It sucks. I go back a few bars and then do a repeat of the riff with a little bit of a dance added on. Still it sucks. I turn to Larry. "You got anything?"

He shrugs, and then does a quarter-ass job of replicating

my riff, but he tacks something decent on the end. Why can he do it and I can't? I refuse to believe that I need drugs to write. There must be another way.

A shadow of a figure approaches from the kitchen. The bright sun behind her makes Laura look like an onyx ghost without a face, yet the boney frame gives away who it is. When she steps into view, she reminds me of a modern day version of a nineteen fifties housewife. I guess you could say she looks like a soccer mom.

She sets a plate of freshly baked, double chocolate, espresso-walnut cookies on the table. Unlike her normal attire, she is tastefully made up. Her long hair falls in waves around her face. Her clothes actually cover all of her female parts, and she smells like baby powder perfume. Our eyes lock, and even though hers are red and somewhat filmy, the skip of my heart tells I have hope for her. My attitude starts to soften, and I feel like the Jensen of recent times again. She smiles, and the light reflects off of her lip gloss, bringing about a fake glimmer to her face. I can't help but smile back.

This moment reminds me of the first time we met, on the day I came to audition. She walked in and stole my breath. But in taking a closer look and seeing the lines around her eyes that make her look ten years older than she is, I'm reminded that this is far from the same person.

Larry grabs a cookie and starts eating. I'm a little more gentlemanly and say thank you. I stand my guitar back down between my legs and force my eyes off of her and onto the plate. My fingers rap at the sides of the guitar again. Laura makes damn good cookies. I nearly ballooned out eating them. Once you start, you can't stop, because the munchies set in. I watched her spend hours learning how to soak out almost all of the taste from weed before extracting the THC in butter. Chocolate helps disguise what little taste is left. The walnuts and coffee would do an even better job of covering it and God knows what else.

Pass, just in case.

Larry grabs a second cookie. "You don't want to miss

these, man. You know how my sister can bake."

Yeah, I know about all the things his sister can do, starting with blowjobs and ending with needles. Now my attitude is getting harsh again.

Larry resumes playing, yet I sense him watching out of the corner of his eye. I haven't even taken a bite and I'm already paranoid. Laura smiles at me and then swallows hard. My heart hurts over leaving her behind. There is a façade here, and she is hiding behind it. She's not as okay as she seems. God, how I want to help her.

Her face goes stern, and her eyes flick to the plate, then back at me. The shake of her head is subtle, but it's definitely there. She's warning me? Why would she do that? Could it be she actually cares? That while she wants me back she wants me healthy too? Maybe it is a message that if I come back, she will make sure things are different.

No, I'm deceiving myself. I must be.

This is lame. Not only have I put myself in the middle of temptation, I'm holding this guitar like it's a shield so that I won't grab anything else. If I could get these people to lay off of me, accept that I don't share this lifestyle anymore, and respect that I have found someone special then—

Then monkeys will fly out my ass.

"Hey, Larry. I'm sorry man, but I've got to go."

"What? You just got here."

"I've got some place to be."

"Yeah, Laura told me you had a stick up your ass now, but I just thought she was enjoying hearing herself talk." More Jack gets guzzled down. Memories of what a nasty drunk Larry can be reinforce everything, so I pack it up. "Guess that new girl is why you want nothing to do with us. Afraid we might fill her in on a few details?"

My body tenses at his threat. Crap. If he knows I met someone, he can find out who she is. I'm screwed.

Laura's head snaps to face me. Her eyes narrow and her features turn hard. By Laura's reaction, I'm guessing he hasn't clued her in.

I'm out the door before he finishes his yammering, only to hear him scream his final words that the band is now better off without me. I don't care if he's right. I am certainly better off without them. Still, I need to find a way to balance music with everything else in life. I took a huge step back by coming here, and then corrected it by leaving before it's too late. I'll let myself think that I'm even. As for that song, I'm done. It's just an unnecessary tie to my past. If I need drugs to write, I'll never write again. I'd rather miss writing than miss Lizetta.

Bertha and I speed off as Larry's words catch up with me. I've been putting off telling Lizetta what a horrible person I was, but I'd damn well better fill her in before someone else does. First, I've got to get to Paul before she gets home from girl's night out with Griffin. Since her dad had an addiction, I need to approach this gently.

Laura

Jensen bails, and it's like he's leaving me all over again, only this time I actually see the door close. He's seeing someone! How could he do this to me?

Fuckin' Larry! He knows how to play me. He also knows the way to get to me is to make me jealous, pissed, and irrational. Springing Jensen's news on me was a failsafe in case his plan backfired. I'm being played, and dammit, it's working. Some little bitch has my man. I need to fix this—pronto!

7

Friday, May 19

Lizetta

Etta's happy bark signals my arrival at Jensen's. The moment the door opens, her paws are all over me. She gets just enough love not to feel slighted before I get my lips on the man that has my heart palpitating simply because he exists. Jensen has given me some amazing kisses, but his embrace reminds me of a bear who wants to drag me into his cave and hoard me. Between this and him calling to apologize for his recent distance, I almost feel that all is right again. Still, after the concern I have felt over the last few days, I cannot shake my weird itch of discomfort over his invitation.

Jensen pulls back and smiles down at me. The tender caress of his thumb on my cheek has me melting. But fear creeps in again when his eyes lose their glow, giving me the feeling that soul-felt pain is surfacing. Jensen guides me to the sofa, and when Etta curls at my feet and peers up with a gaze of sadness, her warning of oncoming hurt sends my stomach crashing.

"There is something that I need to tell you. I didn't say anything sooner because you mean so much to me that I am afraid of losing you, but please believe that it is all in the past. You should also know that I've already talked to Paul about how to approach this."

My stomach ties into a knot. "Why would you be concerned over losing me? What would Paul have to do with something in your past?" I want to tell him that my feelings go much deeper than I've confessed, and it would take a lot to scare me off, but how soon is too soon to open up your heart?

Is that really my concern, or is the nagging feeling that something is wrong keeping my heart on guard?

Wait a minute. He talked to Paul? Paul would be exactly the person to talk to if they were kindred spirits.

My breath hitches. No. That is not what he is going to tell me. Not Jensen.

Jensen closes his eyes like he is trying to halt time. Etta placing her paw on my knee in what looks like an offer of consolation, causes my gut to cramp further. Jensen rattles his head, and then puts his hand to his temple. His building frustration has me on guard for what is one of the worst things anyone could tell me. "I'm not the fitness nut that you think I am; I'm a recovering junkie. Forcing an attitude change toward my health is how I banished my demons."

My mind fights reality. "No. No, you can't be. Not another one. I won't allow you to have been like that." My fingers press into my closed eyes and squeeze while I hope to smother the wave of disappointment that pulls me under. *Please, Lord, not another scarred life. How could he ever touch something that destroyed my family? Something that turned my dad into a raging monster that made us fear him.*

Jensen reaches out to me. "Honey, please—"

I stick my hand out to halt him. I need a moment to process this. Was Jensen like my dad? Did he abuse people? Did he sleep around with every low-life woman in his inner circle? My dad liked to have company when he shot up. Was Jensen like that, or was he a lone wolf? I've so many questions that I have no idea where to begin.

Why can't I have people in my life that have never suffered? It would give me so much hope. It is no wonder why just the idea of something bad has such a heavy effect on me.

JENSEN

All I can do is pray for understanding while waiting for Lizetta to compose her thoughts. Paul warned me to be as upfront as possible and to give her all the time she needs to digest each piece of my news. He's right; she deserves that courtesy. Still, watching her chest sag makes me fear she is withdrawing her heart. The pain in her eyes rips at my soul as the stupidity of my past harms another wonderful person.

Finally she takes my hands. "Why?" she asks. "What happened? Why did someone with your talent and intelligence risk throwing his life away?" The betrayal that radiates from her and Etta's eyes makes me see how I have punished innocents for no reason.

"Before we get into that, I want you to know that I take full responsibility and make no excuses for my behavior. Also, three months before I met you, I stopped poisoning my body, which meant giving up alcohol and all drugs of any kind. I also left every so-called friend that helped me find excuses not to be the person I wanted to be. You haven't met my friends because I don't have any. They walked away once I let them down too many times. I don't blame them in the least."

I give her a moment to absorb that and wait for her nod of acknowledgement before moving on. The poor woman looks ill. I reach out to her and she softly tells me to keep going.

"My older brother, Eddie, started abusing when our dad died. He tried to keep it from me, but when you share a room with someone, it's kind of hard to hide that you are drinking away your pain. Mom had to work two, and sometimes three jobs, to make ends meet. Her dad tried to help, but eventually Granddad had a massive stroke. Everyone's life got a lot harder. I couldn't help but think that maybe Eddie had the right idea to numb himself to how our family was falling apart. It seemed the easy solution. Now I see that it was just an idiotic and dangerous path that only a coward takes, and that the real solution would have been to band together."

She nods. I know she gets it. She's probably heard this part of the story countless times before from Paul. Did she ever hear it from her dad? The tears build because I already miss being someone who hasn't caused her pain. "Hey," I say, taking her hand. "I promise that, if you'll allow me, before the night is through I will tell you every last thing, but first, I have to know if you are okay. Paul told me about your dad."

Her sigh tells me the subject holds sorrow that she would rather keep at bay. "Let me guess," she says with resignation to how things work in her life, "long story short, Paul knew what was up with you. He gave you a chance to prove you were no longer a mess, and then you decided to step forward, possibly because you knew that if you didn't do it soon, he would have words for you." She peers up, and I get a hint of a smirk through her tears.

"Honestly, that is part of it, but I swear I would have told you anyway."

"Sounds just like him," she says while wiping the tears from her face.

"You didn't answer my question."

She squeezes my arm and forces a smile of support. I can only begin to imagine what memories are flooding her mind. "I'm okay," she says. I want to believe her without question, but I sense her guard rising. "Just keep telling me everything. How did it get out of control? What did it do to you?"

Paul warned me about this, too—that she'd likely hear me out while wondering how much I am like her father. But even if our stories are identical in how they started, the similarities will eventually end since I am sober and he is in a grave. I need to remember that, because my immediate reaction to her question about why I lost it is to head to the nearest bar.

The memories begin to flow—horrible memories of the things that drove me into addiction. Memories that bring back images of my brother becoming so ashen, so lifeless, so full of … nothing. I can't fight my closing throat, because what happened to Eddie was only a step deeper into hell than I went. Laura is as bad as he was.

Etta nuzzles against me, offering comfort and showing me love. It makes the shame over the mess Eddie and I made, and the innocents we hurt, sicken me deeper.

"Eddie's band was on the verge of hitting it big when their addictions took over so strongly that they sold their equipment to pay for speed. He had just gotten out of a twelve-step program and was sharing his excitement over building new dreams when we were walking down a rural road. A car came out of nowhere and swiped him, tossing him into the air and smacking him onto the shoulder. The driver only slowed for a moment, and then went on as if nothing happened."

My forehead tightens, and I close my eyes in hopes of shutting out the vision of the past. "Eddie was not only covered in blood, he wasn't breathing. His pulse was faint, so I gave him CPR, even though each press brought up blood. It was probably hopeless from the start, yet I couldn't abandon him. Every breath I gave filled my mouth with gore and made me feel powerless. Being powerless while someone you love suffers is the most soul-scraping thing that can happen. You pray to switch places. You act in desperation. You swear that you will surrender everything good you have just for them to take another breath."

The bile burns its way up my throat, and it's gulped back down. My hands press into my temples, trying to push out the hurt. I've never been able to fight the desperation I feel when it comes to that moment. "Do you have any idea what it is like to watch someone you love suffer while they teeter on the verge of death? To be on your knees, praying and doing everything you can to help them, while knowing it is futile? When do you stop praying for salvation and start praying for mercy? When do you just hold the person in your arms and tell them you love them and wish them happiness in whatever the next step holds?"

Tears flow down my cheeks and onto my hands that Lizetta now holds. Etta's whimper of compassion and Lizetta's eyes that radiate love into mine offer comfort, but the dizziness builds. Sobs break my words as I plea for answers, because someone has got to have them. "How do you forgive God for letting your brother lie there, suffering, and knowing he is dying? It wasn't my fault that I couldn't save him. Still, the shaking in my soul whenever I think of Eddie won't end. All I could do was keep pumping on his chest and praying—afraid to admit that it was useless. Then I felt his ribs give, and …"

My breath shudders. After years of denial, it's time to face the unthinkable. "No one has ever said it, but I probably broke his ribs, sending bone into Eddie's lungs and ending his chances for revival." She reaches out and draws me close. "Dear God, Lizetta, I know that he seemed dead anyway, but what if he could have lived? Were his ribs already broken from the fall or did I push too hard? Were the pulses and breaths I gave keeping him going? What if I could have kept them up a little longer? I can't help but question all of that."

Her grip on me tightens, and she rocks me gently. "Jensen, it is not your fault." She pulls back and looks me dead in the eyes. Finally someone is giving me what I have needed for years. "You were doing exactly what you were supposed to do. Every second of it. You have to accept that." She pulls me back into an embrace, and I catch the gleam of love in Etta's eyes that makes me lose it all over again. She is a pillar of hope in my life.

Still, "I just can't escape the thought that I—"

Lizetta draws my eyes into her's again. "Jensen, if that is what happened, what you did was give him mercy. Practically every day I have to show mercy to animals that aren't nearly as sick. That is done out of compassion for their pain and the desire to give them the highest quality of life possible. Know that in your efforts to save him, you gave Eddie the precious gift of love."

Tingles blanket my skin, bringing about peace to my soul. At last, redemption is upon me. Her words paint my soul with a comfort that no drug could ever match. "I am so grateful for you and Etta. This sounds crazy, but I swear that right after he died, I heard Eddie's voice saying to let the universe be my guide. I tried to understand, but I couldn't get it until I saw Etta on the side of the road. I thought I was living my nightmare all over again, but an angel in scrubs appeared and gave me hope."

"I looked such a mess that day," she chokes out.

My hands cup her cheeks so I can capture her gaze. New tears form because more than ever I see what a gift she was. "You looked like a savior whose only concern wasn't her own. You were the beacon of light that showed me I would be okay. I was so afraid that seeing Etta would send me begging for a needle and a spoon, but instead you both brought me deeper into salvation." I squeeze her hands again to emphasize my plea. "You ground me. For months I have stayed on track because I had this dream that there was something better for me, something that could make me feel rooted. That dream is you."

Lizetta's tears mirror my own. Her eyes are so puffy and red that I worry for her all over again. When she grips my hand, both fear and anticipation fill me over her upcoming words. "Time and again, my father hurt me. When you first said that you were fighting an addiction, my mind went to the time he smacked Jimmy across the face so hard that blood sprayed. After that, every time Mom and Dad fought, Jimmy and I cowered together. I'll also never shake Mom's expression while trying to hide why the cops had come to the door on the day Dad died.

"My dad was a shameless bastard whose womanizing gave Mom Gonorrhea. Thank God she cut him off for good then and there, because eventually a hooker, a fling, or a needle infected him with HIV. The killing blow to our hearts came when Dad's last day was spent in a motel room, dying alone with a needle in his arm. For years I have carried those images of my father, a man who couldn't be bothered to shake a habit—not for his wife and certainly not for his kids. I grew to love Paul because he showed my family that we were worthy of happiness. Now you have basically told me that you got clean for yourself, but are willing to fight even harder for my sake. Do you have any idea how that sounds to a little girl who was hurt by her father, only to go to school each day and be ridiculed about her body? You too, Jensen, are a savior."

I am truly at a loss for words, awestruck by the beauty this woman brings into my life. I've prayed to find salvation and forgiveness, but never have I dared dream to be seen in a light similar to how I see this angel.

Fear ruled me when I began this conversation. Now our hearts entwine through shared tears. How I wish it could stop here, at a moment of perfection. I curl her in my arms, still not knowing what I could possibly say in response to her poetry except for the simplest of words, "Thank you for seeing me as I long to be."

She pulls back, and her eyes go straight into mine. Her hand lends a gentle caress through my hair as she tells me in no uncertain terms, "No, not as you long to be. I see you as you really are." Just when I thought things could not possibly go any better, this phenomenal woman proves me wrong. "With that being said, I need to know if there is anything else you should tell me, be it big or small. I need to know and trust all of you."

She's so sweet that my heart falls for her all over again. I so badly want to say that all is in the open. We've both had enough, and we are at the perfect place to end this conversation. However, she's asked to know everything, and Paul has already warned me that if I add on more at another time, she will wonder if the bad news ever stops. It's either tell her about Laura now or risk losing her trust later.

Why won't Laura go away? I left all my other problems behind, yet she is the ghost who haunts me. "I've walked away from it all. I met you on my ninety-first day of sobriety, and I swear I will never go back to my former life but ...

"You are such a sweet and wonderful person that I don't want the one thing that carries over to hurt you, but you need to know." I take her hands and am sure to look her square in the eyes. "I'm not like your father. Yes, there have been times when I wasn't exactly a one-woman man, but I swear I left that behind with the drugs. However, there is a girl who I keep pushing away. She's had a hard time accepting that my new life doesn't involve her. Please believe that I want nothing to do with her. She's a walking time bomb that's half ex-pseudo girlfriend and half groupie whore that letting back into my life, in any capacity, would be the stupidest thing I could do."

Lizetta gives a demure nod. "So, what does this girl have to do with you now?"

She sounds so broken that I want to swoop her up and fly her off to all the good she deserves. I raise her chin, bringing me into her view. I'm as insistent as can be. "Nothing. Absolutely nothing, except that she won't go away."

But that is not entirely true, and my remorse builds just thinking of how I left someone I care about behind with all the other junkies. There is no disguising the guilt in my voice. "My compassionate side tells me I should help her, because I'm the only one she's ever trusted with what's at the heart of her issues, but I won't subject myself to that environment anymore. She won't take the guidance I have offered, because all she wants is for things to go back to the way they were. If she shows up again, she'll do it in a way that will make you question my fidelity, so I need to be certain that you know my heart is only with you."

The weakness in Lizetta's voice guts me. "But you are telling me this because you want to help her, or because you are afraid she will show up again?"

I cup her face in my hands, drying her tears with my thumbs, and being damn grateful that she is letting me. "Hey, it's okay to question if you can trust me." She looks up with those big green eyes, and I hate who I once was more than ever. "I would wonder the same thing, but I am telling you about her because her suffering rips me up inside.

Even though her problems are not my fault, I hold guilt that I don't think I'll ever get over. With or without you in my life, I can't and won't get involved with her." Her eyes drop. I thought she would at least show a little relief. "Lizetta, please, tell me what you are thinking. What can I do to help you? Do you have questions for me? What about your father? Do you need to talk about him?"

Lizetta

This is overwhelming. I have so much to process about Jensen—being a former junkie, witnessing the gory death of his brother, an ex who won't go away—whom he wants to help but can't—and the burden of guilt for things that are not his fault. His past brings back flashes of my father, yet in all this tragedy I have found that he is someone who can help me overcome the pain of my past.

Obviously he cares about this woman, and I have to question how much he loves her. What is she like? Is she prettier than me? Nicer? What I do know is that for as opposite as our pasts are, Jensen and I have one very important thing in common. We are both deeply affected by the suffering of others.

Etta whimpers and lays her head across our laps. Although I know that a recovering addict can slip, animals know when to trust people, and I've proven with Paul that I can forgive a broken past. Moving past the years of pain brought on by my dad has never been easy. Due to that and Jensen's news, everything inside me is sagging from the weight of my heart. I need to keep a little bit of guard up to protect myself. I want to help this wonderful man so he can continue to see that his sobriety is not in vain. I also want to help that poor girl, even though she sounds like someone I'd rather not meet.

I nudge Jensen to lie back on the sofa, and then curl next to him. As far as I am concerned, there is only one thing to add. "The complete and honest truth is that I would be a liar to say your past doesn't frighten me, but I am also in awe over your efforts to save your brother and your desire to help a friend. I do wish you would cut yourself some slack and move past your guilt. But what is really going through my mind is your compassion. Through my compassion I have learned to see the beauty in myself. I pray that you find the same in you."

With a kiss to my brow, he curls my head into his chest. I tack on another prayer, one that I won't tell him, because I think he needs to feel I am unaffected by that part of his life. Still, I can't help but worry.

Thank you, God, for Jensen's miracles. Please bless the woman he cannot help by giving her one, too.

8

Saturday, May 20

JENSEN

Bertha's roar announces my unexpected arrival at Lizetta's. I'm going to keep proving that I am not the excuse for a man that I used to be, which is why I'm here so early.

Paul stands in the barn, wiping grease from his hands on a red shop cloth. He takes a few steps out to greet me and extends his hand with a smile. "Jensen!" His hand smacks into mine, and his natural charm puts a smile on my face. "How is it going?"

He acts like he doesn't remember our previous conversation about how I was going to tell Lizetta everything last night. From what I have come to know about him, Paul is probably letting me tell things in my own time.

I'm nervous over where things stand. Just because our last conversation ended on a good note doesn't mean Lizetta was still okay once everything had time to set in. "Did Lizetta tell you about our conversation last night?"

He gives a firm nod to the concrete. "No, but she and Judy had a gab fest into all hours of the night, and she was pretty quiet this morning."

My hands turn clammy. Talking it out is one thing, but quiet is not a good sign.

Before I can ask if I blew it, Paul sticks his hand out to stop me. "I got it covered. Everybody around here knows that people have problems. It's not the problem that's the issue; it's how it is handled."

"But what about the stuff with her dad?"

"If she wants to talk to you about it, then be sure to listen; else you keep fixing you, and let Judy and me worry about that bastard. Lizzie knows from me and my friends that not every man who once had a problem is an ass."

The weight of the world flies off my back. Lizetta has a serious lock on me. It's a lock that makes my heart sing, and I hope she never releases it.

A *creak* and a *slam* come from the screen door. Jimmy jogs across the yard. The glow of his golden hair reminds me so much of Lizetta's that my blood warms. I really need to make sure she knows that my heart is with her. How soon is too soon to tell someone how you feel? I'm in sad shape if I get misty just by looking at someone who shares the same hair color as my girlfriend. It's just more proof that the love bug has bitten—hard.

"Hey, man." Jimmy gives me a double pat on the back that he must have learned from Paul. "Today's Saturday, right? Isn't Lizetta at work?"

How do I brave it up? I guess the how of it really doesn't matter because now that I've told Lizetta, it's time to suck it up with everybody else who should know. "Actually, I came to see my sponsor." I give Paul a sly fox of a smile, and it's returned three-fold.

"Sponsor?" Jimmy wags a finger between Paul and I. "You two know each other outside of Lizetta?"

Yeah, I kind of had a feeling Paul has played big brother before.

Paul cocks his eyebrows in a silent message that the talking is all mine. "No, I just filled Paul in with a little something about my past. Lizetta knows, too."

Jimmy's chest puffs, and he eyes Paul with the pride of being his son. After Lizetta sharing a little about her dad with me last night, I appreciate how Jimmy sees Paul more than ever. "Yeah, Paul's good like that."

I hit Paul with the rest of the news. It's also my way of filling Jimmy in without having to hash up the details. "I hit that one hundred and twenty day mark a couple of weeks back."

Paul shoots me with his finger and clicks his tongue.

With all his long hair and scruff he reminds me of a seventies rock star. He drives home that thought when he grabs a pick off of his guitar and scribbles on it. He starts to flick it at me like a Morning Star but stops to walk it over and place it in my hand. The orange pic says "120" with a star next to it. "What's the star for?"

"You're not supposed to get another chip until you hit six months, but last night you reached a different milestone. Congratulations."

Jimmy shoots me a thumbs-up before grabbing a guitar. "Well, with an endorsement like that, I guess you're sticking around a while."

My head rattles. Is he serious? "Wait. You just found out that I have a drug problem, and you're okay with me dating your sister?"

Jimmy straps on the guitar like I've just commented on the weather, not questioned his code of brotherhood. "If Paul and my sister can't scare you off, there's nothing I can possibly say that will. This family is big on trust. However, if you do anything you shouldn't, especially if it in any way endangers my sister, I'll kick your ass."

The hell? First, what's with the calm-as-a-person-in-an-ad-for-an-aromatherapy-candle attitude? Second, I hardly think this wiry guy can take me down, and he has to know it. Paul reads my mind and tells me on the hush, "Careful, the kid's a scrapper." It's said dead seriously, but the wink that follows makes me question what the hell is going on all the more. That changes though as Paul locks his eyes into mine. "Seriously, kid, around here you're okay in everybody's book until you prove differently. Their dad played the same game you and I did. He's in the ground, and they regret the time they spent giving him twenty chances more than they should have. I've shown them time and again that people can change, so they believe that now. They also know that sometimes, no matter how much a person claims they are trying, a person is just not willing to do what is necessary. When you see that, you've got to cut the loser or he's going to bring you down. Lizetta knows the difference. Hopefully you do, too. It will get you further than you realize."

Paul's understanding puts a rock in my throat. He's right, which is why I am here with them now and not reaching out to help Laura.

A familiar melody twists through the air as Jimmy starts playing "Here Comes the Sun." He sounds so horrible that the badness probably vibrates into the earth and disturbs George Harrison's corpse.

Paul's head drops into his palm. "How many times I gotta tell this kid that you don't mess with The Beatles? You can screw around with Zeppelin and The Stones, but the Fab Four and Mott The Hoople are sacred."

Jimmy acts oblivious to Paul's groaning. "You know, for the life of me, I can't figure out why this doesn't sound right."

"Because it's a capo song," Paul and I say in unison, but Paul tacks "you moron" on the end.

Jimmy laughs and wags a finger between Paul and I. "See? This is why I'm not fazed by your news." Jimmy pops the capo around the seventh fret and resumes playing. He also resumes sounding like crap. The capo may have done its job of raising the pitch, but "You forgot to tune it," Paul and I say on cue. This time I tack "you idiot" on the end. Paul just happens to add the same thing. He high-fives me, and for the first time in a long time, I have real friends.

My feet feel firmly planted as Jimmy nails that opening riff. Harrison knew what he was talking about when he said everything is all right, and I send a smile to heaven for him.

I really miss the good aspects of my former life. I used to have a great writing partner. We were no Lennon and McCartney, but we worked well together. Under different circumstances, great things could've happened.

Did I really need to give up that part of my life? I thumb the pic in my pocket that Paul just gave me, the one that is both my one hundred and twenty day chip and my gold star. It doesn't have to be one way or another, does it?

"May I?" I ask of the other guitar. Paul holds his hands out in a be-my-guest gesture, and I give it a go with Jimmy by adding in Lennon's bit. Jimmy kills the sound with the wave of his arm. "No way, man. I'm not even worthy of being in the room when you're playing, let alone you being second fiddle." He then takes off his guitar and then motions for me to switch. As humble as I want to be about it, he's right. He's more Lennon to my Harrison. That's not ego talking; it's reality. This match will do for now, but when it comes to writing, I really need to find the Lennon to my McCartney.

Lizetta's car pulls up. When she walks toward the barn, my grip on the guitar tightens, making me white knuckled. I just want us to truly be okay and to fully put the past to rest.

Lizetta's head is tilted in curiosity as to why I am here when our date isn't for another hour. I remove the guitar while remembering how the last time I held one while tense, I treated it as a shield. I won't hide behind anything when it comes to this woman. I won't even mince words. The guitar gets exchanged for her hands, and right before everyone, my eyes command her attention. "Everything okay? Are *we* okay?"

Lizetta looks to her family, and they nod in acknowledgment that I've proven there are no secrets. Her eyes get misty.

Lizetta

After leaving Jensen's last night, I spent hours talking to Mom about how she came to trust Paul. She reminded me that trust is earned through actions. Seeing Jensen here and being sure that all is out in the open with everyone is yet another way I know trust is deserved.

I've never understood drugs. Why would you put something in your body that will eventually kill you? Is it just for the quick thrill? It's so abusive. What kind of person abuses anyone, let alone themselves?

For all the times I have pondered this, last night was the first time that reality hit. On some level, it's like eating the chemicals in junk food. They hurt your body and damage your mind. It's like eating too much fried food. It clogs your arteries and causes blockages in your heart. It's all self abuse, yet because junk food is legal, prominent, and considered less hazardous, society accepts it. I've taken part in self-abuse for years. When the bullies attacked, it was easier to feed into what they were saying and become consumed in my problems then to fix myself.

I don't believe in abandoning anyone just because the going gets tough. People who care about each other stand together, unless there is good reason to run. Jensen has not given me any indication that he is putting me in danger, so beside him I will stand.

JENSEN

She sniffles, and then looks dead at me, shaking back her head in bravery. The smile that slips across her face helps me to release the breath I didn't know I was holding. "Yeah, I can honestly say we've never been better. I respect anyone who is reaching out for a second chance. Just keep showing me that I can trust you, okay?" I get another kiss, this time a sweet one on the lips. "Give me some time to clean up."

Lizetta heads to the house, and as the screen door shuts behind her, I plop onto the sofa. A spring tries to poke its way between my legs, but right now, I wouldn't care if it went up my butt. I'm just too damned relieved.

Jimmy resumes playing as Paul steps up and gives my back a double pat. "See, kid. She means it, too. You're gonna be just fine."

My thumb glides along the edge of the one hundred and twenty day, guitar pick chip. I should be proud, but I am still ashamed of my previous actions.

I also should have called Mom by now. I've got paycheck stubs gathered, print outs of my school schedule, copies of papers I've written—all ready to prove to her that I'm doing all the right things—yet I have failed to call the woman who sacrificed so much for me, which means I am just as pathetic as ever.

Not anymore.

I dig into my back pocket and don't allow myself to think of what I am doing or the pain I have caused. Instead, I dial the number and wait. A hesitant voice answers. "Jensen?"

Maybe she fears I'm calling to again belittle her parenting skills for having two fuck-ups for sons. Or maybe she is afraid that she will hear that this is the police department calling the person I've listed in my cell phone as the emergency contact. Regardless, I stare at my sobriety chip and let the words pour out—words that start with, "Mom, I'm sorry—for everything."

My tears drop at the shuddering of her breath. I need to keep the conversation going. I need to prove that my apology is real, and that it covers my every action that harmed her. "I'm sorry for all the times I came home in the middle of the night and puked on the floor. I'm sorry for the time I hit your car. I know I claimed that Bertha skidded on some grease, but I was wasted and hit the gas instead of the brake. I'm sorry for hitting you in the head with a bottle on the night you kicked me out. I'm sorry for doing my first line, because *you taught me to be better than that*." Warmth is pouring down my cheek, and the sobbing starts, for both of us. "Your voice rang in my head the entire time, and I'm sorry that I didn't listen. I'm sorry that I didn't have the courage to call you well over a month ago, when I hit ninety-one days clean." Her breath hitches. "I'm sorry that—"

"Jensen." The gentle tone that only a mother can make slips into my ears. I'm not done, but I'll stop, because she deserves the respect. She gulps. "What have you done over those one hundred and twenty days?"

My accomplishments race out so she can see that I've returned to the land of the respectable. "I'm in school, just like we always planned. I have a job assistant managing a warehouse. And as of a few weeks ago, I started making new friends. I found a sponsor, a fellow musician, and … and a really special girl that you would approve of. Mom, she's amazing, and she trusts me." I choke on the word trust. Trust from Lizetta means so much. I need it from Mom, too.

Etta barks, reminding me that she is someone who relies on me. "That was Etta. I rescued and adopted her a few weeks back. Mom, the universe works in really strange ways." That statement holds so much emotion that I can barely get it out.

"What—What happened to that other girl? To Laura."

Is the fear I sense that she'll hear Laura is still in my life, or that Laura took it too far and is no longer with us?

The words are hard to say; yet I force them anyway. "I had to leave her behind." An image of a bloody corpse on a battlefield covers my inner vision. My eyes squeeze tightly to shut it out, but it won't go away.

"Well, then," Mom says. Is that joy in her voice? *Please, God, let it be joy.* "It sounds like we have a lot of catching up to do."

My head drops, and all goes blurry from the heat that washes out of my eyes.

Thank you.

Laura

This new version of the band sucks! I take another swig out of whoever's bottle of cheap crap is sitting on the coffee table. If I'm going to suffer through this racket, I'm gonna need some help.

I can see through Jensen. He's happy now because he has his little girly; yet he's still not able to walk away from what we have to offer. What is it he wants? Obviously it's not me.

Why can't it be me? Sure, it's been ages since anyone has been able to call me sweet but … Well, Jensen knows why. Shouldn't the hell of my past get me a little bit of love? Can't he see that if only someone loved me, I'd be such a better person?

I rub out the water forming in my eyes. Staying tuff is the only thing that keeps me alive. If I gave my reality too much thought, I'd crumble.

The recording contract hinges on him, so he could probably get one on his own. Whatever the reason, he hasn't let us go nearly as much as he thinks he has.

Inside the family room, Jensen's forth replacement gives one of his signature riffs a shot. A two-year-old imitating Slash on a ukulele would be more impressive. It must take some serious talent to sound that bad. It also takes some serious alcohol to tolerate it, so I polish off the last of the vodka. All the other bottles are empty, except for some rum. I hate rum. Hopefully there's beer in the fridge.

Jensen's too far above admitting he wants to go back to his old ways. Who better to give him a push in that direction than his new girlfriend? She ditches him, he wallows back, and my world returns to normal. I just need to plant the magic seeds of doubt in her brain about trusting him. With his past antics and all the girls who can say he banged and ran, that's a freakin' cake walk. I'll also help girly find a replacement and away we go!

The fridge is empty. Damn. I'm stuck with the rum.

She's probably staying at his house. I'll head over just before dawn so I can follow her home and work from there. Easy peasy. Besides, I could use a little fun. What better way than to make a new buddy, even if I am going to screw her over and steal her man?

A bottle that I didn't notice before sits on the coffee

table. Well, what do we have here? Some kind of fancy brandy? No one here drinks this stuff. It must belong to the new guy. Wonder how I missed it? I must have been looking for the old standards.

It gets chugged down, but not before I toast the magic of the universe for bringing me a precious gift.

What's that sick smell? My head feels like little green men are having a rave in it, and that stench makes me want to puke.

I open my eyes only to slam them shut as the sun nearly blinds me. I squint hard to get past the pain, and then slowly creep them open. I'm on the sofa, but God, what is that smell?

I roll over to avoid the light. Something cold squishes when my cheek hits the cushion.

Ah, God! Puke!

Across the room, my brother laughs. "Rise and shine, lightweight! That's kind of impressive for a girl who only had a little vodka."

"Ugh! It was the swanky, French brandy that got me."

"Imported brandy? Man, you really must have hit it hard. No one around here touches that stuff."

I try to get up, but the brightness of the sun glaring in my eyes smacks me down. "What time is it?"

"One-thirty."

"In the afternoon? Shit!"

Larry laughs. He can find it funny all he wants, but I more than missed my chance to spy on Jensen's new lay. Crap!

9

Friday, June 2

JENSEN

Bertha rumbles as we pull up outside of Good Samaritan. Thoughts of Lizetta woke me before my alarm did. Now that she has accepted everything about me, I want more—a lot more.

With the turn of the key, all goes silent except the birds outside Bertha's window. I swoop up the bouquet of roses and head for Good Samaritan. The place is dark inside, so I take a seat on the concrete with my back to the wall and wait.

What do I say without sounding like some crazy guy who's begging for attention or a perv who's trying to score? I just want more with her. Is that what I should say? "Lizetta, I want more." No, that sounds like a proposal. The universe can dictate if and when that happens, but now is a little much.

Two days ago, clean test results came through—again. Ever since the condiment incident, every thirty days I've taken an AIDS test. Again it's pathetic how it took a personal threat to wake me up. With all the women who have cycled through my bed, some of whom have had very questionable morals, I should've had a test sooner for everyone's sake. After hearing about Lizetta's dad, I've made a point of telling her that even though my tests have repeatedly come back clean, there is no way that I am touching her without a hat on. I love her too much to risk hurting her.

Wow … There it is. I was wondering when that word would spring up, though I really didn't think it would be this soon.

Is dating for six weeks too soon? Why does time matter? Love is brought on by feelings and the experiences you have with a person, right? After all that we have shared, not having said those three magic words seems asinine.

A lock clicks next to my ear, startling me back into reality. A man who is built like a sixty-seven Impala, and makes me feel like a Mini Cooper, steps out. I've heard so much about Griffin yet have only met him in passing. I stand to greet him properly and find that I have to grow another four inches to face him, and no one has ever referred to me as being short. The shine coming off of the top of his head makes me feel like I am looking at a deity. Damn! His biceps are almost as wide as the sleeves on his scrubs. Lizetta said he buffs himself out so that he won't get harassed for being gay. It must work, because he is seriously intimidating. That is, until he looks to the roses, touches a hand to his heart, and gasps like Michael Jackson impersonating a little girl.

"Pink? Ah, Lover Boy, this is so sweet of you." He leans in and gives me a whisper sprinkled with fairy dust. "But in the future, if you really want to get my heart racing, red complements my eyes better." He pulls back and winks, and then shakes my hand. Now he sounds like he is impersonating Barry White. Which one is real? Maybe they're both fake. "Hey, Jensen. I'm Griffin, your hot mama's bestie. Come on in."

I take two steps then stop and look around while feeling I'm forgetting something. The flowers are already in my hand, so there's nothing else to remember.

"It's all right, honey," he says. "I have that effect on a lot of men." Griffin gives a back kick and shoulder twist, reminding me of Shirley Temple singing "On The Good Ship Lollipop". I totally get why he and Lizetta are such good friends. He's kind of freaking me out though. A person's lifestyle doesn't matter, but ever since that fateful night, homosexuals have scared the crap out of me. If there's a side of me I don't know about, that's fine, but I'd like to know—yet I also really don't want to know, which is why I'm keeping my distance.

And that's all bull because when it comes right down to it, what I am truly afraid of is how it took something selfish to wake me up. So yeah, Griffin's sexuality reminds me that I'm an asshole. I am also so in my own head that I haven't said one word to him. Say something, dork! "Yeah, between us both being so close to Lizetta, and the fact that I've been here a couple of times now, it seems like we should've at least exchanged more than hellos."

"Life can be like that sometimes," he says, followed by a soft sigh. "We can get so wrapped up in everything going on around us that we miss the little things that are more important. Happens here all the time. It might be the only thing I don't like about this place."

My muscles unclench. There it was. The relaxed demeanor with his arms at his side tells me I am now getting a taste of the real man and the voice God gave him— mellow, likely baritone but borderline bass, and not at all girly. He's just met me, and he's already warming up. It's nice to be accepted by good people.

"Anyway, your Sweet Cheeks just called and said she's on her way, which means she'll leave the house in about twenty minutes. Some lame excuse about oversleeping. You know how the womenfolk are." With that I get a manly slap on the shoulder. Griffin seems to have a well-adjusted personality crisis going on. "You want a cup of coffee? It's not very glamorous, but you can hang out in the back with me while I feed the dogs."

I can hang here for ten minutes and not be late for work. Lizetta won't make it in time, but Griffin's invitation feels like a gesture of friendship over that of politeness. I take him up on his offer to make a new friend and become more integrated in Lizetta's world.

My dreams for a normal life are coming true.

Lizetta

My untied Chucks pound on the pavement as I run into work. Thankfully, my best friend supports me by greeting me at the door with a cup of coffee.

"Girl! Where have you been?" Griffin says before slurping out of the cup. So much for my excitement over chivalrous caffeine. "Lover Muffin was at the front door when I showed up *on time* this morning. He had to go so he could get to work *on time*, but he left you those." Griffin points to my desk where a beautiful bouquet of roses sits. "As much as I like Sir Hots-a-lot, the boy has got to learn that when you go to Safeway for flowers, you remove the wrapper before giving them to a lady. I think you should forgive him though, because he had to drop them off earlier than any florist was open. Still, the boy needs a little bit of schooling. I will *never* understand straight men."

Aw. Jensen is so sweet! As if I didn't miss him enough already, now I miss him all the more.

"I gave him a bad time for not having the foresight to get a card, but he did plan on delivering them in person, you know, had you been *on time*."

Yeah, but he left a note anyway!

"You are the brightest spot to ever enter my life. Each day I realize, more and more, how much I need you. Check your voicemail."

This morning has been so crazy that I haven't turned on my phone. The second I do, there is a message from Jensen. *"Good morning, beautiful. I really wanted to ask you this in person, but ... I don't want to wait until tomorrow to see you again."* His voice softens, and I can just imagine his eyes peering up at me. *"Please come over tonight ... and stay."*

My butt hits the chair. This moment feels a year in the

making. I am so, so ready for this, yet in some ways I am not at all prepared. I have to wonder if he has ever been with a girl like me.

Looking in the mirror hasn't been the same lately. Now I see the glow in my cheeks, the specks of silver in my eyes, and hear the music when I laugh. I'm still self-conscious, but I'm no longer that scared little girl I was when Etta showed up.

But then my eyes travel downward, and I remember Laura's insults. No one's opinion is worth my loss of self, but that doesn't change the damage done.

The heck with it!

Forget you, witch. I bet you're divorced three times before you hit forty.

And with that I toss my gorgeous locks back and swing my hips with pride while heading off to work. Great things lie ahead, and I deserve them!

JENSEN

Lizetta walks out of the bathroom, wearing a baby pink nightgown. There is something about its simple elegance, and the grace of the woman underneath it, that could shame lingerie models into a corner.

The satin sways with the wiggle of each step she takes, sending my heart a flutter. This is the definition of grace. I want to treasure this image forever.

However, it's not what either of us needs.

Lizetta enters the bed, then reaches to turn off the lamp. "Oh, no you don't. Let me see the object of my desires." I roll her on top of me, raise her arms, and send the satin barrier gliding into the corner. I want her—for all that she is, inside and out.

My body turns electric as I roll her down, easing her onto the bed, and start trailing kisses downward. Lizetta reminds me of a voluptuous model—an object of Renaissance art. I want to go to a museum in Italy so a room filled with paintings of her can surround me.

The way her waist flares into glorious hips makes my hormones spark so hard they may fly out the window and jumpstart Bertha. She's radioactive. Just being near her makes me glow inside. This girl has me twisted around her finger, and I hope someone epoxies me down so she can't unwrap me.

My kisses progress downward, and she tightens her abs, sending home the message of why she wore the nightgown.

Why can't she see how much this moment means to us? This beautiful woman has earned the right to release her insecurities and know happiness. I glide up her, and the kiss we share causes my chest to deflate in ecstasy.

No, this is not just ecstasy. This is elation brought on by all that I feel for this woman, because for the first time, I'm about to make love to someone—to truly release my heart and soul. So few get to know what that means, and that joy is happening to me. I am blessed, privileged, and humbled by the honor of being with her, but I too have earned this. I've fought to become a better person, to be worthy of someone as beautiful as she is, and I am so incredibly grateful. This overwhelming bliss is what we deserve, and I won't lose sight of its significance, nor will I let her.

Our eyes lock, and warmth fills me from within. It slides into my soul like honey, causing me to brazenly confess, "For the first time, I've fallen, and it's deeper than I ever imagined possible. I love you, Lizetta."

Lizetta smiles, and a little laugh of amazement seeps out. I seem to have caught her off guard. Good. I don't like how she's trying to hide herself, and she needs to know that she is exactly what I want. She says the words back, and I'm just so damned happy at how wonderful my life has become that I want to howl for the world to hear.

With a flick of the wrist, my boxers land to cover the glare coming from the lamp, casting just enough glow for both of us to enjoy the moment. Tonight we cave to the fact that there is something greater than we can fathom at work.

Lizetta

Jensen drifts off to sleep, and I slip into the bathroom. While standing in front of the mirror, I close my eyes and flip on the light. I'm daring myself to take a serious look at what Jensen just saw. While he didn't say a word about knowing why I wanted to kill the lights, his expression indicated I might be in for a pep talk over my insecurities.

Just like Jensen and his demons, this is a battle that I need to fight alone. For years, others have tried to sell me on a new self-image, but time and again I've chosen only to listen to Laura's taunting and the self-doubt it brings.

Slowly my eyes peer open, taking myself in from the bottom up. My calves aren't bad, but my thighs—Oh Lord!

My eyes slam shut. I don't want to do this.

Okay, try it again.

Light slips through the cracks of my lids. My thighs could definitely use some trimming. Then again … I twist at the hip, and a sleek curve jets from the back of my knee, up my tush, and to the top of my hip. You know, that's not half bad.

"Not half bad" is a terrible way to describe myself. I have got to get a better self-image. Tonight, when Jensen wrapped his arms around me, my brain told me those arms needed to stretch; yet his hands were centered on my back with his elbows hanging at my side. I hate that side of myself—the side that constantly screams the lie that I am bigger than I am. That side shuts its trap, starting right this second! Now, what is a more eloquent way to state what I see?

I twist back so that I am dead on in the mirror again. It's hard not to cringe, but I win the battle.

Deep breath. Okay. Try again.

My thighs flow into hips that crest like waves of the ocean. Little ripples appear at the widest points before the waves rush up, reaching for each other to form my waist and then surging into glorious breasts that I wouldn't trade for anything.

There, that wasn't so hard. In fact, it sounded pretty fantastic.

It's time to force myself to see reality. I'm not a size two, and there is no baggy covering that will hide that fact. Do I want to be a size two? Would it matter if I were?

No, but I should be able to say my size without hating myself.

Okay, here it goes.

I'm a size fourteen—a perfect fourteen, which is exactly the same as most plus-sized models. It is also the average size of the American woman. It's not that big, yet the fashion industry messes with our heads so we think it is. You also can't judge a size by its number, because some manufactures alter them for the sake of vanity. The size on a label often means nothing. However, if you take a tape measure to me, I'm model perfect.

For years I have thought of myself as ugly because I chose to listen to what some people told me. Their hang-ups are their problem, not mine. Bodies are not ugly. Being unhealthy is ugly. Not caring about whom you are inside is ugly. Not long ago I ate nothing but burgers and fries. While there are times that I still indulge, I now censor what enters my body, because I love myself. *That* makes me beautiful.

I'm changing. I've come to recognize that my heart is big, and now, inside this mirror, I see what beauty looks like. It is amazing what you see when you find new perspective. I can only dream what other fantastic things lie ahead!

With a flick of the switch, I finish leaving a part of my old self behind, and head back to my future—my *bright* future.

10

Wednesday, June 14

Lizetta

Jensen's been looking a little shifty since I arrived at his apartment. It's especially weird because ever since we spent our first night together, a couple of weeks ago, he's been nothing short of adoring. Not a single lunch break or drive to or from school has gone without a call ending in him saying I love you, and not a moment together has been lacking in kisses and caresses. Overall, I feel worshiped. However, the walk on the way to Bert's was another story, not to mention that this is our usual, cook-at-home night. Something is up.

"So, uh. There's a special reason why I wanted to come here tonight. It's um, it's pretty important."

"You want to ask me something big, so you brought me to Bert's? Oh, that's right. Allowing yourself to steal fries is big. Healthier eating or not, do you have any idea how crazy I think that sounds?"

"I'm not talking about fries." His thumbs keep spinning in little circles around each other—faster, slower, faster, slower.

"Then you won't be having any?"

"In your dreams!"

Thankfully, he is still acting like himself when it comes to fries, but then his eyes get shifty again.

"I have to ask you something, and I'm a little nervous about it."

My gaze darts to his hands—empty. They then go to his shirt pocket, which is non-existent. The ring must be in his pants' pocket.

Wait. A ring? Already? We've only been dating two months. Isn't that a little soon?

Forget the perception of time, I'm saying yes! Sweet sugar dumplings! Short courtship, long engagement, here I come!

His grip on my hands tightens. Shouldn't he be getting down on one knee? I'll settle for a proposal in a burger joint, only because we had our first date here, but I at least need a ring or him down on one knee. Seriously though, ring or not, how could I refuse this man?

"I want you to meet my mom," he says.

"What?" screeches out of me. Regret quickly hits. My response was cold, but is he really freaking out over me meeting his mom?

"Come on, it won't be that bad. We're not meeting the Pope." He takes a second to think about that. "Huh. Would you even care if you met the Pope?"

This conversation is weird. At least the freak out made him unclench a little. "Of course I would care. Giant things scare me."

"Giant like important or giant like large? I didn't think he was that tall."

"His huge hat freaks me out, kind of like The Statue of Liberty."

Jensen's brow scrunches. "The crown on The Statue of Liberty scares you?"

My hands fly as I rant, cause, well, "No, the whole freaking statue does—especially that face. It's already kind of creepy, and then they had to go and make it huge. Whenever I'm in Vegas, I have to stay away from that fake one for fear it's going to come to life and step on me—or worse, come crashing down. I don't want my last vision to be of a giant nose descending to snort me up."

Finally, he leans back in his chair like he normally would. Still, I'm not buying that me meeting his mom is what has him all rigid. "You've seen too many movies," he tells me.

"Don't sound so surprised by that obvious fact. Does

this body look like it does much other than crash out on a sofa?"

"Well, not to worry. My mom is short. Wear heels and you'll tower over her. You will in no way feel that she is The Statue of Liberty."

"Wrong!" I let my hands fly to the sky in hopes that the more animated I become, the more he will relax; yet he stays locked up.

"Wrong, how?"

"If my son brought home a girl, I'd likely have a torch in my hand. Face it, Jensen, I'm screwed."

He chuckles at me. It's about time. "Does meeting my mom scare you that much?" he asks.

"Don't be ridiculous. I've been dying to meet your family." I've also been dying to see that painting his mom did—the one that matches both my dream and that Tarot reading. "It's just that you are not your usual self. The last time this happened, I got some pretty bad news. If this is really as simple as meeting your mom, I think you'd be a lot less affected."

Jensen takes my hand, but instead of the sweet smile he normally gives, his eyes lock on my fingers. "I swear that I've given you all the bad news there is. Thing is," he takes a deep breath, like really deep, "I can't forgive myself for hitting her with that bottle. Hell, I don't even know how I can face her. But mending our relationship will bring me as full circle as I can get. I've faced everything else alone, but for this I really need some support. Also, with you fully integrated into my life, I'll be in a better space than I have ever been. If I take Monday off, you can still work Saturday and go with me for your weekend. Please? It's really important."

He has to know I would never say no. "Of course, but why did you need to bring me here to ask?"

Jensen dips his head and gives me the most adorable glance. "I love how your hair glistens in the light here."

"Here? You mean, *outdoors*?" Then the obvious checks

me to the boards. "Oh my God! You do just want fries!"

That's it! If we ever get married, I'm making him vow to love, honor, and keep his grubby hands on his own food.

11

Sunday, June 25

JENSEN

This is ridiculous. It's my mom, for God's sake. The facts that the last time I saw her I told her to go to hell while putting a dent in her head, and that I chose drugs over her, are making this pathetic bastard shaky. Actually, even with us having already talked it out, I should be on my knees while begging for forgiveness.

I knock, and then wait while my insides spasm. Never again. Never again will I put myself in this type of position.

Heels click from behind the door, causing my jitters to intensify.

We've already talked it out. I flat out asked for forgiveness, and she, in no uncertain terms, granted it. Now it's just a matter of seeing each other in person. The hard part is done, right?

Then why does it feel like I'm about to meet my maker?

Well, Mom is my maker, but still—

The lock clicks, and I expect Mom to peer through a crack to make sure it's safe. I wouldn't blame her in the least. If she doesn't answer with a baseball bat in her hands, it will be a miracle.

The swing of the door creates a breeze, and I find myself facing a beautiful woman who looks slightly apprehensive. She gives me a full body once over and then focuses into my eyes. A smile comes. She recognizes me this time. She didn't before. Hell, *I* didn't recognize myself before.

The whole sizing-me-up thing takes fewer than two heartbeats, and then she's out the door and yanking me into her arms. I've made it! I've come full circle! All my hard work is being rewarded!

Thank you, God. Even if her anger surfaces and she chews me out for everything that I did, which she would be totally justified in doing, I'm good.

 Lizetta

Jensen's mom clings to him while mouthing, "It's a miracle. It's nothing short of a miracle." Watching Arlene's fingers as they dig into her son's back, like she's afraid to let go, drives home the magnitude of all that happened. When she does release him, she looks straight into his eyes. She's crying so hard that the words barely come out. "Yeah, that's my boy. I've missed him."

"Mom, I am so sorry for—"

"You've already said it, and I've already accepted it. Now I just want to see my son and get to know this woman who means so much."

The tight cling I am drawn into forces me to accept that the demons that once possessed Jensen are real. Visions of my father passed out on the floor after my mom clocked him with a skillet flash before me. *"People can change,"* Paul has always said. *"I'm living proof. Just be careful, because we are human, which means we can screw up, too."* Why do his warnings still sneak up on me? I guess he just taught me well.

The smell of lemons and freshly baked cookies hits me as I step into the house. Yumm! I will totally forgo healthy eating for one of those!

To the right, an unheard voice beckons my attention. The presence is warm, yet its call sends shivers up my spine. Just two steps away hangs destiny. While Jensen and Arlene are locked in another hug, I make way to the artistic interpretation of my dreams. My lips part as I stare and try to decipher the image. It turns my heart weightless with joy, yet my forehead aches from being smacked with fear. How well this image matches both my dream and that Tarot reading seems unreal.

A beam of light bursts into the room, and then disappears. My heart races at what feels like a flash of lightning. The Tarot reading! The lightening bolt on The Tower card!

The front door clicks shut, and I turn to find myself alone and feeling stupid for being frightened by sunlight that seeped through the door when it was opened. I look back to the painting and my stomach twists. What does it all mean? Arlene painted this for Jensen, so one of them must be tied into the meaning behind my dream. The light flares again as Jensen and Arlene return from grabbing our bags out of Bertha.

Arlene invites us into the family room for cookies and lemonade. I follow, walking away from the painting, yet feeling drawn backward into fate.

The photos on the family room wall repeatedly catch my eyes, but my inner vision is all kinds of murky. I want to pay closer attention to Arlene's funny stories of Jensen as a child and the pranks his family would play on each other, but only one thing is on my mind. "Arlene, Jensen told me you painted the starlit landscape in the foyer. What inspired it?"

Arlene sips her lemonade and reclines in her chair, yet I expect dramatic music to fill the background at my inquiry of forbidden knowledge. I've seen too many soap operas.

"It came from a dream that Dad had when Jensen was little. Maybe it was because Native Americans can become captivating when we talk about visions, but the way Dad told it made it seem so significant that I wanted to capture it."

"I miss Granddad," Jensen says with downcast eyes, "but I am kind of grateful that he missed all of the bad things that happened. Eddie and I really let him down."

Arlene touches her hand to his arm. "Honey, we are past that now, remember?"

He squeezes her hand, and his eyes gaze to her in earnest.

"There are some things I'll never get over, but I want it that way. Sometimes remembering you were once an idiot can keep you from becoming one again. Just because I've found my way home doesn't mean there isn't more for me to learn." Jensen looks to a photo on the wall of a man and two boys. The man has that same air of dignity and strength that I saw in Jensen the day we met. I take Jensen's hand and give him a smile. He forces one back.

I'm being selfish. As much as that painting haunts me, it was done for Jensen. Maybe there is something in there that can help him move forward. "Arlene, do you know what the vision meant?"

Arlene speaks directly to Jensen. "The ground represents the paths we walk every day. Some patches bring us happiness, others blight. Sometimes you have to walk through the bad to get to the good."

He nods while giving a little smirk. I hope I can keep his smile building. "What about those stars?" I ask. "Why are the center ones so bright? Is it his future?"

Arlene's demeanor goes through an odd transformation. She sets down her glass with care and blinks slowly once, then again. It's how I might look if I were pondering the meaning of life. "Dad said, Jensen will have two sources of light that are heaven sent. The first he would stumble across, and that would be the one to ground him. It would then return to the center of the sky so spirits could be released to their full potentials. Though he is never to seek them out, he is always to be open and to accept them for what they bring into his world."

"Sounds like Lizetta and Etta to me," Jensen says.

Yes! This makes so much sense! The Tower was Etta on the side of the road. Jensen stumbled across her, and she became the grounding force that led him to me. Simple.

But if the grounding force returns to the sky, doesn't that mean death? That sounds really bad for Etta. Maybe we should have brought her with us.

What am I thinking? She's safe as can be with Griffin,

and her health is improving everyday.

I reach for a cookie when a centipede crawls up my spine. There is no bug, but that doesn't stop me from scratching. The night Jensen told me about his past, he said that I ground him. Then it was a beautiful thing to hear. Now the memory freaks me out. If I am the one who grounds him, who is the other woman? In my dream she claims glory, meaning Jensen and I are doomed.

Nah! Etta is both the first woman and The Tower. It's simple.

Yeah, if it's so simple, why did a pang just grip through my gut? And why is Arlene shifting in her seat? "Did your father say anything else?" I ask.

Her brow scrunches. "Come to think of it, he had me do something odd with the ground. Then he rattled on about how it held the key to the prophecy."

"Prophecy?" That word is freaking the living monkey poo out of me. "Your dad didn't say when all this might happen, did he?"

"Umm … Not that I remember. I wanted to write it down, but he said that since he saw it in a vision, only the vision should remain." Arlene cocks her head, then shakes it. I feel like she is dismissing a thought. Suddenly her hand smacks the arm of her chair. "I just thought of another funny story! One morning, Dad turned back Eddie's clock by an hour. Once he was ready for school, Eddie realized what time it really was and went back to bed. Then Dad reset everything to the exact position it had been in before Eddie woke. When the alarm went off again, Dad convinced him that he dreamt getting up. Dad would have gotten away with it too, if Eddie hadn't shaved the first time around."

Jensen laughs at the memory, and I do my best to play along. "Jimmy would freak if I did that to him!" Ugh! Why can't she give me something concrete? The cards were right. I'm going to die, but it will be because all this stressing out will cause a brain hemorrhage.

I finally get a bite of a Rocky Road cookie. It's flavorless to me. In my mind, that just reinforces there is something very, very wrong.

Laura

It's dark as sin as I leave the house. If Jensen's home, I'm gonna hang out there—again—and see if I can catch *her*.

My heels remind me of a pounding hammer as I head for the car. I miss the click of stilettos. The heels on these boots I found at the thrift store are clunky, but at least they are tall and way better than combat boots. Now I feel less like a dork.

The streetlights around here suck. I can't see shit as I fumble through my keys while on the approach to my car. The toes of my right foot step on something thick and soft, and my ankle twists out. Shit! My left foot trips over the heel of my right. I throw my arms out, but my right elbow smacks the pavement. Fuck, that hurts!

Massaging my throbbing ankle does nothing to ease the pain. I catch sight of what tripped me and scamper up. "Holy shit!" It's some furry, dead thing. Gah! Is that a rat?

I put my weight on my left foot, and then kick the thing with my right. Fucking shit that hurt! The thing sails into the light.

I hobble over and look down at the stuffed pig that has likely sprained my ankle. How the fuck am I going to drive over there now? Crap, I need a drink!

12

Tuesday, July 4

Laura

Larry has his ass firmly planted on the sofa while watching *Attack of The Killer Tomatoes*, smoking weed, and drinking Jack. I wish there were another way to get what he's got. A respectable job, another source—anything so that I don't have to beg him for the fix I don't need. Thankfully, it only took a few days for my ankle to heal; else I'd really be in a state.

I only allow myself to use that stuff on the weekend. Even though it is a Tuesday, it's a holiday and some people took yesterday off. That makes today part of a long weekend.

Larry doesn't even look at me when I step up to him. His eyes stay on the TV as he hands me the goods. I reach out, and he yanks it back. "Talk to Jensen recently?"

"No. He's made it clear that he's finished with both of us, so I'm done." I am so not done. I just want to do this my way, because Larry's way sucks.

He tucks my fix under his butt. "Yes, you are."

Shit. I've got nothing. No fix. No money. Not even a leaf of weed or a shot of booze.

He fakes a sigh of pity. "Well, I suppose there is another way."

Now I get eye contact, just before his eyes go to his zipper. "Oh, hell no!" Related or not, the guy is vile. I'm not touching that rod of syphilis for anything.

He shrugs it off with a laugh. "Maybe you should pay your ex a visit then. You get him back, the band gets to sign on the dotted line, the money rolls in, and you get a modest salary as backstage manager. Simple. Else …"

His eyes go back to his zipper. Gross! "What the hell am I supposed to do that I haven't already done?"

He looks to his pants again.

"I've already tried that with him. How about you let me come up with a real plan?"

Larry shrugs and unzips his pants. I make for the door, and I swear to God, I still hear his laughter as I drive off.

I don't know what makes me more of an idiot—wanting a fix, considering succumbing to Larry for it, or watching the outside of my ex-boyfriend's apartment while trying to get the courage to exit the car. I still have no idea what type of car his girlfriend drives, but the only car I see here is Jensen's monstrosity. That thing is the sickest color Satan ever puked up.

This is so not going to work. Why am I even bothering with this lame attempt?

Because Larry has what I want. There. I admitted it. Big whoop! If this fails, then I'll go back to my plan to become besties with whatever piece of trampitude Jensen is banging.

I make for the stairs. What do I say? "If you don't come back to the band so they can sign that contract, *if* the record company still gives a crap after all this time, I'll keep being used like a blow-up doll by your former friends?" Better yet, how about the truth. "Dammit, Jensen, I loved you. Your leaving turned me into a mess. That little experiment we did with heroin is now a lifestyle for me. Please help, because without you I may not make it."

Now I'm on to something. I started earning his trust last time. I'll stick with the truth, because now that he has seen that I can be on his side, maybe he will believe me when I tell him that I need his help.

I don't need his help. I need Larry's.

Fuck, I need Jensen's help.

Shit, when am I going to accept that I just plain need help?

I'm about to hit the first stair when the door opens. Jensen steps out with that mutt of his.

JENSEN

Etta and I plan to go for a quick bathroom walk before heading off to Lizetta's for what Paul called a *family* barbecue—just him, Lizetta, Jimmy, Judy, and me. Naturally, I'm to bring Etta, because, as Paul said, "Lizzie would roast us both if you don't. Besides, I think she sees it as a celebration now that Etta's all healed up."

Once I cross the threshold, a woman in what can hardly be called a mini-skirt and long sleeved T-shirt with half of if ripped away to show her skeleton heads up the steps. Ah, shit! Laura. But long sleeves? Ten bucks says she's gotten so sloppy about her habit that she shooting into her arms now.

Etta gets sent back inside, even though I really want to ask her to sink her teeth into Laura's throat. Thing is, I'm so embarrassed by this girl that I don't even want Etta to know I talked to her.

Laura glances up at me, and every bit of joy inside me shatters on the ground. God help her, she looks used and discarded. My gut twists at her sight, but because her shallow eyes and weathered skin scream heroin, I can't let her near me. "Stop. Stop right there."

She halts, and those empty eyes lock into mine. I take one step down, and then two more, then stop. I'm two steps away from taking her into my arms and begging her to stop using. I want her to move in with me so I can watch over her. I want to become her savior. But none of that can happen, because if I get near this girl, I will compromise myself, and I will lose every gain I've spent months making.

Why is it that everything always comes down to me being selfish? I quit using for selfish reasons, I freaked out over Eddie while talking to Lizetta because it could have been me who was killed, and now this. Being selfish now may be justified, but it still breaks my heart. "Whatever it is you came for, the answer is no." I don't even give myself the option of thinking further about it before heading back inside and locking the door. My new family can wait until my old hell is long gone before I leave this apartment—which is again, selfish.

Goodbye, Laura. My heart bleeds for you, but I can't tell you that, or I'll crumble.

Laura

The door shuts behind him. It's not the respectful click of last time, nor is it the quiet walking away of when he left. It's a slam—a loud, punctuating slam. It happened without a hello or a how are you. We were two steps away from each other when he turned his back on me, again.

I take two steps forward and whimper out the plea I should have made before he shut the door. "Help me. Please. I can't find the strength to stop abusing myself."

Jensen has left me no choice but to take those two steps back, and then several more while accepting that I may soon fall. He could not have made it any clearer. We're done—for good.

Tears burn my eyes so hard that I can barely see the road. With nowhere to go, I sit in my car outside of the place I used to call home. It's now hell, and it's the last place I want to be.

I want to be safe at home.

Home isn't safe.

I slip off to the liquor store and abuse the tab Larry has for when he sends me on runs. I park in a shaded spot a block from my house, crawl into the backseat, and wait for seemingly endless hours in the summer heat. My hand goes to the door, and then retracts. Again I try to sleep. How much time will pass before I start to cave again? An hour? Five minutes? I unlock the door, and then lock it again. I drink more before trying to sleep off what my brain is screaming for me to do. He was kidding, right? He would just give it to me. I wouldn't have to …

Why should he be different? I have to do it with everyone else.

Again I go to open the door. Could I really do it? It's just a blowjob. It wouldn't be the first time I closed my eyes and dreamt I was elsewhere.

I chug, and then try to sleep again.

I keep playing the game until I pass out. When I wake, it's no longer the weekend, and I have three more days to find a new trick with Larry so that I can load up again.

13

Saturday, July 8

JENSEN

It is dusk. This field is the same place that I always go when I need to think, only this time the grass looks more like streaks than blades. I must be dreaming about Mom's painting that now sits in my living room. "This is a part of you, Jensen. It belongs in your home."

The deep blue sky is partially obscured by clouds. I catch a glimpse of golden hair as a figure dashes past and into the distance.

Lizetta!

I'm on my feet and running towards her, yet she is already out of view. The sun begins to set. As the sky grows dark, its texture changes from a three-dimensional eternity to a wall of brushstrokes. Stars pop into the night sky, as if being dabbed on.

Did I imagine Lizetta? My body quakes at the thought of even a moment where she isn't real.

The sky loses its brushstrokes and becomes clear again. Footsteps race up from behind, and I turn in hopes of greeting my love—but it's not her.

Laura has always made my brain hazy, and in my dream, it's no different. The closer she gets, the more my heart races. It must be fear of what she represents, but as her lips approach mine, I can't help but cave.

"No!" my brain screams. "You cannot succumb, no matter how much you love her." Bliss consumes me. My bones melt, and I collapse. Laura looks down, and with her building smile, crackling erupts from her skull. Rubble falls, and a needle rises out of her brain. Golden light beams from her eyes and engulfs me. A silver tail trails behind as I sail upward, but my body turns gray and shatters when it drops to the ground. Medusa has reduced me to stone.

Laura runs into the distance. Her arms are open to the world while she twirls like a kite and is raised high into the wind. I'm yanked up and pulled behind her, destined for the stars.

The sensation of being pulled jerks me awake while gasping for air. Etta goes up on all fours with her ears up while fully alert and sensing threat. There may actually be one, because when I look down, a part of me is standing up and saying hello. "Don't even think about it. There is no way you are entering that Pandora's box again. We've got it way too good now."

The sheet becomes a towel for my perspiration before I roll to a cooler spot. The red glow of the alarm clock tells me that it is three thirty in the morning. Fear still runs through me. I need to hear Lizetta's voice and know that she is not an apparition, but it's far too early to call.

That's crazy. This love thing is constantly proving it's deeper than I think.

My body sinks back into the bed. I'll focus on something else. The field was peaceful. I'll put myself back there.

My mind lays me down in a sea of green and wildflowers. I imagine drifting away …

I spring alert. My brain told me that I love Laura.

No, that can't be right. That has to be caused by the guilt of telling her to go away without letting her get a word in.

But in my mind, I kissed her. My body reacted.

She also turned into a syringe and injected me with bliss.

It must have been a warning. That's all. And guilt. I feel guilty for pushing her away again, but I had to do it for self-preservation. Still …

I settle into the bed, then get edgy and toss over, then do it again. I look down at the reason. "I don't know what got you started, but you are on your own."

Still, he won't let me sleep.

Self-embitterment groans out as I head for the living

room. Etta stays behind. Smart dog. I don't even want to be around me right now.

With my trusty axe in hand, I whip through some Stones and some Zep to loosen up, and then zip through some of my favorite, self-written gems. They sound pretty good.

Now that I'm back among the sane, I pull out my latest endeavor, a song for Lizetta. I'm so close, but I can't get it to work. The melody is a mess—but it's not. The chord progression is wrong—but it's not. I need help—serious, freaking help.

Five hours later, I place a call and pray I can make magic happen.

How loudly Bertha's door slammed when I arrived at Lizetta's reflected a lot of things. One of them is how pissed I still am with myself for what happened with Larry over a month ago. Forgiveness for my stupidity is not an option. What did I hope to accomplish that was so important that it was worth risking everything for? After that dream last night, I think I know, and it is not cool.

Another reason for my edginess lies in approaching Jimmy. He actually stammered when I called and asked if he wanted to hang out and play today. Shoot, his voice even cracked, reminding me of a pubescent boy, when he said, "Sure!" I've got to tread lightly with my intentions. He deserves that.

The way my brain is flying reminds me of being on coke. That's the level of agitation I'm trying to conceal. I don't want Jimmy to know that I am looking for someone to be Lennon to my Harrison and get his hopes up. Not only is he the brother of the woman I'm realizing I need like air, but I refuse to return to being a selfish bastard with a devil-may-care-so-screw-you attitude.

It's amazing how much space is in this barn when the Bel Air is out. The more time I spend here—surrounded by the tools of the gearhead trade, memorabilia from old gas stations, and a sofa that looks like putting it in a dumpster would show it mercy—the more I wonder what is in store for Lizetta and me. Will I have a life like Paul's? Surrounded by nice things and the need for a man cave such as this haven? I'm surprisingly cool with that. In fact, after the hellhole I lived in with the band, "domestic tranquility" has a beautiful ring to it.

Jimmy and I give harmonizing on "Rain" a shot. We sound surprisingly listenable. So far, I've only suggested playing Beatles' songs because they are such church-worthy deities around here that if we played "Good Morning", the chickens and dogs in the backyard would probably chime in at the right spots. Jimmy deserves every advantage possible during this stealth audition.

Jimmy's singing is a little sharp. It could be the nerves that have his words speeding out, or he could be feeding off of my anxiety. Instead of pointing it out by encouraging him to relax, I goof it a bit so I have an excuse to correct us both. While we don't nail it like The Fab Gods would, it's close enough for today. Fresh air seems to breeze in as I see that this arrangement might work.

We get a little more daring. Our rendition of "Everybody's Got Something to Hide Except Me and My Monkey" sounds halfway decent—that is, until Jimmy tries to mirror me doing Harrison's licks. It sucks—like big time. He can't keep up the pace, but that is fine because I just need a rhythm guy. He can easily handle that.

Jimmy is insistent that he gives it another shot. He takes a seat on the sofa, grabs determination, and dives in. As much as I respect that, his second time sucks too. He still has no idea what is going on, yet he tries again, like he wants to impress me—and he is. It's unfortunate that it hasn't helped his playing. It's also making it hard for me to finish relaxing. He then gets this crazy air about him where he kicks his dweeby self in the ass and mans up. It sucks considerably less. This kid knows how to earn respect.

The fourth time, he stands, grabs a stance, and nails the riff! Like, dead freaking on! Then he nails it again, and again. We start getting creative, and soon we've re-arranged the saints known as The Beatles. We're so good at changing it up together that I'm half afraid Judy's going to run out here with a knife and off me for blasphemy.

I'm going for the impossible. If I can find someone to compose with, I'll be golden. I don't know which is getting me more riled, not being able to finish a song or how it drove me to re-expose myself to Larry's world. The memory of that stupidity makes me tense to the point where my face gets stern, and I roll my neck and shoulders. Now that he's come into his own, Jimmy sees through me and puts down the guitar. "Hey, man, you okay?" He's got that suspicious, sideways look he and Paul get when they want the straight truth and don't you dare give them a line of baloney. What I fear he really means is, what are you on?

Not cool.

I try to play it casual by leaning against the workbench. "Do me a favor. Put the guitar back on and try something for me." Jimmy cocks his head. I can't avoid the question for long, but he nods, telling me that he'll see where this is going. There is that second chance thing rearing its head. "Listen to this." I slip him a few bars of the song I've been working on. It's the first love song that I've ever written.

Huh. Maybe it's not me that's the problem. Maybe it's the building realization that my feelings are out of control. Being in love is one thing, but the intensity at which I am feeling it is another.

When I reach the place that keeps stumping me, my head rattles. "I can't put a finish on it. I'm missing a critical puzzle piece." I scrub my scalp in frustration. It reminds me of a junky itching for a fix. The truth is, I don't want a simple finish because a song that represents feelings like I have for Lizetta requires something special.

Jimmy's tension over playing with me has stepped aside so that a greater concern for my health can waltz in. That's bad. I'm not cranked out; I'm just lost. I try to emphasize how serious I am by giving him the bars one more time, and then shoot a look requesting help that I hope doesn't make me look like a scared little girl. Seriously, I need to get past this hurdle.

He strums a few cords like he's just trying to appease me enough so that we can talk about whatever the real problem is and—

Holy, God! What did he pull that tune out of?

He starts to remove the guitar strap.

"No. Play that again." He re-shoots me the notes with a scrunched face that screams he is doing it so we can move on to talking. It sounds like angels guided his fingers. "That's perfect!" And it really is. Now that the kid's head is in a different space, he's golden. That's what I need. I'm a different person now. Everything needs to be approached differently. Music is no exception.

"All right, Jensen, you better level with me, because something weird is going on with you."

I set my axe down and look straight at him. If I'm going to expose myself, I'm doing it fully. "I've come to understand that one of the reasons why I was always wasted was because I couldn't find balance. After watching my brother die, I threw myself into a band of junkies instead of getting the emotional support I needed. When I walked away from them, I put myself at zero. Then I met Lizetta. She helped my emotions balance, but that did nothing to bring back the other half of my soul that had been torched out. Do you realize what you just did?" He shifts his eyes like he's afraid to find out. I'm surprised my excitement hasn't clued him in. "You went on instinct and nailed something I've struggled with for weeks."

His eyes go from stern and concerned to wide. He gets it. A smile creeps across Jimmy's face, and I can swear the kid is starting to blush. I feel like an idolized God, and it's damn cool. It also makes me choose my words carefully. There is no need to go into the part about really attempting to compose together yet. Even though we may be onto something, once I come down from the stress-induced high, I may ask myself what the hell I was thinking. "We have the potential to work well together. Do you want to start up a band?"

Jimmy's face goes from red to white. He jets out his chin like he's sizing me up. "You're serious. Like, you're really serious."

"Yeah, I am." I take a seat on the sofa, that longs to send springs up my butt, because I want to really talk to the guy, like true friends. "You should know something else. I'm just as serious about Lizetta." As soon as the words come out the pressure in my veins releases, and my brain says, "Ahh ..." It's really going to suck if Jimmy says no.

He's not going to say no.

Then again, he hasn't said yes.

His steps toward the sofa are hesitant. Slowly he sits, implying he is uncertain about pretty much everything right now. "You really think I'm good enough to play in a band? With you?"

I shrug. "Why not? You were able to pick up the pieces on that song, and you only partially suck at singing." I give him the typical nudge that shows I am joking.

"Yeah, I'm totally stuck on rhythm guitar, aren't I?"

"Oh, hell yes! There's no way you're touching lead with this wizard around."

His features go deadpanned. "Can I at least name the band?"

This kid is killing me. "Oh yeah, sure. We'll be known as Jimmy and The Frickin' Rainbows! That'll bring in the chicks."

He leans back and crosses his arms, still playing with me. "Hey, you just told me my sister has you whipped, which, by the way, has been *blindingly obvious* for months, so you can forget about other *chicks*. And while we are on the subject, I would not exactly be heartbroken if she moved. I've been dying to get my hands on her room."

My smile gets so big I must look like a cartoon cat that found some lasagna to scarf. I don't think the song my heart is beating out can get much happier, but then Jimmy proves me wrong. "Yeah, man. You're on." And with a firm handshake, we put the finish on it.

Now it is time to take on the really scary battle of the day. I hoped that working with Jimmy would get my mind off of last night but ...

Why would I have a dream about Laura that makes me wake with a hard on? Not being able to find Lizetta was about as scary as Laura turning into a huge needle. Still, why would I wake in a way that—

No. I can't possibly still want Laura.

I look down to my zipper.

Can I?

My head slams back against Bertha's headrest, bringing Laura's house into view. If I wanted to see Laura, I'd be knocking on the door or have parked in the driveway where the roar of Bertha's engine could command attention. Instead, I'm halfway down the street, tucked between two cars. Laura would have to come outside to see me.

Please come outside.

No! Don't! Stay inside, or away, or wherever the hell you are. Don't see me!

My hand is on the key and about to turn over the ignition when I stop and drop it to my lap. No running. I'm going to face this. I face four beers in my fridge each day to remind me that I am stronger than they are. I've earned the right to have a good life and am embracing that, so I can certainly face this last hurdle. There is a hold on me here, and I need to escape it.

I kissed Laura in my dream last night. I kissed her, and it felt amazing. It was bliss. Pure, unadulterated bliss—just like heroin.

A needle came out of her head, and I died. Even just a moment with her can take away every gain I've gotten—the perfect woman, my mom back, a second family, and a new partner. So why am I here, risking it all?

Because I don't want to admit what I still want.

The last time I saw that garage, I pulled my stuff from there and bailed without looking back—or so I've told myself.

Though Bertha was packed to her headliner, she felt empty. That is, until the corner of my eye caught the passenger seat. Then my heart jumped forward in an attempt to escape my chest.

In the seat sat an amp and a bunch of cables, yet the way it was loaded reminded me of a person. "Laura," I whispered.

The guilt of abandoning her on the floor like a heap of laundry pulsed through me. Pain came to my forehead from it meeting the steering wheel, and out poured the tears. Laura had once been such a natural beauty. The day we met, she stole my breath, despite the fact that my brain yelled that she was bad news. It's been nearly two years, and my head still screams it, yet I remember how her eyes shined like shooting stars that I wanted to catch. To this day, even with all of the ugliness she has shown, that is how I picture her.

I pulled out of the driveway, about to go back for her, but as soon as I started to turn the wheel, I jerked it in the opposite direction. The movement was so swift that I'm still not sure that I was the force that moved it.

Laura, I'm sorry. You are a star in your own right, but my guilt for leaving you behind has to end. It's not you I'm hot for; it's for another taste from that needle you stuck in my arm. That stuff is so bad that sometimes once is all it takes to get you panting for more. I hate you for what you did, but I also love you. I'll stop lying to myself about that, but loving you does not make you the woman for me. I never told you how I felt because I knew we'd end either by my leaving or my dying. If there ever was any hope for us, you killed it when you stuck that needle in my arm.

I thought I had come full circle when I made amends with Mom, but I was wrong. Now is when I finish facing everything. My declaration is stated out loud, because I want to absorb every bit of this moment as deeply as possible. "Goodbye, Laura. Most of all, goodbye, heroin. I won't let the urge to try you again ever sway me into nightmares, or let it draw me back here. I am stronger than you, and you will never be capable of giving me the happiness that I have given myself."

Bertha and I make our escape. We're rounding the corner when I hear The Beatles playing "Blackbird", Lizetta's ring tone. Her timing drives home what I already know; my future is calling. I've finished leaving behind the crap and am flying into the light of the life I have earned. I hit the speaker button and tell Lizetta I'm driving towards my angel. I'll hang out in the lobby of Good Samaritan for hours if it means catching a glimpse of her.

Happiness radiates from me. I am on the right road.

My foot depresses the pedal and—and—

Nothing.

Bertha stalls. Just like that. Bam! She stalls on me. White smoke blankets my view from the rear view mirror. Yeah, nothing will stop Lizetta and I, except maybe a blown gasket a few blocks away from Laura's house. Roadside assistance better come fast and get us out of here. How would I even begin to explain this if I ran into one of the wasteoids that float in and out of that house?

This is the problem with trusting the universe. Sometimes you can't be sure if you are getting a mixed message, or if you are just the victim of bad luck.

Screw this madness! I'm taking matters into my own hands.

Bertha's door gets slammed after I step out. That was

dumb. I need that open.

I yank the door so hard that I'm surprised that I don't dislocate my shoulder. Then I grab the wheel with my right hand, place my left on her frame, and push.

The strain is heavy on the first step, then a little less on the second. No one ever said being on the right road was easy, but four steps in, I have Bertha going at a tolerable pace.

Bertha gets light. I look behind me, expecting to see someone helping, but I'm as alone on this journey as ever.

14

Saturday, July 15

The near demise of Bertha has made Jensen's week stressful. If he hasn't been working or studying, he's been under her hood with Paul. I've missed our dates, but staying with Jensen every night, taking him to work each morning, and cooking for him while he studies, have turned us into a team. Now that Bertha's repairs are finished, I dread the perfection of this week coming to an end.

The sound of the shower stops and is followed by the *whoosh* and *splash* of a filling tub. I grab a glass of orange juice and head down the hall. He may not even want it, but bringing Jensen juice is a great excuse to hang out with him while he's naked.

As he lounges, not a single sud covers his perfect-to-me body. In my eyes, his toned yet not over-built torso, and flat abs that lack a six-pack, make him look like a real man. The scruff from skipping a day of shaving nearly has me purring. To complete the picture of perfection, the faintest amount of steam curls around him. He's beautiful.

"Did you come to join me?" he asks.

Not long ago, I would have said that it doesn't take a physics major to compare the size of that tub to the glories that are me and conclude that Jensen's idea is a terrible one. While the thought still crosses my mind, my inner voice smacks it down. All I really want to do is love him, and that is more important than self-doubt or the few extra pounds I carry.

Yes, *a few*. Not a ton, or a hundred—a few, and those are diminishing because I am taking better care of myself—and because Jensen always steals my fries.

I crouch down and hand him the glass. He spins to sit in the center, grabs my face, and gives me a luscious kiss before taking a swig. His eyes glide down and he craves a hefty helping of dessert. "Come on. Join me."

As enticing as the bad boy gleam is, all I want is a moment to enjoy the peace he brings to my soul.

Warm water drips onto my knees as he takes my hands. "Come on." He winks, and instead of my hormones going haywire like they normally do, I feel grounded. "Nah, I'm too busy sitting here, loving you."

His playful smile leads way to eyes filled with warmth. As much as the naked body before me is amazing, it's the love that Jensen gives me that makes him the picture of perfection.

JENSEN

Seriously, God, why did you choose to make me so lucky? So many people struggle to earn redemption and never feel they accomplish it. I simply surrender my life to the ways of the universe and get rewarded many times over.

Truthfully, the surrender wasn't that simple—not by a long shot—but man, was it worth it.

The water swishes as I set the glass on the edge of the tub and replace it with her hands. The pang of love swirls up and locks in my throat, causing me to try to swallow it down. "How is it that any time any other girl has even remotely hinted at love I have freaked out, yet you say something like that and all I want to do is curl you in my arms and surrender everything?" I love this woman so much that my eyes actually start to show it with moisture. "Maybe it is because with you I know that surrendering my heart doesn't mean surrendering who I am."

But I do want to surrender, not just to her, but also to us. Etta comes bopping in and completes the picture. This is what I tried to convince myself I had before with people who were bad influences. Now it is real, and each day that Lizetta spends here drives home that this is what is meant to be.

Not long ago, I watched a man die. He was a man with dreams—a man who had let the amazing moments he could have had slip away, only for them to be replaced with actions that led to his downfall. I was almost that man, and because I am not, I need to do what is in my heart. I'm serious about her, and I know she feels the same. Spending this last week with her has been nothing short of perfection. Jimmy is right; it's time she moved in. But how do I ask? I don't want to just spit it out. It should be something special. Maybe I should just let my heart talk. So far, every time I have put faith in a higher source to guide me, it has led to happiness. Surely this will be no different.

"Lizetta, only you can take a mundane moment and turn it into something so beautiful that it alters how I see my life. Times that people strive to have come so easily to us because we stop and smell the roses. Will you marry me and spend the rest of our days finding joy when it is most fleeting? Please say yes, and build a garden of wonder with me."

Holy … What did I just say?

I need to retract that, pronto! It's too soon!

My mouth springs open so I can back peddle. I won't be able to save face, so I need to suck it up and …

And look at that beautiful face. Look at those green orbs of heaven that are filling like pools at the top of a waterfall in a Greek temple. They steal the breath I need to form words, and I realize that while I was thinking something else, what I said was exactly what I meant.

This moment right here, this is what life is about.

Lizetta

Did he just …?

From the time we are little girls, every woman dreams of

the one who will sweep her off her feet with words of love in an opulent setting. Only Jensen could touch my heart in such a way that would turn a bathroom into a palace.

Lights flash as I blink away the tears filling my eyes. Jensen has left me dumbfounded.

"Lizetta? Baby, you still with me?"

I want to scream my yes for the world to hear, but it's locked deep in my throat. Instead, I nod rapidly until my voice finally cooperates with my heart. "Yes! Yes, I will marry you!"

Etta starts barking and jumping in excitement. She may not understand the fine details, but she's well aware that something amazing just happened. I toss my arms around Jensen's neck and smack my lips into his, which in turn sends him slipping down the side of the tub, crunching his neck. His glass gets knocked over, and the cold juice that splashes on to his leg makes him jerk and laugh.

Jensen fakes going in for a kiss and instead twists his body so that I tumble into the tub with him. I scream like a delighted five-year-old on Christmas morning.

His scruff tickles my cheeks, and kisses that would normally have me smiling, have me giggling. With a squeal, I kick and send splashes flying into the air and raining down on us. "Holy snapping turtles, we're engaged! Wait, this is real, right? Please tell me this is real."

"Oh, it's real. Hey, hon, I'm kind of going under here, not to mention my legs are cramping. Can we take this elsewhere?"

"No!" I kiss him again, then get up and futilely dab myself with a towel before peeling off my clothes. He stands, and the water rushes off of him, reminding me of a waterfall over a statue of hotness. He barely dabs off the water before he drags me into the bedroom and onto the bed, and then wraps me around him. "Will you ever forgive me for proposing in the bathroom?"

"You forgot the part about being naked and just having invited me to have sex with you."

His hold on me tightens, and he nuzzles his cheek to my ear. "You make it sound so dirty."

"Tell you what, you make it up to me with the size of the rock you put on my finger, and I'll leave that part of the story out when I tell it to our children."

"Hmm ... Children with you. I want an angel of a girl with silky blonde hair and a dark-haired little brother to terrorize her." It all purrs out of him, that is, until he jerks back. "Please tell me you don't expect that to happen anytime soon."

"And ruin this perfect figure? Are you kidding?"

His seductive purr returns. "I love you and your perfect figure."

I savor the peace of the moment. Things like this happen to other people and you hope, dream, and pray it will happen to you, but it often seems impossible. Yet here I am, lying in his arms. I want to pause time and hold this moment forever.

15

Thursday, July 20

Lizetta

I'm engaged!

I'm freaking engaged!

I'm engaged to a man who adores me and loves hockey! He, Etta, and I are going to live happily ever after with a slew of kids, and cats, and God knows what else. We are totally saving money and buying a farm!

The glistening of the engagement ring that Dad gave to Mom keeps catching my eye. "This family has a gift for taking the bad and making it good," Mom told us. "The harder we fall, the higher it gets us to climb. Take this as a reminder to keep climbing. You can keep it and save the ring money for your future, or you can sell it and use the money anyway you want. Just keep climbing."

Sell a one-carat, Marquise cut diamond for half of what it is worth so we can buy something a fraction of the size? No way! I've had my eye on this baby since I was a little girl. It's mine now!

My feet race all over the pavement. With how much I have been shopping, and packing, and carrying boxes around, I'm surprised by how little I notice their ache. Just a few more days until I move in with Jensen! Saturday can't come fast enough!

Like a flash, I dodge through the lunch-hour madness of suited business people and nearly run down the street. I know exactly the dress I want and where to get it. I've marked a huge part of my budget for it, but it is going to be so worth it! Between my savings and the check Mom and Paul gave us, we are going to have the best wedding ever.

I'm getting the dress of my dreams! Jensen is the man of my dreams! This is amazing!

With the last sip of my special treat, a hazelnut mocha, I slam dunk the cup into a trash bin and resume humming a tune that Jensen's been working on. The boutique is just a block farther, and although they don't open for another fifteen minutes, my pace grows faster. I called in sick today because I couldn't wait any longer. The dress in the magazine is perfect! A plunging neckline to show off my killer boobs, and it is just form-fitting enough to make these curves sing. A girl's gotta work what God gave her! And oh! All that beaded, French lace!

My heart thunders with excitement. I'm so wired on life that I should have skipped the caffeine.

"Stop!" someone yells. "Stop! Lady you need to—"

Something crashes on to the concrete. Pieces of it fly up and into my face. The pain that shoots through my forehead sends me propelling backward. Another dose of agony gets me from behind as my head smacks to the ground. Gray haze coats my vision, and then my world fades to black.

Laura

Larry strolls into my room with no regard for the shut door. A bunch of twenties, some heroin, blow, and a bag of weed hit the bed. Whatever he wants, it's gonna suck for me. I haven't gotten heroin handed to me without a fight in weeks.

"What's this for?"

"Good news! Your boyfriend's about to come back." Larry strolls out like he hasn't a care in the world. "I heard it through the grapevine that Jensen's girly is in the hospital and gearing up to die. Go do what ya gotta do to comfort him."

The door clicks shut, and I'm left staring at my

ammunition, awestruck.

Oh, thank you, God! Thank you, for my second chance.

The only limits our heart knows

are the ones we give it.

16

Thursday, July 20

I used to be afraid of the dark, but this black, this absolute void of all, brings about a sense of peace. A white light cuts through the darkness and enrobes me. My heart tells me that the melody that plays is the song of angels. Am I dead? If I no longer have a body, how do I feel the physical comfort of lying in a tub of warm water with whirlpool jets massaging my muscles into bliss?

No! I can't get comfortable!

I'm not ready to leave Earth. Jensen and I are getting married!

The light pulls me upward. Questions spiral in my brain. Will I go to heaven? Are the pearly gates actually made out of pearl? Will I wait in a line to spin a giant wheel that decides my fate? Maybe there's a test. If there is a test, I am so hosed!

I thought you either went up or down. I'm being pulled up and back. Going up is good, but going back? *God, please help!*

Is it dumb to ask for help if you are already dead?

The force grows stronger until it spins me around and plops me back into darkness. Silver light slips in, bringing life to a world of fluffy clouds. My feet stand on a flat surface, and there are walls. Is this a glass room above Earth?

Before me is a desk that is made of pearly wood. On it is a silver keyboard and a huge monitor, along with a stress ball shaped like the devil and an Oakland A's bobblehead. At least whomever I'm about to meet is a homie.

Silently, a woman seated in a silver chair, pops in behind the desk. My heart jumps and I gasp, causing me to giggle with embarrassment.

The woman twists back and forth while tapping a pencil into her palm. She acts as if she has been here the entire time.

"Miss Lansing?" She stands and extends a chocolate-toned hand that looks so buffed and polished that it almost dazzles. She's intimidatingly tall—like the guys on *Supernatural*-type tall—and her grip is strong enough to make sure I know that she's the one in charge. She's also got the coolest, swirly purple and pink beads in her braids. "I'm Alvara. Welcome to the gateway. Won't you have a seat?"

She motions behind me, and a silver toadstool appears. Am I in Wonderland? That seat is ridiculously small. Oh my God! Maybe I'm—

My eyes flash downward. My body is the same as when I woke this morning. Fish paste! I thought life on the other side would be different. I take a seat. The stool turns fluid and grows to conform to my tush and back. Crazy cool!

Wait. "The gateway? I can't be dead! Not now! I'm at least about to enter heaven, right?"

Alvara's eyes are locked on the monitor as she types with the efficiency of a secretary on *Mad Men*. "Think of this as where we review your files to verify that you qualify for the next round."

Next round? What the hell? Whoops! I don't swear. I *never* swear! Why did I do it here of all places? Did I just doom myself? Oh no! Lord, please don't let me be butterscotched before I even get started.

"Relax," she assures. "You are not *butterscotched,* as you so eloquently put it. If you were, you would have gone straight down. Now, let's see what we have here." She looks at the screen while letting out the occasional "umm hmm" and raising an eyebrow. I claw my nails into my arm and scratch. How can I itch when I have no true body? My actual body is waiting to be reunited with Jensen while what I have here is a ghostly shell. But I shook hands with the gatekeeper. Man, death is confusing!

"You've done a lot of wonderful work with animals. Your compassion has been exemplary. I see no reason not to move you on to the interview."

Interview? That means going further into the process. "No! I'm engaged! This can't happen now!"

"Relax, Miss Lansing. I assure you that soon you will be at peace with the situation."

Alvara resumes her typing while I scan the room. There are no doors, no windows—nothing but glass inside clouds. Impossible. If there is a way in, there is a way out. I just have to find the key.

That's it! The Return key, just like in that TV show, *Drop Dead Diva*. She pressed Return, went back to Earth, and landed in a different body! My dream doesn't mean I'm being replaced. I'm coming back in a different body and escaping my old issues!

I bounce up and reach for the keyboard, only to get my hand slapped. Alvara's eyes flare in warning, and she stares me back down into my seat. I am definitely on to something, but now she knows that I am aware of the Return key trick. "Miss Lansing, there is no escape from fate."

That's it! I'll reach to the other side and hit Escape! That can't be much different.

I smack the key. Alvara's "No!" screams through the air. A boom rings out, followed by a golden flash. Darkness sucks me in and drags me through a rollercoaster of motions—flying up, plummeting down, corkscrewing around. I tense in fear of this ending in a painful crash. Oh God. What have I done?

My reflexes have me screaming as the painless impact bounces my butt into a cool sea of tan. Have I made it? Is this one of the patches in the painting?

No, this is tile, not sand or dry grass.

"Code red, room five three three," a woman's voice blares above me. "Code red, five three three."

What the—

A defibrillator cart zooms past as orderlies and nurses race down the hall. A few feet away, Griffin stands with his hand on Mom's back, looking helpless as she cries onto Paul's shoulder. Jimmy's head hangs low as he exits a room.

"Mom! Paul!" I run to them. "It's okay. I'm fine. Mom!" I tap her shoulder, but my finger doesn't hit anything.

No! This can't be!

Heavy sobs come from the room Jimmy just left—sobs that send me racing to find Jensen kneeling next to a bed. I try to throw my arms around him, but they whip right through, leaving them tingling. "Jensen. Honey, I'm here. Talk to me. Please."

"He can't hear you," a baritone voice, laced with the tone of compassion, says. Behind us stands a young man in a black suit and white shirt with an open collar. His orange hair is so vivid that it's practically psychedelic. His eyes are deep blue while his skin is pale as snow. Except for his sculpted features, he reminds me of a statue of a clown in a drive-thru.

"What?"

"He can't hear you. You're not here to him."

"Yes, I am!" My arms flail.

"Are you trying to signal a passing ship?" Oh, this guy is not only odd looking, he's witty—or so he thinks! "Your soul may be here, but your body isn't." He points just beyond me. "Your body is there."

I whip around, and an unforgiving wave of nausea sweeps through my stomach and up my throat. Time and again I've nursed injured animals, but never have I seen a sight this disturbing. Lying under the rows of bandages and tangles of tubes is my body. That face, that figure that I have such a volatile relationship with, that golden hair that is my personal pride and joy—it all seems so impossible, yet my heart breaks in knowing that it is my body that lies under the attack of tubes and wires. We expect to see those in movies and nightmares, not in ourselves.

My heart weakens further when I absorb Jensen's pain—watching him resting on his knees and releasing the tears I fight back. I drop to his side with my soul sinking at his suffering. Even if I can't comfort him, that doesn't mean I can't give him all the love I have. Somehow, love always comes through, doesn't it?

A wave of grief washes over me at the thought of losing Jensen, of never seeing my family again, and of never getting another kiss from Etta. Tears threaten to flow as my throat closes in, but I hold them back. I will not collapse. My broken body may be before me, yet somehow I am still here. Clearly I am meant to fight, which means the tears have to wait for another day.

"Please, someone tell me that this is a dream," Jensen begs.

"What happened?" I ask the man behind us. Is he the Grim Reaper?

"My name is Harold, and you were obsessed with shopping for a dress."

"Why would that land me in the hospital?"

"You failed to notice that you were walking under a piano."

"So?"

"It was falling from twenty stories above." He makes a dive-bombing noise while giving me a plummeting thumbs down.

Oh, there is someone with a sick sense of humor around here. One person says that death is not like a TV show, and now Harold tells me I am in a cartoon. I notice a silver tail coming off of me and going into my disabled body. What is going on here?

"If it were a cartoon, you would have a keyboard shaped head. This is real, and before you ask—no. No one is dreaming."

My stomach gets swishy. I don't like that these people can hear my thoughts. Are they undead, too? Is this guy a Zombie Angel?

I get an *Oh, please!* look. "No, I'm a run-of-the-mill angel, just like the ones who sing in Hark the Herald." He waits for me to laugh. I don't. "Herald and Harold, get it?" I stare. "Oh, come on!" He rolls his eyes at my lack of humor, and then gives up. "Things didn't work out as orchestrated, but in our defense, our guys did warn that you were too far into the danger area."

"Nobody warned me!"

He raises an index finger. "They yelled for you to stop. You were supposed to have a life-altering moment to lead you to ... Never mind. It's pointless now. Instead, you tuned us out, chowed it, and died. But then—"

"But then I hit the Escape key and sent myself back the wrong way."

Harold leans back against the wall and examines his nails. "No. Then you pissed off the gatekeeper and insulted the Big Guy by rejecting Heaven. Thing is, just because you screwed up your destiny doesn't mean you should screw up Jensen's. He deserves peace, so you must still be involved in that."

"So, I am coming back!"

"You know what I like about you? You believe in miracles." Harold looks to my body in the bed and chuckles. "This isn't one of those wacky TV shows on Lifetime. That silver tail coming off of your rump means you are tethered to that body. When it goes, so do you. Don't think of this as your soul returning to Earth, think of it as Purgatory dropping by for tea. You and Jensen were brought into each other's lives to fulfill destiny. That part hasn't changed."

Harold fades, and I'm left kneeling next to Jensen as he sobs. "Honey, I'm here. I am not leaving you." The defeat in not being able to throw my arms around him cripples my soul.

Jimmy joins us on our knees. "You okay?" he asks Jensen.

Jensen's irritation sprouts through his sobs. "They say Lizetta can't hear us, but I swear she's with us now. It's her who can't be heard. It's crazy, I know."

"It's not crazy," Jimmy says. "I didn't feel that way before, but I do now." Jimmy helps Jensen up, and the guys take seats beside my body. Griffin comes in and pulls up another chair, joining them in vigil. I lie down on the bed so that when Jensen grabs my shell's hand, mine is right there with his.

Don't worry, honey. I promise that I am coming back to you.

17

Friday, July 21

Lizetta

Jensen sits with his mom, staring at my body in silent vigil. It's so sweet that she has driven all this way to be with him for just a few hours. It is hard for her to get away from work, but she wants to be here for us all.

Before Arlene arrived, my night was filled with watching Jensen twist in that chair while struggling with sleep. When he found it, he also found nightmares. Why was I so determined to come back when the only thing I can do is watch the people I love suffer? If I can get through to one person ...

They say the more open you are to things, the more likely you are to sense them. Griffin believes in psychic stuff. It's certainly worth trekking over to work to see if he notices me.

My hand passes through the handle of the door to Good Samaritan. Since forgetting that I can't touch anything doesn't make me feel like enough of an idiot, I try knocking. I am so lame! I decide to embrace the madness and not only walk through the door, but also through the receptionist's desk.

I plop down on top of my desk, swaying my feet over the edge while nervously waiting. Considering that I can walk through closed doors, I can't even begin to fathom how I am sitting on an object. How do I even stand on the floor without falling through? This whole dead/undead/ghost/not a ghost thing is confusing.

When Griffin arrives, his expression reeks of hopelessness. By force of habit, I try to cheer him. "You must have had a sucky date last night. Oh, let me take that back. If your date had sucked, you'd be in a much better mood." His eyes float to my desk. He closes them and sniffles. Tears fall, and my heart breaks for him.

There has to be something that I can do. Maybe I only need to create a big enough disturbance.

I stand on my desk and wave my arms. "Come on, you big pansy! You claim you're all into psychic stuff. Here's your real ghost. Look at me!" He wipes away tears, then closes his eyes again as more fall. Still, I have to keep trying. "Seriously, Griffin!" I jump off the desk and attempt to grab his arm. "You keep telling me all this stuff is real. People who believe are supposed to be more in tune. If that's true, why can't you see me?"

His eyes go to mine, and then they narrow. Yes! "Griffin! Oh, thank God! I'm here. Well, I'm not physically here but—"

His head rattles, and he rubs his eyes. "I need more sleep."

Oh, come on! I need to shoot a rubber band at him like I used to do when we were kids and I wanted to get his attention. I head to my desk and go for the drawer handle. Of course my hand passes right through it. Gah! How many times am I going to forget? This doesn't make any sense. If I can stand on a solid object, I should be able to touch one.

Maybe it's just my state of mind. I try again, focusing on actually feeling the handle, which I don't, but I convince myself I do. When I pull, nothing happens. Like zero.

Dr. Leopold walks in and asks Griffin to give her a hand with something in the back. Griffin's eyes are hazed over, and he's as oblivious to her as he is me. Again she calls his name, and he snaps to. "Sorry," he utters, and then follows her out the door.

Pickle farts! I start to make the trek back to the hospital. There has got to be a way to communicate with someone.

Being filled with fear in the afterlife and the horror of seeing myself in a hospital bed were nothing compared to the sadness that watching Jensen brings to my soul. How can I be in Bertha's passenger seat and he not notice?

"Please, God," he prays. "You have enough good people with you already. Leave her with us so the world can benefit." His grip on Bertha's wheel tightens, and he gathers a shuddered breath. Jensen's pain rips at my soul. "Again I am selfish, I know, but what will happen to me if she dies? Please don't test me, and please show us all mercy by keeping her here."

Jensen shuts off Bertha and then rests his head on her steering wheel and cries dry tears. I try to hold my hand on his shoulder. "Baby, please don't cry." He pauses. Hope that he has heard me hits until he shakes his head and gets out of the car. I race to join him.

JENSEN

I stop at the foot of the stairs to rub my eyes. They feel like sandpaper. I've lost so much fluid from crying that my blood may have turned to powder. Even Bertha sounded like she'd been crying.

Bertha is fine.

I am fine.

Lizetta will definitely be fine.

What the doctors think doesn't matter. They don't know my girl.

Etta's barking so loudly that I'm surprised the neighbors haven't called the cops. My speeding off without a goodbye last night must have put her out of her mind. God only knows what she thought when Griffin dropped by this morning to feed her.

She's all over me the second my foot crosses the threshold. Immediately, I kneel down to her eye level, but her avoiding my gaze deepens the hollowness in my heart. I need to feel her connection, to know Etta is in this with me, but she keeps yapping towards my right with her tail and ears raised. She must be so pissed that she won't face me. I failed her.

Yeah, but she also knows something is wrong. Etta knows everything.

I touch her jaw and try to persuade her to turn my way. My forced words nearly gag me. "Lizetta will be back soon. It's going to be okay."

Etta continues looking away and barking like crazy. According to the doctors, I'm lying to both her and myself. "Okay. You got me. Things suck. However, we are absolutely, positively, not giving up even the smallest amount of hope, got that?"

Oddly, the barking continues. It's not even her normal acknowledgement bark. Lizetta's situation is freaking her out as much as it is me. Hopefully she just needs food, because I can't deal with this now.

Pulling a can of dog food out of the cabinet brings back the tears as memories of Lizetta showing up on my door step with bags of the stuff on the day we met fill my heart. That's the day my life became complete.

It will stay complete. This is temporary. She will be fine.

The smell that hits my nose the instant I break the seal on a can causes my stomach to turn. Normally Etta races over at the sound. Instead, she stays by the door, barking. "Come on, girl." I can't deal with both my sorrow over Lizetta and the tension that barking is causing me at the same time. Maybe I should take her to Lizetta's where she can be with other dogs.

Lizetta …

My butt hits the sofa. My head, my heart, my stomach—they all feel destroyed.

Etta runs into the kitchen and starts flapping her tail like crazy. She swings it so hard that it *thunks* on the cabinet to her right. Just above her is the box of cereal I left out this morning. Again she is barking like she's begging for my attention. She's right. I need to eat. I haven't ingested anything since breakfast yesterday—not even water.

Cereal sounds vile. Actually, all food sounds disgusting. I try to appease her by looking in the fridge. There's barely anything in there except for the same four beers that have stared at me for months.

Fuck it! If ever there was a time—

My hand goes for a cold bottle while my brain screams something about it being five months. Why can't everyone around here shut up and leave me alone?

I sit on the sofa with my head hung low from the guilt of just holding the bottle in my hand. Dammit, I hurt! This will make me hurt less. The pain of knowing I am about to blow it hurts too, yet somehow it all feels justified.

I should call Paul.

Paul, my sponsor. Paul, my future father-in-law.

Fuck it!

I crack the seal and toss the cap onto the coffee table. It bounces next to a stack of bridal magazines and a tiara.

That tiara … My eyes close off the world as my pain reaches new depths. Lizetta wore it all night last night, because even though I'm not supposed to see any of her stuff before the wedding, she said I made her feel like royalty.

My chest gets heavy and starts heaving. Somehow my body finds more water and the tears flow again. *God, please don't take her. People like me need beautiful souls to guide us. I may have survived before, but now that I've known her, how can I face an empty world?*

My head hangs low, and the tears get smeared onto my sleeve before I raise the bottle. Etta races toward me. She lets out a growl that is deep with bared fangs. Her tail is smacking to the right again, only this time it is freaking me out, because the wags are sharp and threatening. Dogs usually flap their tails to the right when they are happy. The last time she did it she seemed to be pointing to the cereal. I've no idea how to read Etta now.

Etta growls again. The bass in it vibrates my veins, sending a chill through them. I swear she's just doubled in size and is challenging me to see who is bigger. She butts her nose to the bottle, and that growl threatens me again. The bottle goes to the table, and I retract from the poison.

Now that she has my attention, Etta heads for the kitchen. She's right. The sink is where this belongs. I dump the thing and then pull out the remaining three bottles with the intention of dumping them as well, but the smell is so vile that they get chucked out the front door so they shatter on the concrete and are rendered useless.

I've got to get my head together. My body needs nutrients and water—lots of water. The glass I down makes me want to hurl. Still, I force myself to start on another because I need to stay strong and healthy to make it through this.

The sudden ring of my cell phone causes me to gag on the water while jumping to answer Paul's call. My coughed hello reeks with distress.

"Hey, sorry. I didn't mean to ruffle your feathers by calling. Just wanted to let you know there's no change."

I nod, even though he won't know I replied. Talking seems futile.

Paul groans. "We both know why I am calling. You *okay?*"

He didn't need to put stress on okay for me to know what he meant. "The house doesn't have a drop in it, and neither do I."

"Good. Same here. You call if you need to. I made Jimmy take Judy home, so I'm on watch at the hospital. I swear, I'll call if she makes even the slightest movement. Get some sleep."

I take a moment to gather my wits and calm my heart. The stench of the beer hangs in the air and reeks like a seductive dance partner who hasn't bathed in weeks. As much as being near it makes me nearly hurl, the sink gets a thorough scrub before I head off to the bedroom. The sight of the bed makes all of my senses lock up. In just a few days, this is to become her bedroom too. She's already brought over some clothes and a box of dog ashes. Being here without her is so wrong that I don't even know if I can do it.

I force myself to lie on the bed. I have to, because I just saw what will happen if I don't stay strong.

This is temporary. She will be back soon.

Etta jumps up and doesn't lie next to me like she does when Lizetta isn't here, but where she would if we were all together. As disturbing as it is, I find a bit of peace. Eventually we both drift off to sleep.

18

Saturday, July 22

JENSEN

Bark! Bark!

"Hang in there, sweetie," Lizetta tells me. "I'll figure something out."

Knock. Knock. Knock. Bark!

"Hurry, honey," I say. "I miss you. This waiting is killing me."

Pound! Pound! Pound! Bark! Bark!

My eyes pop open, and I scramble to rip off the sheets. That knock sounds like the hounds of Hell are on their way.

Etta sits by the door with her tail stiff as a bottlebrush. I should heed her warning, but maybe something happened and Paul came over instead of calling.

I jerk the door open.

Crap! I really need to listen to Etta. With the way this girl loves to pop in, you'd think I'd at least learn to use the peephole.

Lizetta

Behind the door is a woman in a tank top and a microscopic skirt. Maybe it is the weird lighting from the angle of the sun, but her skin is yellow. Are her arms covered in makeup?

The aura she radiates is one of concealed pain. Is that why the moment the door opened I felt emotionally drained? The dark circles that peek through makeup make my heart ache for her, yet I also feel conflicted. She looks like a junkie, and I can't shake the feeling that she has chosen her own path.

Is that horrible of me? People choose to start taking drugs, but they don't choose to become addicts. Did this girl who looks so emaciated choose—

Is that? Oh, no way! Is *Laura Muler* groupie girl? The one that Jensen—

Oh, gross! Let me go get a knife and slice myself so God can pour more salt on me.

Dear God, what happened to her? She used to be so pretty. Just the thought of her used to fill me with jealousy, but now ...

Now my heart bleeds for her. What could possibly cause her to plummet so deeply into hell? What a terrible waste of beauty.

JENSEN

Etta stands at my feet, continuing to bark. I should *shh* her so the neighbors don't flip out, but I'd rather Laura feel threatened. Etta then butts my leg with her nose as if saying, "See, I warned you not to answer the door. Why don't you ever listen to me? Idiot."

My sigh rings in my head like I'm hung over. Maybe my brain is too clouded by what is happening with Lizetta, but I foolishly refrain from slamming the door in Laura's face. "And to what do I owe the pleasure of your charms? This is the worst of all times. I also told you to leave me alone."

Her teeth nip at her lip and she raises her brows. It's not in the seductive way she usually does it. Instead, she seems resigned to the fact that she can't blame me for my attitude. "I heard what happened."

What? "From who? Never mind. Please, go away."

"I thought you might need someone to talk to. We can do that, you know?" I start to shut the door on her, and she jabs a paper bag into my chest. "Here, I brought adult milk and cookies."

Etta warns me as I open the bag. She's right. It's filled with future regret. "Tequila and limes? Really?" I push Laura aside so I can chuck the thing out the door.

"What are you doing?"

"Putting it with the last of my beer."

"That stuff was expensive."

The bag bounces off the pavement. Plastic? "Glad you sprung for the good stuff."

"I also heard you got engaged." Laura tosses her purse on the coffee table, and then plops her butt onto the sofa. I glare at the purse until she moves it to the ground. I don't want anything of hers even remotely near the stuff that Lizetta and I are using on our wedding day. Lizetta's been shopping with such urgency that you'd think the wedding were tomorrow.

Pain gets choked back. I would give anything to marry that woman tomorrow. Hell, the second she wakes I'm grabbing a preacher. I'll marry her in the damn hospital. Were we engaged too soon? Hell no! I'm not letting another moment of life slip past without her.

"You heard? How? That only happened a week ago." And how long until you let that skirt ride up and flash me? "Never mind. I don't want to know how you, or anyone else, knows anything about my life now." Man, being around this girl makes me punchy as sin.

"News travels. Is this her?" She picks up the engagement picture that we had taken the night after I proposed. Lizetta couldn't wait, and I am so, so incredibly grateful that I listened to that inner voice that tells me never to waste a moment and put off having it done. God, how I miss her.

Laura blinks, and her mouth drops to form a void. "Wow!"

"Wow, what?" If she makes one comment, one tiny comment, I'm going to rip the anorexic bitch's throat out, regardless of the hell that makes her that way.

"She's pretty."

Laura then has the balls to start thumbing through the

stuff on the coffee table. Her grubby hands dare to reach for Lizetta's tiara. Is nothing sacred to this woman? I snatch it from Laura's hands. "No one touches her stuff!"

She puts her hands out to tell me not to get so testy. If she doesn't want to see me testy, she should leave.

"Jensen, do you remember the time my dad showed up drunk and pissed after losing a bunch of money and tried to take it out on me? You saved me by fighting that asshole off. I thought I'd return the favor by helping you fight off this."

And there went the last of my compassion. "Fight it off? Fight off the pain because my fiancée is in a coma and will likely die?" No, I did *not* mean that! It just croaked out from anger. Ugh! I hate how Laura truly brings out the worst in me. "I really need you to go."

She nods in acknowledgement that she has blown it. When she stands, she actually puts her hands on the hem of her skirt and tugs downward. Is Laura showing modesty? What the hell kind of trick is this? First the warning over the cookies, now this. If she didn't bring a bottle of liquid coffin nails, I'd think she was trying to be respectful.

"I'm sorry. I get it. It's just that—" She snickers. "Lately you've looked better than I have ever seen. Even before all the bad stuff happened. I thought that maybe if I was here for you, you could be here for me and show me how you did it."

Does Laura really think I'm that stupid?

Then again, this is reminding me of the few times when Laura actually opened up to me. The times when she told me about how her father had abused her. The times when she said he would starve her in retaliation for acting out. That pain radiates off of her, but I've also seen her fake it. I won't let my own tragedy blind me to reality.

There is water in her eyes when I hand Laura her purse. Fucking tears. The fall of each one scrapes through my heart. I can't take her pain, because the only thing helping me hold it together is how angry I am. "I'm sorry," she says, "for all of the things that happened." I have to fight off losing it. Laura's words remind me of when I called Mom, and it's making my insides crumble.

She reaches out to hug me, and Etta barks like crazy. My chest caves and tears start falling all over again. I cling to Laura because I'd give anything for this to be Lizetta.

Etta growls at me to knock it off, but I don't let go. Maybe I am still a junkie, because even if Laura is as poisonous as crack, I need something.

She's gotten so frail that she may shatter if I squeeze her. I was the only one that gave a shit about her. Now something about her reeks of being a bag of garbage that only gets picked up when someone needs something to puke in. She's pouring her heart into this hug, but I have to turn myself off to her. I can't get sucked back into her world.

Etta helps me come to my senses by butting her head into my knee. I don't let Laura leave before stating what obviously needs to be said. "Knock off the heroin."

Laura's eyes go to her makeup-covered body. She nods in acknowledgment that she's heard me but not necessarily that she'll listen. "Remember," she says, "you can call me if you need to talk. After all we've been through, I know you pretty well."

I close the door behind her and lean against it. "Not anymore you don't."

Lizetta

How my family clings to the hope that I will wake warms my heart. My poor mother. I can only begin to imagine what it would be like to watch over your dying child. She tries to focus on her knitting, but her eyes keep peering up, hoping to catch a sign that I'm coming to.

If there were just some way to let her know that I am here. The entire ride over, I tried to show Jensen I was with him, but every effort failed. I miss my body—that body I hated for so long. How is that for irony?

Instinct says I can pull myself back inside it, but something is warning me that it has been wrapped in caution tape. Is the fear that accompanies that the reason why a moment ago the world started twisting?

A nurse dashes in. She's got that look—that look that comes from being taught what to do in situations where there is a problem with the patient but you are not to panic. She checks the activity on the monitor, and then instructs Mom to clear her stuff and go for a walk.

"What's going on?" Mom asks in panic. The nurse tells her I'm having a seizure and ushers her out. "A seizure? But she's not shaking. How can you just come in and claim she is having a seizure?"

"We saw it on the monitor at the nurse's station. Non-convulsive seizures are not uncommon for coma patients. Give the doctor some time to make sure everything is okay, and we will come for you in a minute. Meanwhile, try to relax."

"Relax?" Mom screams. "My baby's having a seizure, and you're telling me to relax?" The doctor comes in and does nothing other than watch the machine as its needle flips out. "Why isn't anybody doing anything?"

Jensen returns with Mom's coffee, hears the news, and then ushers Mom out to calm her. I'm torn between following them and staying to find out what is wrong. The decision is made when a familiar voice comes from behind. "Good afternoon, Lizetta."

The carrot-topped man in the suit has returned. "What in craziness is going on?"

He sighs. "Why is it I never get the smart ones? You were hit in the head with a piano. Your body is in a coma."

"I know that part! What's the deal with the seizure?"

He shrugs. "It comes with the territory. I know you are not a doctor, but you must have studied at least a little of this in school."

He's so nonchalant that it compounds my heartache. While he hasn't told me I am not coming back, he has implied that it would take a miracle. Doesn't he understand the pain I'm experiencing over how I may never be with my family again? Maybe that means little to him, but the thought of no more camping trips, no more Christmas mornings, no more long evenings gathered around a dinner table, means more than I can place value on. Fear of losing that is keeping me in the fight. He has to help me. "If you are my guardian angel, then you know how much it breaks my heart to see my family suffer. Can't you put me back in my body so we can be done with this mess?"

"You can pop in right now, *but* that body is toast."

"What do you mean, toast? I'm not coming back?"

"Not in that busted body."

What? No! He can't—

Wait a second. That was some interesting wording.

Harold takes a seat on the edge of the bed while nurses come and go. "What is it with your obsession over that body? For years you hated it. Now you are clamoring for it back. Funny what a little perspective can do. Well, if you get back in it, in this condition, you definitely won't be around anymore to help Jensen."

My words come out with hesitation as I stare at my former shell. "Dear God, this can't be." He's right. I used to hate that body. Now I'd give just about anything for it.

Harold's eyes show that my pain hits a chord. He swallows back sorrow, and the sensitivity that I so desperately need comes through. "Look, dear, I really am sorry, but there is only so much that can be done." He looks me straight in the eyes while taking my hands. Part of me doesn't want him near me, but the other part appreciates finally feeling someone's touch. I just want to hang on to him and cry. "I wasn't kidding about how things went differently than they were supposed to."

"What was supposed to happen?"

Gently he shakes his head. Empathy fills his eyes. Even with all those jokes, he can't hide that he is hurting for me. "Trying to make something happen because someone told you to does not address your problems."

"If I am going to die anyway, what does it matter?" This means I can't be meant to die!

"Bodies die; souls don't. That is why we are always so concerned about them. How else can you explain the level of compassion you show others over that which you show your body?"

He reminds me of Jensen on the night of our first date. I hate to admit how right he is.

"Lizetta, even if you could go back in time, you have knowledge now. A little knowledge can change how we see the world. The seizure was the first of three warning shots. Please, use your time wisely. There are people who need the understanding that only you can give. Save them, and in the end you will save yourself."

Harold fades out, and I'm more sad and confused than ever. Some lousy guardian angel.

19

Sunday, July 23

JENSEN

Moments gathered around a picnic table should be reserved for happy occasions, not for discussing the termination of a loved one's life. No one wants to admit that is the real reason why we are here among the peace of the lake. Is this really the right place for a conversation of this magnitude? Then again, this conversation doesn't belong anywhere on earth, which makes me wonder if we are actually in Purgatory, even though the situation makes us feel like we are in Hell.

After a series of small seizures, the doctors pulled Paul aside and gave him the gentle suggestion that the family consider taking action. How can they overlook the passion with which we are praying? How we spend every second we can by her side, holding on to hope and begging God to grace us with even the slightest twitch of her finger? It's obvious that, in the doctor's eyes, Lizetta will never recover. I absolutely loathe us all, because we are starting to accept that diagnosis as well.

How can I let myself think that for even a moment? It must be because this whole situation has me feeling so lost that I'm crying one moment and then ready to scream the next. Or maybe it's because I've been losing track of the days since both Lizetta's accident and when I last ate. I'm sure it is also tied into how my brain flips between screaming for a drink and sending messages of things that may not exist, like the sensation on my right that tells we have company. How can there be no hope for Lizetta when I feel her here?

Then again, if she is here, she couldn't also be in the hospital, meaning …

The thought sends waves of cold through my body.

Lizetta's mom sits across from me, staring at the water. Judy's blonde hair is clipped up, and little tufts of it flutter in the breeze. It reminds me of how lovely Lizetta's looks in the sun, and I want to puke. It's not because the love of my life looks like her; it's because the entire family has signed medical directives, and the woman who gave Lizetta her life now has the power to take it away. They claim I have a say, but I have to face that I am powerless over whatever decision this woman makes. All I can do is pray she does the right thing. Lord, what I would give for a miracle right now.

Jimmy's head has been down the entire time. He is probably the reason why I think Lizetta is here. Every now and then I catch a glimpse of his golden hair and swear Lizetta's next to me. Etta's exactly were she would be if Lizetta really were in that spot, sitting behind us both. It makes it harder to believe the screaming in my gut that Lizetta is among us is wrong.

The tug of war of my emotions is becoming unbearable. Paul's eyes keep turning to me with concern. I shoot him a forced smile and nod that I'm still among the clean and sober. He gives me a subtle thumbs up, telling me it's the same on his side, yet our eyes scream that neither one of us knows how we are managing to hold on.

Paul takes Judy's hand and then looks straight across the table at Jimmy and I. "Anyone want to make this a little easier by starting? If it's on your mind, say it. No one is going to get bent at anyone."

Judy whispers so quietly that we almost can't hear her. "I don't want my darling to suffer anymore." Her eyes remain on the lake, and my lungs lock up in fear of what she means.

"What are you saying, honey?" Paul asks.

"Nothing. I'm not saying a thing. It's more of a prayer."

I breathe again.

"I seem to be praying every moment," Jimmy says, "but I

don't even get the slightest sign that it's working. Except …"

"Except what?" Paul asks. "Does this go back to what you were telling me the other day?"

"It's just that I can swear she's here with us, but I can't tell you why I feel that way."

Paul looks to me for my piece. Maybe I'm just wiped out, but my thinking she is here can't be an illusion brought on by hope and the occasional glance at like-colored hair. "Jimmy is right. It's easy to think that it is all in my head, but since we sat down, the feeling that she is here has been so strong that I swear my side keeps buzzing."

We may be here to talk about options, but I know where this conversation is headed. We either wait and do all we can to keep her, or we take away her nourishment. If the feeding tube is removed, she will shrivel up from the inside and die a grotesque death.

Maybe it's selfish. Maybe this is just me imagining how it would feel and how I wouldn't want to go that way. The reality is that my poor girl is suffering, and I can't decide what would hurt her more—waiting it out or starving her.

My gut grips at the thought of how much pain starvation must bring. But what if she is in some other type of pain? Is she in mental agony until she gets to move on? By keeping her alive, have we thrown her into misery? Does she hate us for our selfishness? Or does she cherish how we fear losing her? If Lizetta isn't staying on Earth, why should our selfish desires delay her finding peace in Heaven?

This is crap. I want my girl back, and I will never have her again if we starve her. I'm done with this conversation, and I let everyone know the subject is closed. "May twenty-seven," I stand and state in no uncertain terms. All eyes go to me. "Lizetta set that date, and that's the day I'm marrying her. By then she will have fully recovered and will be ready to proceed with the wedding of her dreams, which we are all going to make sure she gets. You told me I have a say, and I insist that she and I marry on May twenty-seven."

Jimmy slams his hands onto the table and seconds my

motion. "May twenty-seven!"

Paul gives a firm thumbs up as Judy nods in agreement. She then looks up to me and mouths "Thank you" for allowing her mind to relax a little longer over the struggle it faces. With that endorsement of my declaration, the hope that was so fleeting for all of us just a moment ago now covers her face. It puts a knot in my throat, because she looks just like Lizetta did on the night I told her about my past, right after the crying stopped and her acceptance set in. As much as I feared that after she had time to think about it she would leave me, the comfort she brought that night had me feeling as if I had been bathed by the compassion of angels.

I need out of here, because if I keep looking at Judy, I'll either lose my composure with tears or head off to the bar to lose my sobriety.

With Etta's leash in hand I head home—straight home— to mark my calendar and drop off Etta. Then I'm off to be sure my future bride knows the wedding is still on.

The lamp's glow puts me in the spotlight as I sit on the sofa and stare at a bottle of tequila. The cap hasn't even been cracked, yet defeat weighs my heart. I held fast to the belief in miracles and that May twenty-seven will be the happiest day in my life, until I got another look at Lizetta in that hospital bed.

I should have dumped this crap Laura brought down the drain so I couldn't dumpster dive for it later. Worse, I actually watched her when she left and saw her trash it. She isn't even here, yet she's still an enabler.

Judging by how my eyes are locked on it, this tequila must hold the key to the universe. A shot is all I need—just enough to take the edge off.

A clean glass sits in front of me. If I use a glass and don't drink directly from the bottle, I can monitor myself. It's not like I would be chugging and not paying attention.

 Lizetta

Jensen reaches for the bottle. Yelling at God may cheese Him off further, but something has got to give! "Please, can't you see that we need you?"

Etta barks as Jensen grabs the bottle. "I love you, too, honey," he says. "And yeah, I know, I'm an idiot." He cracks the cap, and just the smell of the stuff seems to make his muscles unclench; yet he swallows hard, like it also makes his stomach sour. "A know-it-all doctor told me the love of my life only has a few days to live," he justifies as he pours. "I'm entitled to this and a lot more."

Don't you dare take on that tone, mister! I am going to make it back, and if you've fallen off the wagon, you are going to be in for one Hades of a surprise when you realize that I know about it! "Please, God! You have got to do something to help him!" Again Etta barks, this time while staring straight at him and whipping her tail to the right. He pauses to look at her, but it doesn't stop him from raising the glass. "Son of a dang it, Jensen! Stop!"

Etta's growl steals enough of his attention to slow him down.

Wait a second. She's angry, yet she's whipping her tail to the right. That's supposed to be a sign of happiness, yet Jensen says she only does it when I am around.

The last time Jensen almost drank, Etta was the one who stopped him. I got riled up and ... and so did Etta! I wanted to get Jensen food, and she moved to the kitchen when I did. She growled at him when I got upset. When he dumped that beer, I was standing next to the sink. Was Etta trying to show him that I am here? Animals are good at sensing emotions. Many people believe that they are also good at sensing supernatural beings. Maybe I can make this undead ghost thing work for me after all.

Jensen brings the glass to his lips. I take to running around the room and screaming gibberish while letting my sense of panic build. Etta chases behind as I run across the sofa and over Jensen's lap. Her tail whips him in the face when she darts over him and lands on the coffee table. When she jumps off, her back paw hits the bottle. Jensen saves it from wobbling over, then slams down his glass. His fists are tight enough to tense his shoulders. Crap, he looks pissed! Fear creeps through me. He reminds me of my father.

He breathes deeply once, twice, and after the third time, he releases his tension. I sigh in relief when he sits on the floor and nurtures Etta like a newborn. "*Shh*. It's one in the morning, and you're going to wake the neighbors."

JENSEN

I love Etta, but son of a bitch, she's making this harder! My hand smooths over her with the softest touch I can give. This isn't her fault. Etta knows I am in danger and is trying to help.

God, I want to strangle something!

I pop up and turn away from Etta. She deserves better than to think my anger is directed at her. It's aimed at the only one who deserves it. I look straight to Heaven and tell off the guy who thinks he's such a big shot. "God dammit! How the fuck could you let this happen to such a wonderful person? You want us to be good, and when we are you strike us down! How could you let this happen to me after all the months we spent working together? I would beg, and you would give me an inch, and I would say thank you. Every inch you gave I would turn into a yard before I would beg again. That was our deal! Now you fucking do this!"

My voice turns scathing, because I now loathe the man it is directed at. "You hurt the sweetest person on the planet. Was that the problem? That she's an angel and you want her back? Are you testing me like you did when you took Eddie right in front of me? Is that it? Are you saying that it is my fault? That you will keep fucking with me, time and again, until I destroy myself? How dare you!"

I grab the glass and throw it at Him. It smacks the ceiling, and then shatters on the floor. That smack wasn't loud enough. I need something bigger, something bolder to convey I have had it with this guy! "Do you think you can make her happier than I can? Bullshit! Screw you! Screw you and your supposed compassion. If you gave a shit about either of us, you never would have allowed this!"

I raise the bottle to toast the prick who thinks he is such hot shit. "Screw you, and cheers!"

Panic sets in and makes me forget my limitations, so I run to Jensen and swat at the bottle. "Jensen! No! Don't you dare!"

Etta springs into action and goes into a sprint, giving her enough momentum to knock Jensen on his butt. Tequila sprays across the room. The bottle flies and hits the coffee table, causing more to spray. Jensen rushes to protect my wedding magazines, budget, and tiara, but it's too late. He takes the sleeve of his shirt to the papers, wiping frantically. "No! No! No! This did *not* happen! I swear to God, Lizetta, I am not like your dad." He drops to his knees, and I'd give anything to tell him I understand why he is crumbling, and that this is even more proof of how he is nothing like my father. "I've ruined her. I've destroyed the last that she left behind." He clutches the magazines to his chest while doubling over into sobs.

He's right, God. I want to defend you in this, but I can't.

Jensen takes the tiara to the sink and rinses off the alcohol before drying it with a touch so delicate that you would think it were made of paper-thin glass. "What have I done?" he questions over and over. "I'm so sorry, Lizetta.

Please don't hate me when you see this. Really, I haven't drunk a drop of it." Tears fall into the tequila as he mops it off the table, nearly buffing it dry before meticulously returning everything. He stares down at my belongings, and I would give anything to be able to dry the tears that rain. "I swear that I'll tell you the truth, that I almost drank. I'll tell you, because you are going to make it back here."

Finally, he grabs the bottle and sticks the neck directly into the drain. "I swear, Lizetta, somehow you are protecting me. That scares the hell out of me, because if you're here, then you are not in your body. Every time I feel you with me outside of the hospital, I fear that no one's called yet to tell me the bad news.

"I can't stay here anymore. I need to be with you for real." He bends down to Etta, resting his palms over her cheeks and smiling. "Again you save me. Thank you." He looks to God. "I'm still pissed, but thanks—I think." With a kiss to Etta's head, he grabs his coat and keys and heads off to stand vigil over my body.

20

Monday, July 24

As the clock across from my bed ticks over to four in the morning, lethargic steps approach my hospital room. Griffin enters, rubs his eyes, and slumps into a chair next to Jensen, who has finally calmed enough to sleep. Griffin curls onto his side and shuts his eyes. Knowing that I'm okay as can be seems to be as soothing to them as counting sheep.

He shifts so that he can curl into a fetal position as best as his tall figure can in a crappy hospital chair. You would think hospitals would have recliners for such horrible occasions. Would it be so difficult for the staff to get these guys cots? I sit on the floor between them, because it's all that I can think to do.

Griffin peeks at my body and shakes his head. He then extends a hand toward Jensen, only to retract it when Jensen snores. "Never mind, you'll just think I'm nuts. Lord knows I already think I'm crazy enough, I don't need you adding to the concern over my sanity." He looks to my body while shaking his head. "I swear, Lizzie, you may be in that bed, but so often it feels like you are one hell of a lot closer."

"I'm right here," I say while looking up to him.

"Weirdest damn thing," he mutters. "Even for the briefest moment at work right after your accident ..."

I kneel so that we are face-to-face. His eyes give little blinks, and a bit of water streams down. I've come to accept that it is futile, but I won't feel like a friend unless I try to dry his tears. "That's because I am here, Griffin. I really wish you could hear me." My hand tingles as it passes through him. His nose crinkles like it's itching. That's interesting. I touch the same area. "Griffin?" His face twitches, and he reaches his hand around to rub it.

I pull back. "Griffin, can you feel me?"

He fails to respond.

Another tear forms and falls. I reach to it while saying, "You're gonna ruin your eyeliner." His brow scrunches, and he rubs his nose again. His eyes search the room. "Weirdest damn thing."

My hand goes to his knee. "Griffin, am I getting through to you?"

He looks down and shakes his head. "Losing my damn mind."

Am I imagining this, or is he responding whenever I touch him while speaking? How can I get a definitive response?

I suppose I could ...

I'm blushing just thinking about it.

Sorry, Jensen, but I'm really doing this for us.

My hand goes to the most private of all of Griffin's places, and he fails to respond. Then I speak up. "Griffin, do I have your attention now?"

He jumps up and looks down to his crotch. "Something *weird* is going on here." He almost has his hand on Jensen's arm before he high tails it out of the room. "No way I'm waking Mr. Sex On Legs and telling him that something in this room is making my crotch vibrate. It'll freak Straight Boy's shit out. I have *got* to get some real sleep!"

Sweet kitten whiskers! I gotta go with Griffin. I may have just found another key!

"I need this psychic to either tell me I'm nuts or convince me I'm not," Griffin says. "Must be losing my mind!"

I can hardly keep pace with Griffin as he dashes out of

his car to rap on the door of The Great Zolta's home. The woman who answers looks like Amy Winehouse, minus the bouffant, while modeling yoga chic. Her eyes lock into Griffin's kohl-lined ones before going down his intimidating body. Her feet creep back so smoothly I almost miss it, but Griffin is well aware. He puts on his Miss Manners voice. It's deep and manly, yet also soft and polite. He could easily sweet talk someone into bed with it. "Hello, is Miss Zolta home?"

The woman looks through fake lashes that are so dense it's amazing that she can open her eyes. The corner, just inside the door, holds her attention. Wasn't a baseball bat kept there? "Do you have an appointment?" she asks.

Griffin lowers his eyes to his hands to appear less threatening. "No, I'm—I'm sorry. I saw her about a year ago, and something in the cards came devastatingly true. We need her advice, pronto."

She tucks jet-black hair behind her ears and avoids making eye contact regarding the bad news. Griffin is so upset that she's already changed her demeanor. "Sorry, my sister's on vacation. You want to make an appointment for next week?"

"Next week!" The words squeal out of him, and I expect him to stomp his foot like a little girl. "Psychics can't go on vacation! They are like public servants. How would she like it if the fire department said they would show up in a month? She should at least be on-call!"

Her expression goes flat, like cheesed off, comedic straight man type flat. "That is what happens when you make five times the money I do from my *legitimate* job. It's not even like she went to the Bahamas. She's on a culinary tour of France. Four weeks of eating her fat ass deeper into a chair while I house sit."

"Son of a bitch!" Griffin's hands fly into the air. "What the hell am I supposed to do?" Now I get the foot stomp I expected earlier, and his hands land firmly on his hips. I freaking love it when Griffin flames out! "I don't suppose you have any special abilities?"

"Oh, sure. Of course I do." She reaches inside the house, grabs a deck of cards, and tells Griffin to draw one and not show it to her. "Now, how about I tell you which card you are holding?"

Griffin's brows cock. "Uh, sure ..."

Her fingers fly to her temples while she squints. "The three of hearts."

Griffin tilts his head and eyes the card. "That translates to what in Tarot? Cups?"

She yanks the card back from Griffin. "I don't freaking know, because I'm not some crackpot psychic!"

Griffin wags a finger at her. "Oh no! Let me tell you, that woman is no fake! Sister nailed it big time." The sag of Griffin's eyes show the fun and games are over. "Is she really not coming back for a week?"

The woman's gaze drops in empathy. "Well, she'll be back late Friday night," she says, sounding like she is hopeful that it will help.

Griffin talks to the steps as he heads down the porch. "Geez, I hope Lizzie holds on that long. Thanks anyway."

"Hey, you okay?"

"Not really, but thanks for asking." Griffin heads off with his head down. Again I'm faced with watching the people I love hurt over my misfortune.

Suddenly my tension releases. Coolness blows at me from behind, not like air conditioning, but more like a sense of peace. My silver cord is fading. Harold's previous words ring in my brain, "That silver tail coming off of your rump means you are tethered to that body. When it goes, so do you."

I've got to find my way back to Jensen.

JENSEN

Bertha's V8 roar is like a brain massage. "Don't worry about this part of life," she says. "You are safe with me."

Though her ticker may have its trials, her armor surrounds me in the comfort that even if I careen into a ditch, she's got me covered. Had I been in her instead of at work when Paul's call came, that may have happened. That call was a kick to my head, but his words jumpstarted my heart.

"Too much fluid."

My foot presses harder on the gas. I not only need to hurry, I have to drown out Paul's haunting words.

"Emergency surgery."

He tried to give me the news like it was a baseball score I didn't give a crap about, but some of the words spoke far louder than the tone used to convey them.

"They have to drill into her skull—"

Then he started to lose it.

"to remove the pressure—in more than one spot."

Which means multiple holes—like three of them.

They want to turn my angel's head into a bowling ball.

Nightmarish visions clog my brain like a cheesy horror film filled with screams of agony and a whirling drill. My bowling ball analogy doesn't help. My head needs to clear. I can't let devastation rule me, or I won't be able to do what I know Lizetta would want. We need to stop feeling helpless and take matters into our own hands. Tonight, I'll be the one to do it.

My work boots thunder down the hospital corridor. Although everyone is going about their business, all eyes seem to be on the bag I carry. Is this how terrorists feel while on a suicide mission?

Inside Lizetta's room her family paces, twiddles their thumbs, and is generally freaked out over the impending surgery. I don't bother with hellos for fear of causing my resolve to falter. I bring Lizetta's bed into a seated position.

Paul and Jimmy come in to assist. Either they can read my mind or they just trust me that much. No one raises a question as I grab a rubber band out of my pocket and tie her hair back. If anyone flinches when I pull out the scissors, I don't notice.

I can barely get the words out. "If we are going to lose even the smallest part of her, it is going to happen with dignity." I dive in with the intention of cutting as close to the root as possible, and then retract. I can't do this.

No. Don't think; just do. Lizetta's suffering does not need to be in vain.

I suck it up and make the first cut. I once told Lizetta I wanted to create a little blonde haired girl with her; now we will. With each snip of the scissors, I banish the pain of our loss. The first cut represents Lizetta's love of life. The second her compassion. The third is for the peace she brings into my world. Each snip is another reminder of how special this woman is.

The hair goes into the bag and my emotions lose all peace. I pull her head into my chest. Hot tears pour as my eyes squeeze out the guilt from having been the one to rob my girl of the locks she loves so much. The doctors may try, but I truly will find a way to keep Lizetta alive, even if it is in the form of a wig on a cancer patient's head.

My sobs grow loud. I don't give a shit who hears or what they think of a man who is falling to pieces. *Dammit, God! This is so fucking unfair!*

"Thank you. Lizetta would want this." Jimmy reaches for the bag. He gets it. He gets me, and he's sobbing just as damn hard and just as without shame. "Here, I'll take in the donation. Let me share this burden with you, brother."

How the hell did you allow this to happen? I'm serious, God. What the fuck were you thinking? And what makes us all so unworthy that you won't answer our prayers?

21

Tuesday, July 25

JENSEN

The news from the doctors is always conflicting. One says Lizetta has only a few days, no matter what we do, while another says that if we continue to take action it could be weeks. One says she's aware of what's going on around her, while another claims she hasn't a clue. The only thing they all agree on is that the surgery was a success—for now.

Mom says there is an old belief that people in comas are straddling the line between here and the afterlife. I choose to believe that Mom is right and that Lizetta can understand everything I say, so I'm going to make damn sure she knows it's time to stop straddling and come back.

How is it Lizetta is in front of me, yet I feel like she is next to me? Right now I swear my cheek is buzzing with her touch. Pretty much the only time I ever feel like she isn't by my side is when I'm in the bathroom. I press her hand to my heart. "I miss you, baby. I stopped by the florist after work. Some of those bright daisies you want for the wedding are next to your bed. I also put down the deposit for the wedding." It took everything I had to keep from losing it when I handed the woman my credit card. I got this far in my new life on faith, and I'm not going to stop believing now.

The bandages on her head feel like they are clogging my throat. It's hard not to stare at them. I'd much rather stare at her eyes, and I would give my legs if it meant she would open them. She's gonna be pissed when she sees the scratch near her left one. First thing she'll probably do when she wakes is go for her makeup bag. Any minute, she is going to freak out and look for that thing.

I kiss her engagement ring before pulling her makeup bag out of the nightstand. I should bring her a mirror, because if she has to deal with the tiny one in that compact, it'll make her crazy. I resume my position of holding her hand next to my heart, then smile at the thought of Lizetta waking in a panic over how she looks.

Heels click down the hall. They slow, stop, and start up again before black boots cross the threshold. The vibe goes from depressing to chaotic. Laura puts her hands out to stop me even though I haven't moved. "Don't get upset."

Is she serious? My pseudo-ex-girlfriend has suddenly popped in on my comatose fiancée. Of course I'm upset.

"Since you've been avoiding me, I had to catch you here. I found something you will want." Before I can tell her there isn't anything that she could possibly have that I would ever want, she scuttles over to hand me a stack of photos. Great. I didn't realize she had blackmail material. I guess it's not surprising.

I'm afraid to look for fear of what compromising position these show me in. Maybe it's shots of the condiment incident, in which case I want to know but ... Dear God, I really don't want to know.

My eyes hit the photos, and that feeling you get when you see something surprising, painful, and pleasant, all at the same time, creeps up my insides. These are pictures of girls playing on monkey bars. One of them is a blond who looks to be giving it her all. "Is that—Is that Lizetta?"

Laura pulls up a chair next to me. "Yeah. Recognize that sandy blonde?"

"You know Lizetta?"

"We grew up together."

"Why didn't you say something sooner?"

"I didn't realize she was your girlfriend, until I saw that engagement photo. It kind of threw me. Also, you were so against my being around that it just felt like more drama for you. Then I found these and thought you might want them."

Liar! If I were in my body and had blood, it would be boiling. Laura has always been full of hooey, but this really takes the Snickerdoodles!

I catch a glimpse of the pictures. Is she kidding? That's not me! That girl is too thin. What kind of trick is she playing?

I take a closer look. That's me all right, but I thought I was at least twice that size. Even then, was I really not as big as I thought?

Son of a monkey! I never thought I was huge until Laura came around. Why did I let her distort my view? I know exactly when that photo was taken. It was the day I lost my self-esteem, and I've never fully recovered.

Laura could swing and flip like a ballerina on the monkey bars. Her eyes were so determined, yet her smile was bold. I loved how her hair danced in the sunlight. I imagined mine doing that, but the best I could do was jump and grab the bar. I hoped that if I could do just one pull-up, Laura would show me more.

Every morning I'd get to school early and fight to bring my chin up. Some days I saw big gains, while others I struggled. Finally, my chin went over the bar and I was elated in the hope of becoming athletic!

That afternoon, I scarcely had a bite of lunch, not wanting to weigh myself down. It took forever for Laura to nibble down half of her sandwich before heading off. Sure enough, she went straight for the monkey bars. I walked behind, but my heart raced like I was sprinting. She jumped and grabbed the bar, flicked her legs up, and hung. "Hey, Laura, would you please show me how to do some of that stuff you do?"

"What? Like this?" She pulled herself into a double spin.

"Yeah!" Anticipation filled me!

"Umm … Can you even do a chin-up?"

"Yes! I did one this morning." I jumped up and grabbed the bar, ready to show her.

"One? I can do twenty. Do you really think that because you can do one chin-up you have the strength to flip yourself around?" The verbal slap would have been fine, if it was politely stated, but her arrogance came through loud and clear. Even if it hadn't, her glaring eyes that scanned my body and landed on my stomach spoke volumes. "Besides, you'd never be able to bend back enough to get your legs past your gut and over the bar. Talk to me when you lose thirty pounds."

What? The doctor said I only need to lose five! I looked down to the roll of gut that was exposed from my shirt being drawn up while I hung. I felt sick and immediately released my grip. The moment I landed, I covered my flesh. How dare the doctor lie and say I only needed to lose five pounds! The burn of shame welled in my eyes. I grabbed my lunchbox and headed for the bathroom to hide in a stall. Food was shameful. If I didn't think I would get in trouble with Mom, I would have tossed the box in the trash.

Still, the depression didn't stop my stomach from grumbling. Sitting in class while the whole room mocked my noisy gut would lead to more embarrassment. I nibbled at my sandwich, intending to eat only half like Laura did. Meanwhile, the Ho-Ho in my lunch box glared at me. Laura's judging eyes were glued in my mind, filling me with self-loathing. I had to lose weight, and I would never do it by eating Ho-Hos.

Did Laura eat Ho-Hos, or was she some health food nut? The thought of her nibbling on a salad and dreaming of sinning with chocolate thrilled me. It turned my image of her hazel eyes sad. Bet she would be jealous!

I smiled as I devoured the first bite, but during the second my heart ached of loneliness. By the third, tears came. Even as a little girl, I realized I was a junkie who couldn't say no. How different would life have been if I had given that Ho-Ho away and told mom to never give me another one?

Laura puts her hand on Jensen's arm. Why doesn't he jerk away? "You okay?" she asks.

His eyes stay on the photo. "No. Not at all. She was so adorable. I can't believe we may never have the children we dreamt of."

No. Don't think that way. It *will* happen.

Laura's hand goes to his leg in an offer of sympathy, but this time he tenses to her touch. He looks into her eyes while shaking his head in disbelief. "Lizetta being friends with someone who was going through all that pain, while wanting to hide from her own suffering, reminds me of how selfless she is. I need some air."

Laura gulps. Did his words actually get to her?

"Why don't you get some coffee?" she asks. "I'll keep Lizetta company. Maybe hearing some old stories will help."

Jensen nods and heads off, leaving me with the horrible woman. The moment he's out of earshot, she seems to forget how Jensen hit one of her nerves. She puts her feet up, not just on my bed, but also on my pillow! "Seriously, how the hell did *you* nail Jensen?" She takes her feet down so she can lean in and rub my misery in deeper. "I really need to thank you, because with this little stunt here, Jensen is turning vulnerable again. He's perfect for me now—like really perfect. I can finally have my happily ever after."

Oh, no! Not her! Absolutely not her!

That painting. That Tarot reading. My dream. They all pointed to another woman coming in and taking the glory. That absolutely, positively, will not be Laura Muler! If I can't come back and get him, I will find someone else for Jensen—*anyone* other than this horrible person.

JENSEN

The coins *clank* down the slot and into the bucket. The

cup drops, and the smell of coffee rises.

How the hell were Lizetta and Laura friends? Laura's been screwed up since she was a little girl. Would Lizetta really have a friend like that? Lizetta fights her misconception that she's three times her actual size. Maybe Laura's reality is distorted as well. She told me she didn't have anyone she could trust. Lizetta would never be less than the perfect friend.

The sound of pouring ends and coffee waits. What the hell am I doing? I gave up coffee when I gave up alcohol, because it was part of my hangover cure. Having no crutches for the morning after makes staying sober a little easier. Right now I need every drop of help I can get.

The cup stays in the machine. I'm damn near broke and just shy of maxing out my credit card due to wedding flowers, yet I plunk down more cash for some juice. Dammit! All Laura did was suggest coffee and it gave me the notion that it's what I need. Man, that girl clutters my mind.

Shit! I left her alone with Lizetta! I almost hope Lizetta hasn't woken and they are laughing it up, because the last thing I want is Laura on the guest list to our wedding.

Inside the room, Laura is whispering to Lizetta and giggling like she's part of the girlfriend brigade. She looks at me, smiles, and giggles again. I guess it's good that some girl talk is going on. Anything to help, right?

I look to my girl, hoping to see a hint of a smile that shows her friend is getting through. Instead, I swear, I freaking swear that there is a disturbance in this room, and Lizetta looks just as lifeless as before. I'm about to hurl my juice.

This is too much.

"Hey, Laura, would you mind taking off? I need some alone time with my fiancée."

Laura

Good enough. I've done about all I can here.

"See you later, old friend." If she can hear me, she's fuming. If my lies don't bring her out of the coma, nothing will.

At the foot of the bed, I turn to give one last pout of sympathy, but the unexpected hits as I get a solid look at the full picture—the wires, the tubes, the bags of fluids. My stomach feels like the bottom has dropped out. I've been so wrapped up in the goal that I've missed the direness of the situation. That's Lizetta under all those bandages. My old, childhood … schoolmate. She's a good person who always tries to do the right thing, even when people hurt her. Good people shouldn't suffer.

I used to think I was a good person. Then I suffered too much. I had to do something to take the focus off of the pain, so I became me. Jensen did the same thing.

Lizetta doesn't deserve her fate.

JENSEN

As soon as the door closes, the room seems to brighten. I go to my side of the bed, the side where I keep the chair and the same side that I sleep on at home. I kick off my shoes and curl up next to Lizetta.

Come on universe. Work this one out. We need a miracle.

22

Wednesday, July 26

JENSEN

Outside my window, the rest of the world carries on with worries of their own. Most of the people around here are probably in a deep sleep. I lie in bed, staring at the ceiling. I should have stayed at the hospital, because I can't feel Lizetta now, and even though Paul assures me that she is fine, it's making me crazy.

Why are there times when I can't feel her? It's rare but …

Maybe she's normally with me but is now off taking care of something important.

That's crazy. My mind is frying.

My fingers press into my eyelids in hopes of making my eyes water. They are so dry that it hurts to move them. My mouth is also one huge cotton ball.

Pain shoots in my gut. My weakened state is only partially the result of a lack of sleep. I can't remember the last time I had a real meal, and my intake has consisted of small amounts of water, a sip of protein shake here and there, and an occasional piece of bread. Anything else makes a return appearance.

Etta whimpers when my feet hit the ground. I rub her belly and assure straight into her droopy eyes that I am okay. I need a vegetable, a piece of fruit—anything to give me nutrients before I keel over. What happened to the man who was so healthy? How ironic is it that while Lizetta has to be fed through a tube, in some ways she is healthier than I am?

It's a clear night, yet all I see is fog. Somehow Bertha manages to get me to a grocery store. I turn off my thoughts about how queasy my stomach is and let the colors guide me through the produce section—carrots, kale, strawberries, blueberries—nature's rainbow of health. My knees buckle when I grab a gallon of milk. The liquid splashes in the plastic and the bile in my stomach goes with it. I try to ignore the queasiness and move on, but instead of seeing nutrition, I see acid reflux. If I eat this, I'm going to need something to counteract how sick it will make me.

No.

No drugs of any kind are allowed in my body. Antacids weren't acceptable a few weeks ago, so they shouldn't be now.

I stare at the groceries, and my stomach burns. The weakness that makes this basket seem far heavier than it should becomes mentally draining. Will this ordeal ever end? Is there a way out other than the unthinkable? Am I only waiting for the inevitable, just like the doctors say?

Oh dear God, why me? Why Lizetta? Why the challenges? I can't do this anymore. I can't go on without food, without support, without something to ease the pain that gets harder to face each day. My face scrunches, and my chest heaves. Dry sobs—again. *It's too much.*

I have too many decisions to make. Whether it's about food or the love of my life, someone needs to tell me what to do, because I can't live like this anymore. Hell, with the way things are going, I won't be alive much longer anyway. Please, God, help me, because I am not as strong as you seem to think I am.

A moment later, I have to will my hand not to shake when I give the checkout woman my credit card, and then walk away with a bottle of vodka and two six packs of Ensure.

Lizetta

There has to be a reason why I was allowed back other than to get Etta to stop Jensen from drinking. What was it that crazy angel said? That I'm not coming back "in that busted body." Then there was that shady comment, "For years you wanted to trade it in for another, and now you are clamoring for it back." It sure sounds like he is implying that I need to find a new shell.

Man, this really is like *Drop Dead Diva!* She had a useless guardian angel too; only hers didn't look like a fast food mascot. The woman died, hit the Return key, and then popped into the body of someone else who had just been revived. Perfect! I'm in a hospital. People die here all the time. I just need to hang around until somebody awesome passes on, and then jump into her body upon its revival. It'll be like a self-serve dessert bar!

Yeah, a creepy one filled with needles and diseases. What happens if I pop into the body of someone with something incurable? I'll probably get Jensen convinced I came back just before I die again. This is tricky.

Room upon antiseptic-smelling room holds one heart-breaking story after another—coughing, puking, moaning—heart disease, cancer, AIDS. I'm not in a ward where babies are born. This is where people go to die.

I'm pretty sure Jensen doesn't have a gay bone in his body, so everyone male is automatically removed from the candidate list. I come upon a room with a woman who appears to be in her mid-thirties. She has medium-toned skin and long, dark hair. I like its flow. She and Jensen would be beautiful together.

My heart drops into my stomach. Even if he is still with my soul, I don't want him with any part of anyone other than me. I miss my life. I miss my body—my beautiful body that is a reflection of my experiences. If I take over another one, will it remain as it was when I inhabited it, or will the habits of my spirit take over? Will it someday feel like a home, or will I always feel as if I am renting a room? What if I jump into someone's body too soon and they can't get back in, even though they are supposed to? That would turn me into a killer.

This is morbid.

Beside the woman is a picture of her with a man and two children. I've no choice but to cross her off the list. I can't let her family watch her die and return only to leave them for Jensen. There sure are a lot of factors in this. Why does returning from the dead need to be so complicated?

In the next room lies a lady whose advanced age takes her out of the running. Even though she is asleep and surrounded by gifts showing overflowing love and support, her being alone tugs at my heartstrings. I touch my hand to hers, wishing I could hold it. Her body remains still and with a bit of a smile across her lips. This lady is old, like great-grand-matriarch type old. *Lord, please let me know what it feels like to be her someday—well-loved and having lived a full life.*

Suddenly, the machines around her start screaming that her heart has stopped. "Are you an angel?" a female voice rings out from above.

My eyes go heavenward, where the spirit of the old woman floats. "You can see me?"

"Yes, honey, of course I can see you." Her chest expands with her inhale. Her skin turns smooth and free of the signs of aging. Along with it, her grey hair turns cherry cola red. A white light beams down upon her and she faces it in awe. "This is the moment that I have waited my whole life for! Goodbye beautiful people of Earth. A new adventure awaits!" The light draws her away as I stare, forgetting to breathe in the presence of perfection.

That's not how I looked when it happened to me, but it is how it should be for all of us—to depart when we are ready in a moment of glory. It is no wonder why I upset God.

The next time I go, I will give myself that gift of happiness, but first God, please let me fulfill a life of compassion that extends to all creatures. When it comes right down to it, that's all that matters here. Without boundless compassion, we are nothing. Please, let me help make mankind something.

A Code Red alarm sounds over the loudspeaker, sending me racing to the Emergency Room. My feet can't hit the ground fast enough. What if this is it and I take too long?

Faster! Faster down the florescent-lit corridor I go!

A car crash victim, of about my age, is being wheeled in. "We're not getting a pulse," a paramedic yells. The doctor calls for a crash cart as I watch her spirit rise. She looks down upon her body in sorrow, then smiles to the light and lets it consume her. Unlike the woman before, this one leaves a silver cord trailing behind, much like the one attached to me.

"Clear!" someone yells. The body jerks, but her heart doesn't start. They try it again with the same results. Still, there is no sight of the woman, just a cord ascending toward Heaven. Is she being given a choice? That means her body is capable of living! This is perfect!

"One more time," the doctor says. The cord begins to fade, and my excitement builds. She's going to Heaven! You go girl!

I close my eyes and dive toward her body. This is it! "Oh God, thank you! Thank you so—"

Bam!

I'm cold cocked across the room. The woman gives me the stink eye before being sucked back into her body like it's a Hoover.

Harold's laughter rings out next to me. "You didn't think that lame stunt would work, did you? How many times will I have to tell you that this is not a TV show? There are rules here—like actual rules—not Toon Town rules."

I point my finger in his face. "You never said that I couldn't come back. In fact, you've implied—"

A nurse runs through Harold on her way to assist the girl who's just been revived. Harold motions me out of the emergency area and leads me to where the ambulances arrive. "You have the most interesting way of interpreting things. Now, I'm sure you've noticed your body isn't doing so well. You might want to try to think of something constructive, else I'm going to have to shake you by the shoulders."

"Huh? But I don't even know what I am supposed to accomplish!"

Harold takes two steps back into an oncoming ambulance. He fades, yet his voice hangs in the air. "You've said your prayers, now discover how you can make them come true. Observe and learn, dear girl. Observe and learn."

JENSEN

Last time I pulled poison from the trash. This bottle came from the grocery store. I grabbed it without a thought, but an altar boy buying his first nudie magazine would not have felt as guilty and excited as I did when I whipped out the credit card.

I went for vodka. I never drink vodka, which shows that I'm not returning to my old ways, right?

Yeah, that's a bunch of horse crap, and I know it.

Etta growls as I crack the seal so I can dump the booze down the sink; yet I'm still seated on the sofa. I have no intent of dumping this anywhere but down my throat.

I can't keep getting like this. I'll call Jimmy or Paul. They will be more than happy to talk me out of it.

Shit. Jimmy's studying for a test that he is probably going to fail, and Paul's at the hospital. I can't risk Paul answering with Lizetta in earshot and have her worry.

God, why can't I feel her? Jimmy said he's felt her before, too. Maybe she's floating around and is helping Jimmy with that test.

This is crazy. I'll call Griffin. He wants what's good for Lizetta as much as I do. He can talk me down.

Without even a ring, the phone goes to voicemail. Crap. I'll call Mom.

No, she'll freak, and I'll get defensive. Bad combo.

There is one other person.

Laura is shocked when I call. She should be. It's three in the morning, and the last time I called her was back when I was still vulnerable to her ways. She also sounds a little afraid I'm about to tell her some really bad news. "How is Lizetta?" she asks.

"Worse, and I'm about to lose it."

"I'm on my way."

I hang up and realize that I just invited my bed buddy over for a drink—a bed buddy that reminds me how badly I want to ride the heroin dragon again. I am so, so screwed.

Laura

Perfect! I knew pulling the, I've-got-stories-about-your-comatose-girlfriend card would sucker him in. I've got a fifteen-minute drive to come up with more bull shit about my childhood pal that I miss so much.

I get on the freeway and gun the gas. A shot rips through my leg.

Motherfucker that hurts! Son of a bitch!

I pull to the shoulder while using my left foot to brake. As soon as I am off the road, I pound on my leg to loosen the cramp. It only gets worse, and walking on it seems impossible. The pain goes from burning to itching. I yank up the leg of my jeans and scratch, and then scratch more, harder and deeper each time. The streaks grow redder—bloodier.

Blood …

I've got to get another fix.

JENSEN

The reflection in the bathroom mirror is of someone who is

ashen and hollow. The dark circles under his eyes scream that he is lonely and lost. That figure can't be me.

I try to breathe in every molecule of goodness the universe will grace me with. If I get enough grounding air, that figure will look like me again. Though there is not much good in my life, there is much good in the world. The true me knows that, and doing the right things will bring him back.

With another breath, I tell myself I am sinking into the ground. If I can become one with the earth, then so can Lizetta, and we can become one together. When it boils down to that, collectively we are still but a lone unit.

We are always alone, aren't we? We hope to find someone to spend our life with, but the image you see in the mirror is always yours, even if it has company.

There is no escaping you.

Laura doesn't need to knock. The second she steps into the driveway, Etta sounds off like an earthquake is about to hit. I open the door and am not at all surprised to find that, even at this hour, Laura looks like her trampy self—except for the jeans.

Jeans? Holy shit, her legs must be bad.

The part of me that wants to slide backward is relieved to see that I have somebody I can do it with, but the part of me that wants to move forward is disgusted. Laura is too far gone to be only a weekend junkie. She no longer looks skeletal—she looks hollow.

"Jesus! This place reeks of vodka and tequila. How much have you had?"

"Not a drop, but the floor and sink had their fair share. I just dumped the entire bottle of vodka, but I left part of the mess from an accident I had a few days ago with some tequila as a reminder not to fuck up." I take Laura to the sofa and push her down by the shoulders. "Sit!"

"Yes, sir!" She gives me the dirty once over. "Stop!" I raise a finger to halt her right there. "No funny ideas! I'm engaged to a woman who may have some problems right now, but I love her and that is the end of that, okay?" Laura nods. It isn't good enough. "Tell me you respect it."

She tosses her hands up. "Fine! I respect it."

"You still using that shit?" She shakes her head, and my glare shows I don't believe her.

"I'm chipping back."

"That's useless, and you know it. When was the last time?"

"Last weekend. I used to ride Saturday and Sunday. Now I'm down to Saturday."

"Stop lying. That shit don't fly with me. We both know you take it whenever you can get it. Let's change that. What I heard you say was, 'I just quit.' To which I replied, 'Good, then I'll help you.' Don't move."

From inside the fridge I grab a pitcher of strawberry protein shakes I made five minutes before she got here. I pour a couple of glasses and set one in front of her. "Drink."

"The hell? What is this crap? Pepto-Bismol?"

"You and I have spent way too much time getting the other to drink, and in some ways that's not such a bad thing. We were just drinking the wrong stuff. A few days ago you said you wanted me to show you how to get better. If you really meant that, down that protein shake and then drink another one. Come back tomorrow, and we'll do it again. We are back to being drinking buddies, and when I know I can actually trust you, we will start talking. *Like, actual talking.* But not today. One step at a time."

"Is this a challenge?"

My glare speaks that if anyone here is doing any challenging, it is Laura with my patience. But yeah, it's a challenge for her to shape up, just like it is a reminder for me to stay clean.

Laura raises her glass. "Cheers."

She chugs while I sip. My stomach tries to squeeze the shake back up.

Once she downs her second shake, she gets the boot. "See you tomorrow. Swing by at six o'clock every morning for breakfast. If you have to do that, you won't be up partying all night. Meanwhile, eat something! Eat a lot of something and drink a lot of water or juice with nothing in it, okay? Don't screw up!"

When I shut the door, Etta glares at me to say, "That goes double for you." I start to thank her, then make for the bathroom to say hello again to the protein shake.

Laura

Yes!

Yes! Yes! Yes! My insides want to burst!

It takes everything I've got to hold back my scream until I drive away. "Score!"

23

Thursday, July 27

Lizetta

Paul and Jimmy stare at each other. Mom paces while repeatedly slapping her hands on her legs, like she is trying to beat herself up. At Paul's touch, she puts out her hands in a signal for him to stop. "I'm fine, but I need more answers than that so-called doctor, who just strutted out, can give me. How can it be that my daughter has survived like this for so long, yet they are giving me this line of bull? It doesn't make any sense. The fact that my baby is obviously fighting must mean something!"

"June Bug, have a seat and calm down for a moment."

Her hands sharply cross in front of her. "No. I'm fine. I'm going for a walk. There's a man upstairs who owes me answers. Clearly no one here has them. I'll be back in a minute."

Paul and Jimmy resume staring at each other. "Which of us is going to tell Jensen?" Jimmy asks.

Paul's shoulders drop in acceptance of the weight. "I'll handle it as soon as he gets off work."

"Maybe we should call Arlene and ask her to do it."

"Nah, she'll want to come down, and if he's not up to company, it will add stress. Jensen likes to handle things his own way. She and I had a good talk. The best way to be there for Jensen is to let him call the shots, but when you have to tell your kid bad news, you want to be there to smother him. Besides, this isn't the first time I've had to give news regarding someone in a coma. That time sure was different though."

Paul strokes my cheek with his thumb. The reduction in

my number of bandages has taken me from mummy-like to resembling a crash victim in a cheesy, made-for-TV movie. The good news is, the people in those movies always recover.

"Let's just say the accident that guy had was self-inflicted, which is all the more reason why it should be me who talks to Jensen."

Thing is, no one else seems to know I'm going to make it back.

JENSEN

For the last week I have spent a good chunk of my life in this chair while staring at a woman in distress. First the coma, then seizures, then holes in her head. Now, because of the results of her latest MRI and EEG test, the neurologist has changed her diagnosis to Persistent Vegetative State. The doctor tried to explain what that really means, but all I heard him say was Lizetta's chances of recovery are slimmer than ever.

You allowed this mess, God. You probably think I should be grateful that she is still alive. I could justify you taking her because you were jealous and wanted to spend time with her, but to cause her this suffering is senseless.

My stomach lets out a roar. I promised I wouldn't allow that to happen again. I promised Lizetta I'd marry her. I promised to never touch drugs or get wasted again.

I am really sick of promises.

The can of strawberry Ensure I grab out of my backpack seems appropriate. This is the crap they give people in hospitals and convalescent homes—the food of the geriatric—the food for those too sick to eat. I raise the bottle and toast its followers. I swig down the goo. It almost comes back up when I put it all together. This is the thing we are considering depriving Lizetta of so she can pass on and be at peace. How ironic is it that my decline puts me on the same treatment path as someone who can't care for herself?

The bottle gets stashed under my chair so I can't smell it. There is no way I can drink that stuff now that I see it for what it really is—the same stuff that is in that disgusting feeding tube.

When it comes down to it, I need that bottle to help me hold it together, just like alcohol once did. How much healthier am I now? How much have we all suffered since Lizetta's accident? Hell, her family and I all look like walking zombies. What good is a bottle that keeps you alive when you're dead inside?

The doctors' constant hints that we are prolonging the inevitable are their way of saying that we have only succeeded in adding to her misery. Then again, some of them say she is not even aware of what is happening. If we are the ones hurting, and Lizetta's condition is hopeless, why are we doing this to ourselves?

Am I really thinking what I think I'm thinking?

Maybe it would be best for everyone's sake.

But I can't imagine life without her. I need her here.

There I go being selfish again.

I didn't just promise to marry her; I promised to make her happy. She can't possibly be happy now.

I give Lizetta's hand a kiss, right where the reminder of a promise sits, and I get defensive over my desire to run. "I need some sleep, honey. I'll be back in a few hours. I love you, always, no matter what."

I bolt out the door, leaving Lizetta and the Ensure behind.

24

Friday, July 28

JENSEN

Lizetta stands inside a field of green.

Knock. Knock. Knock.

I run to her.

Knock. Knock. Knock.

Her hand reaches for mine and—

Pound! Pound! Pound!

I rip the covers off and sprint for the door. Etta dashes along while barking. With a snap of my wrist and a yank, the door flies open. "Looks like you couldn't sleep either," Laura has the balls to say.

Before I can ask her why the hell she is here, she's plopped onto my sofa. She's in pink fuzzy slippers and black PJs with little pink kittens on them. Laura owns pajamas? If she were a normal person, I'd think going out like that was ridiculous. However, this is Laura. Only one thing seems to explain her. Ten bucks says the outfit gives her the excuse to fall asleep on my sofa. Being the gentleman that I am, of course I would offer her my bed, and—oh, no possible way!

"I couldn't stop thinking about Lizetta, so I pulled out some photos from prom. I thought you might like to see them."

Yeah, I'd love to see pictures of Lizetta, but not at two in the morning. Especially not when I was finally getting a little sleep.

Laura makes herself all kinds of comfortable by snuggling into the sofa. She has the audacity to put her furry feet up on the coffee table. When they nearly bump into Lizetta's tiara, my death glare tells her to remove them. "You are not supposed to be here for another four hours. Can we please do this at another time? Despite the facts that my fiancée is in a coma and I've left school, I do still need to go to work."

"You quit school?"

Lizetta

"Yeah, you what?" How can I take time to find a solution when I need to keep watch on Jensen every second? Then again, how could I have stopped him?

Also, prom pictures? Is she freaking kidding? Boy is she going to be sorry when all this gets fixed and Jensen hears the truth. Jensen is in for a rude awakening as well. Obviously they are friends, even though he is in denial of that fact. I've been pretty forgiving so far. Either I am going to come back to the land of the living and let him have it, or I am going to learn how to move stuff around so I can be one of those ghosts who complicates people's lives. I may be an understanding person, but there are limits!

JENSEN

"No, I put it on hold. I'll go back next semester when I can focus." Laura mimics the look I give when I call her a liar. "No, really. I'm going back next semester, no matter what happens with Lizetta. She'd never forgive me if I didn't."

Laura returns her eyes to the photo and she nods. "I get it. If I were you, I wouldn't want to disappoint her either."

There is no way she gets what I am up against. Those fuzzy slippers have yet to hit the ground and walk their way out, so I just keep staring while willing her to leave.

Finally, she clues in. "Sorry, I had a bad night and needed a diversion. I thought you might, too." She's slow in standing while hoping I get it. This could be Laura being the manipulative tramp she is, or it could be Laura needing not to escape her reality and leave the drugs at home. We are supposed to help each other.

"Sit. Let's see what you got." I'm not sure I'm ready for this. I'd be fooling myself not to think that there are heavy decisions regarding Lizetta ahead. If we decide that all is said and done, I don't know if I'll be able to allow myself to think of her again. After taking part in such a decision, I might pull my own plug.

I sit a good foot away, and Laura leans in like we're buddies. Etta starts whipping her tail while giving me the look of a woman scorned—much like Lizetta would if she were here.

No worries, Etta. Laura is not my buddy, though in many ways she's the best friend I've got right now. Paul may get what I'm up against, but nobody gets my past like Laura.

Also, no one makes me as edgy as she does. I hate how I sound to myself when she is around yet …

Frankly, I want to wrap my arms around her, solely because I need someone to still love me despite my being a heartbeat away from blowing it. Fortunately, Etta jumps up between us. I owe her one.

Of course, the top picture is of Laura, looking all kinds of hot in a black dress that reveals just enough skin to be alluring. The Laura I've always known has been pretty, but here she was gorgeous. It's hard not to be invasive and ask for details on what the hell happened, even though I kind of know. *"Dad finally made sure his little girl can't be seen as innocent anymore. It's okay. I've been waiting for it."* As much as I deny what that must mean, it still makes me shiver. If the bastard wasn't in jail for his third DUI, I may have killed him by now.

"Well, what do you think?" Her eager eyes remind me of a little girl who is seeking daddy's approval. Considering all the ways I have shown her how I have approved in the past, and what her dad did, her turning to me as a father figure is creepy.

I play into her want for praise and tell her the truth. "You looked fantastic."

Laura flips through a few pictures of her friends. All of them show staged goofiness. She giggles, and I fake amusement. I don't give a crap about these. I just want to see photos of the future mother of my children. Finally, she gets to one. Lizetta stands alone while looking out onto the dance floor. Her golden hair drapes over her shoulders and down to the top of her strapless dress. Her skin glimmers. God, how I miss everything about her. I'm speechless at her beauty, and because I want to be with her for a moment without interruptions.

"Check out that dress!"

Don't you dare go there, little Miss Anorexia. You always have my compassion until you open your mouth.

"I always thought that dress was a little … Umm …"

"Perfect for her in every way." It comes out like a sigh of longing. Man, the girl has me whipped.

"I was going to say, teal."

Sure you were.

The dress is the perfect color for Lizetta. Still, the brightness of the satin makes it a bit to take in.

"I tried to talk her into a little black number, but for some crazy reason, she wanted that teal dress."

Of course she wanted teal. She wouldn't be Lizetta if she didn't. "Well, she is a hard-core hockey fan."

Laura's expression goes flat. Now that's interesting.

Lizetta

The picture surprises me. I expect to see rolls of fat. Instead I find a pretty, young woman with curves that glide like those of a model—which was how I felt when the night started. When it ended, I was a crying wreck of blubber, all because I let myself be influenced by Laura.

How dare she claim we had been friends enough to go shopping together! God! I didn't even want to go to the prom. Thing was, if I didn't, I would be branded a loser who couldn't get a date—and I was until salvation came from my best friend. "Hey, you know how you keep bitching about your prom? Since Prince Charming has yet to show up on his white horse, how about you settle for a crappy date and let me take you in a rusty Nova?"

Seriously, how could a girl refuse such a charming offer? "Sure, but I'm not putting out, so don't go getting any funny ideas."

"No way. Even if you strapped something on, boobs scare the crap out of me."

I tried not to think of all the bizarre connotations and see it as a man telling me I had awesome tits.

A couple of weeks later, a tuxedo-clad Griffin and I were inside the San Francisco Galleria, surrounded by three levels of balconies. I swore the world was staring down. I wondered if the attention was out of amazement that I had a date, caused by my gloriously low-cut neckline, or because Griffin looked delicious enough to be on the cover of an erotica book.

Griffin was the most amazing date. He even asked for a fabric swatch from my dress so he could match a corsage to it. He skillfully spun me during the fast dances, and then romanced me through the ballads. If I didn't know he was gay beyond a doubt, which he proved by not being able to look me in the cleavage, I would have popped the question.

My perfect night may have stayed that way, if I hadn't stopped on my way out of the rest room for a quick glance in the mirror. No wonder why Griffin kept his eyes on mine. My boobs were lethal!

A group of giggling girls staggered in with Laura at the helm. "Lizzie!" Laura smacked me on the back. "Nice dress! Your cousin's kind of hot!"

The other girls giggled.

I didn't expect kindness, but that cheap jab took her teasing to a whole new level of disrespect, and it pushed me too far. After years of sucking it up, I let her have it. "Aw. That's cute of you to be jealous." I smacked her on the back like she had done to me. "Don't worry. Your date may not get the best date of the night award, but Brad's good looking in his own special way."

Her entourage sang a chorus of "Oohs."

Laura's eyes flared. I thought she was about to deck me. Instead, she did something far worse. She hit my gut with a glare. "Great come back, *Liz*. I always underestimate how witty your kind are in order to make up for their physical flaws."

My brain froze, just like her eyes had on my midsection. It was far worse than a threat made to my face. This one was made into my soul. She looked up with the unfortunate timing of seeing the first tear fall. Then I was out the door. One of the girls called, "I thought you were a cow, not a chicken!"

I fled to the second balcony and grabbed a seat in a corner, literally biting my tongue so I could focus on the physical pain and fight the sobs that would ruin my makeup. When Griffin found me, he read the story in my eyes from across the room. Like a real life Prince Charming, he made a beeline for me. "Let me guess. You ran into Queen Bitch."

Griffin practically dragged me into the center of the dance floor. He tucked his head down into my shoulder and pressed his fingers against my back. The embrace that showed the world I was worth holding brought back my pride as we swayed in half time to the driving beat. Once we had drawn enough attention, he raised my chin and whispered, "You owe me for this—*big time*." His kiss was impassioned, but the butterflies in my stomach were brought on by the shock that someone cared so much that he would do something that went against the core of who he was to help me save face.

The crowd cheered, but his next kiss nearly brought the house to its knees. He tucked me in his arm and paraded me off of the dance floor. I caught a glimpse of Laura's face as we strolled past. Her dropped jaw showed shock, but that didn't stop her from getting in the last word. "Guess her cousin likes 'em hefty."

I barely managed to make it out with my head up. Now this witch is claiming to be my friend in order to steal my fiancé while I am helpless. For years she has been stealing my soul, now she's going for my heart.

JENSEN

Laura flips to the next photo, and it's one of Lizetta dancing with Griffin. It figures that they would go together. If he were not so man-happy, I'd feel threatened by him.

"You know," Laura says, "for the life of me, I can't remember the name of her date. Nice guy. I wish I hadn't lost track of her once high school ended. Apparently they had an epic break-up."

The hell? No friend of Lizetta would not know who Griffin is, let alone think they dated.

I've always known Laura was full of shit. Now this filthy, little liar is fibbing about how well she knows Lizetta. Griffin told me he knew about his sexuality in grade school and has been honest with everyone from the start. Laura is the one who lives lies. I can't help her if she won't face herself.

I nudge Etta aside and take Laura's hands. I can't shake the feeling that Lizetta knows and is pissed, but dammit, I've got to reconcile this crap. Like it or not, the universe keeps showing me that I am in this with her. "Laura," I look deep into her eyes—deeper than I ever have before. She has really beautiful eyes. I've always known that, under the right circumstances, I could get lost in them. "I need you to be honest with me."

She slides her hand behind my head. "About what?" she whispers, and something in her tone nearly steals my breath. I'm reminded of all the times we have been like this and why I always caved. I despise how this girl constantly conflicts me.

I snap back to reality—harshly. "You've lied about your relationship with Lizetta. These aren't pictures of your friend; they are trophies. The more you hurt, the more you hurt others. It's time you faced what caused you to hurt in the first place."

Laura yanks her hands away and starts to make for the door. I nab them and pull her back down. "You need to talk about this."

"No!" she snaps. "I don't need to talk about anything."

She has got to get out of fantasyland. This whole crock of crap about knowing Lizetta isn't just her way of trying to gain approval. She may be so far gone that she is creating an alternate reality. Lord knows that if I were Laura, I would want to. Hell, in a way I did. "You need to let this out and be honest with yourself. I can't help you until you take the biggest step of all."

The way she jerks implies my touch stings. Her tone stays sharp and bitter. "What? And tell everyone that my dad raped me? There! I finally said it. Ya satisfied now?"

Not in the least, and the tension in my neck reinforces the power of my voice. "No. You were like this long before that happened. I can't help you fight lies unless you face the truth."

I expect her to crumble, but she pops up and stares down at me while holding ground with a tone that almost pushes me back. "Fine! Dad beat my mom to a pulp when she couldn't lose the baby weight—baby weight she put on when she was pregnant with me! Did he bug her after she had Larry? No, and she never let me live it down. Finally he caved to his sick fantasies, called her a cow and raped me. If she hadn't been fat, he never would have abused her, and I never would have been raped. Now are you happy?"

Happy about this? Never. But I will get satisfaction tonight when she hits rock bottom, because that is the only way she can head back toward the top. There is also fire in my veins because she lied to me, not to mention that I have a sneaking suspicion that there is a lot more to this story. I've seen Laura in action with chubby girls before. She's ruthless, and Lizetta has emotional scars brought on by bullying. I stand up and call her out on behalf of the woman

I love. "You and Lizetta were never friends, were you?"

She stays up in my face. Neither one of us is going down easily, and I'm fine with that. "How can you see her as some beauty queen? Your idolatry is disgusting!" Laura grabs the engagement photo and screams. "Fatetta! She was a pig who always acted above everyone else!"

I rip the photo from her scrappy hands. "Don't you dare! Tell me you never called her that!"

Laura's eyes get the wild look of a rabid animal, yet they are also reddening. Good! She deserves to feel the sting of the pain she's inflicted. "Oh, I did. To her face even! How dare she parade around like she wasn't the problem!"

That's fucking it! I'm a quarter of a second away from smacking this bitch's head against the wall and cracking her skull open. It radiates in my eyes that scream I'm gonna rip her fucking voice box out!

Her tears begin to pour. The rare times she really cries kill me, because Laura is tough. Real tears only happen when she has been kicked too hard. Like it or not, this is what I asked for. Spit flies out from the hiss of my words. "*She* was never the problem. *He* was." I put the picture of Lizetta in Laura's face. "Apologize to her!" Laura turns away, and I shove it back into her view. "Apologize to Lizetta and every girl you have ever insulted because of *your* issues. Then face the real problem!"

She turns on me. "What about you, Jensen? When are *you* going to face the real problem? You can't let me go, and you know it."

"You're right, I can't. And you know why? Guilt. I feel guilty for leaving you behind so I could take care of myself. I feel guilty that you are killing yourself because of your inability to find the same strength I have. You know that I hate you for bringing me that damn rig when I was too spaced out to stop you, yet I still see your potential when no one else does. You also know I am not as selfish as I think I am, and you play that against me. How you are turning this situation around is proof. I'm facing that now. Can you face you like I am facing me?" I grab the photo again. "Look at the woman in this picture. Know that you gave her self-esteem issues that she battles every day and that you are lying about your friendship with her to get to me. Then catch your reflection in the glass and face yourself!"

Laura falls to her knees, and I go down with her. I may hate this bitch but I also love her, and I am not letting her face this alone. I know she is not strong enough, and I would be selfish to abandon her now.

"I'm sorry," she whispers. She shakes her head and buries it in my shoulder. "Oh God, Lizetta, I am so sorry. You don't deserve to die."

Laura's words make my throat tighten. She's right. Lizetta has been in a coma for over a week. One way or another, she will soon be gone. If I am going to finish facing my demons, I have to face that one too.

I raise Laura's chin. My gentle tone compliments my touch. "Now, tell me who you are really angry at."

Her eyes lock straight into mine. "My dad."

"Whose fault is it really?"

"My dad's."

"Come on." I extend my hand. "As long as you are willing to fix this, I'll do anything I can to help you. But Laura, there are boundaries, okay?"

Lizetta

Laura nods. Jensen guides her to the sofa where he curls her into his arms as she sobs. I should be jealous. I should want to rip her eyes out and kick Jensen to a pulp for holding her. But for the first time, I am thankful that I am not Laura. If my death leads to someone with her troubled past finding peace, maybe her claiming my joy isn't so bad.

She raises her chin, and looks to him with adoration. He returns the gaze, and the grin that drags across his face shows he's resigning himself to the comfort of the moment. Jensen has always looked past my body to see the real me.

Now he is looking past her baggage. She truly is my replacement.

25

JENSEN

"Anyone have anything to say?" Paul asks with his eyes locked on the table. None of us want to look at each other because it would be acknowledging defeat. The last time we were here, at the lake, I had such high hopes. Now, part of me—

Part of me is giving—

This is crap.

Paul's sigh is filled with vibrato. "Being the leader isn't all it's cracked up to be."

Judy puts her hand onto Paul's. "No one blames you, honey. None of us want to start either. Thank you for trying. We all know where your heart is." She then sucks it up and braves moving forward with balls like those that I have only seen on one other person—my mom when Granddad had a stroke that left him blind, half-paralyzed, and unable to live on his own.

Judy's eyes scan evenly across the three of us. "Okay, without determining when it would happen, it is time to decide if we are even willing to consider extreme measures or if that option is completely off the table."

"I don't want us to do it," Jimmy blurts out. The rest sounds sheepish. "But it shouldn't be off the table."

Paul chimes in. "We have that damn medical directive, but Lizetta always avoided talking about the conditions. Jensen, the two of you were planning a future. Did this ever come up?"

This is such a nightmare. In hind sight, I see how this is one of those things you should talk about with your partner for life, but why would two people in their twenties, who are planning a wedding, talk about dying? How could you even begin to expect something like this would happen, especially when you are so young and full of love and hope? "Every word between us was about growing old together. The thought of what comes after never crossed our minds. We were too busy focusing on living in the moment. That's why …"

Dammit. If I hadn't proposed, this never would have happened.

"Wait," Jimmy chimes in. "How do they look at this stuff where she works? We should call Griffin. They must have talked about this a thousand times over." Jimmy goes for his phone.

I shiver. We did talk about this once, when I told her about Eddie. She called taking away his suffering a precious gift of love. Is that what she wants, for us to show her love through mercy?

God, this situation sucks! How can we be sure we are doing the right thing?

Lizetta

Jensen jumps up, grabs a stone, and hurls it into the lake. He then paces the length of the picnic bench, scrubbing his hand through his hair and then smacking the back of his head.

This is ridiculous! Just because I am starting to accept that I may not make it doesn't mean I am ready to leave my family. Even if it gets their hopes up in vain, they need to know I am still trying. I've been so afraid of not playing my cards right that I've neglected doing what I should have done long ago.

I jump up on the table and run back-and-forth. It whips Etta into a frenzy. Then I let fear overcome me for no reason other than the fact that I'm about to die. As my emotions build, Etta barks and circles the table. "That's my girl!"

Jimmy's eyes go up. He's looking at me without knowing it. "Remember that thing I said about how sometimes I feel Lizetta? Anyone think that Etta's acting strangely?"

JENSEN

How have I missed this? Etta is smart, but she's reacted to the alcohol, she sleeps in the same spot she always did when Lizetta is there, and she often wags her tail to the right—just like she does when she sees Lizetta!

Jimmy's words match my thoughts. "This may sound crazy but ..."

I pop up from my seat. My hope is senseless, but so is this whole situation. "Lizetta, if Etta is reacting to you, can you get her to go to that pine tree?"

Etta's head follows as if someone has jumped off of the table and is heading for the tree. She runs along, yapping like crazy. Euphoria rushes through me as my hope surges to new heights. This might be the most beautiful sight I will ever see.

"Now come back," I yell. Etta dashes back to the table. Paul has a tight grip on Judy, whose hand covers her lips, and Jimmy's mouth is agape, all while I hold my breath. Tears fall from every one of us. My words race out in excitement. "Lizetta, we need to know what you want us to do. Should we let you find peace, or do we keep fighting to get you back? Run back to the tree if we should let you go. Run to the water if you want to stay."

Etta makes for the lake and dives in. For a moment I freeze in awe, but then my spirit sends me running. Each thump of my feet makes my heart pound faster, just knowing that I'm getting closer to Lizetta. I don't even bother taking off my shoes before letting the water embrace me, while knowing that by some miracle I am in the same space she is.

Granddad always said there is more to life than we could

ever hope to see. My mother was the only one who didn't think he was crazy. When my brother died, I fought the universe, thus throwing my spirit to the ground. Then Lizetta came into my life and while she has always brought me hope, right now she is making my spirit soar.

Lizetta

Diving into the lake was just the beginning of my marathon. Once out, I run for my life. My dash takes me blocks away—through the lobby, past the exam rooms, and out to the back where Griffin is washing out the kennels. I go through cyclone fencing and into the cage of a German Shepherd. He flips out to tell me he's not happy that I've invaded his domain.

"Sherlock!" Griffin warns. He points to the Welsh Corgi in the next cage. "You'd better shut your mouth, or I'm gonna let Smiddy at you."

Once I get Sherlock good and riled, I pass through two cages and coax a Dachshund into chasing her tail. Griffin takes a stance with his hands on his hips. He reminds me of his mama. "Frankenweenie, what the hell is wrong with you?"

Inside the next cage, I stir up more trouble with a poodle. Naturally, it nips at me. Griffin heads over, and it snaps at him through the fence. "Oh, that's just it! I've had it with everyone around here!" He throws down the hose and struts into the building. When we get near a cat getting a flea bath, it scuttles across the room and slides in front of Griffin. "What the hell is going on around here? Are we about to have an earthquake or something?"

Griffin stays on target toward the front. The door of an exam room opens, and a woman exits with a Dalmatian. I dance around it and then around Griffin. The thing comes unglued to the point where his owner can barely contain him on his leash.

"Did I take a bath in something funny?" Griffin asks.

I stay where I'm at and let him walk forward. A lady exits the next room with a cat in a carrier. The cat looks in my direction and hisses. Griffin turns back in disbelief. "What is going on?" The head-shaking Griffin goes into the office area and takes a seat at his desk. How can he be so oblivious? "Nothing's been the same at this place without Lizzie."

Come on! Make the connection!

A tinkling in the lobby signals divine intervention. Hopefully my favorite, slobbering hound will give me a break. Griffin opens the door to let Socrates in for his appointment. Socrates tugs at his leash in a request to visit me. "Come, boy," his owner says while tugging back. "She's not here now."

The hoodels I'm not! I do jumping jacks while meowing. Socrates tugs harder and begins barking. I pop up on my desk and he breaks free. Griffin chases him, but when Socrates jumps up to get to me, Griffin stops dead in his tracks. "Girl, what is going on?"

"Excuse me?" Socrates' mom asks.

"It's nothing ma'am." Griffin stares at my desk, and then guides Socrates to an exam room. A few minutes later, he returns with a cat. The closer he gets to me, the more the cat smacks its tail against Griffin's bicep. Griffin backs off. The cat still glares in my direction, but now her tail just swishes. "Lizzie, are you here?" He gets close, and the cat tries to claw out of his arms.

Griffin's face goes void of life. "Lizzie baby, knock once if you're here, twice if you're not. Never mind, that's crazy talk. Just knock."

Gah! If I could make noise, I'd have done it ages ago. Griffin waits with bated breath as I scramble for a solution. I jump toward him and yell, "Boo!" The cat's fur stands on end, and she hisses.

"Sweet Baby Jesus! I'll be a—" The cell phone on Griffin's desk rings, causing him to jump, which in turn causes the cat to shriek. "Five missed calls from Jensen. Lizzie, what's going on? Are you ... Oh no, you are *not* dead!" He answers the phone, and his "Hello?" crawls out. "Etta jumped into the lake like she was going after Lizetta? No, no. Not as weird as you may think." Through the earpiece, Jensen's voice rattles on. "Hold—Hold up, Mr. Big Bulge. Stop panicking about not feeling her anymore." Griffin calls out, "Lizzie, you're here, aren't you?" I do the only thing I can count on to work—take a step towards the cat and it claws at Griffin. "Stop pissing off the cat!"

"Sorry."

His words are aimed at the phone. "You catch that?" He then calls out, "Look, Casper, after work we are all going to see that psychic—you know, the crazy woman that said something bad was going to happen to you. Maybe she can figure out this madness."

Yes!

Despite Griffin being far from anything resembling a gearhead, he actually named this trusty, old Nova. Giving this Fire Engine Red baby the name Peaches seemed absurd, until he told me that driving a beater was the pits. Though my logic said the car should be named Cherry, he replied, "Nope. Some things just ain't worth popping." Then my brain shut off because I couldn't handle all the weird connotations.

Peaches bounces into the driveway and scrapes her tail on the way up. Seriously, new shocks are not that expensive. It's a wonder Paul is fine with me hanging out with this guy.

Griffin doesn't even shut off Peaches before Jensen has his head inside her window. "Is she still with you? Paul said there's been no change."

I touch Griffin's arm and hum. He looks to me in the passenger seat and rubs his jaw. "Yeah, she's here. Either that or I've completely lost my mind."

Jensen opens Griffin's door. A smile the width of the Grand Canyon crosses Griffin's face as he eyes every inch of Jensen and bats those lashes that practically reach his brow. "You know, if you ever want to cross over to the dark side …"

Jensen takes two steps back and jerks his hand off of the handle. I laugh at how his being gentlemanly is suddenly a sin.

Jensen's arm gets a girly slap. "So sensitive! Brother, we have got to lighten up because we are both on the verge of madness. We can't let stuff get to us too much, or they are going to put us in a couple of those pink padded cells, and pink is just not your color." He heads off with his hips swinging in a full woman's swagger. "What are you waiting for, Sugar? Enjoying the view?" Jensen snaps into a sprint to open my door. This time Griffin's once-over calls Jensen out as being a prime cut of meat that is buttery, rare, and ready to devour. "Always the gentleman."

The Amazing Zolta answers the door. "Did I forget an appointment?" She snaps her wrist over to check her watch. "Sorry! Closed for dinner! Come back in a few hours. Oh!" Her finger goes up. "A moment." She scuttles over to a Day Planner and smacks it with said finger. "I'm booked for the rest of the evening. Now, tomorrow morning—"

We follow her inside, and Jensen steps up to her. "This is urgent. Someone's life could depend on it."

I take a shot and touch her arm. "Hi, Zolta. Remember me?"

Zolta's torso retracts. "You did not come alone. *She* is with you."

"Oh, we are *so* not alone," Griffin sasses. "You remember Lizetta?"

"The one with the terrifying reading? How could I

forget?" Her gaze goes to my direction. "Oh, dear. What happened?"

"The Tower," Griffin says.

"But she didn't die," Zolta mutters. "Death feels cold."

"No, she's in a coma."

"Can either of you see her?"

The boys shake their heads. Zolta circles me. "How did you learn that she walks with you?"

"Animals react to her." Jensen says. "Don't they only freak out over ghosts?"

"No, no, no. Animals react to energy." She swipes her arm back and forth. Each time she does, it passes through me, and the buzz of her energy interacts with my own. However, she feels no reaction until I hum. Then her fingers flutter to the sky. "Fascinating! Are you sure she's in a coma? Usually, the living stay within their bodies."

Jensen perks up with words that are firm. "I just checked with the hospital. Lizetta is alive."

With a bounce of her knees, Zolta's hands clasp together. "A traveler! Oh, this is wonderful! How did I ever miss that she was a traveler?"

Zolta keeps swiping her hand through me. The constant buzzing is uncomfortable. "Would you please stop that?"

Her hand drops. "Oops! I seem to be annoying the girl. Sorry, dear."

Griffin's eyes go wide in reaction to Zolta talking to me. His words crawl out. "Miss Zolta, what is a traveller?"

"An astral traveler! It takes a very long time to master—if you are going about in a normal existence." With her hands landing squarely on her hips, she juts her head in my direction and squints. "Something must have knocked her out of her body."

"But her body is going to die," Griffin says, sounding panicked. Jensen shoots him a death glare before swallowing back the acceptance that Griffin is probably right.

"What happens if she doesn't make it?" Jensen asks.

"Not to be blunt, but if she dies … Well, then she dies."

She flicks her hand at the boys. "That's not our concern. The real question is, why is she outside of her body?"

Jensen's words go to the floor while hiding his guilt-ridden face. "She was looking for a wedding dress. It's my fault. I was too impulsive. If I had planned a proper proposal, she wouldn't have been—"

"Hold on!" With the stance of a proud warrior, Zolta's hands drop onto Jensen's shoulders. "Fate would have intervened regardless of where she was." Her eyes grow firm. The voice that comes out is strong and deep. It also makes Jensen's muscles freeze. "You must continue your life exactly as you have. Do not waver!" With an unheard snap, Zolta turns to Griffin and resumes being her animated self. "Now, what else happened?"

"Lizzie was walking near a crane that wasn't properly blocked off. The latch failed and a piano came crashing down. Several pieces stabbed her chest, but two large ones upsided her to the ground."

"Did she go directly into the coma? What state is her body in now?"

"Boy Friend and I don't understand half of what they are saying. All we know is she's been experiencing seizures and hemorrhages. The doctors say there's not much more they can do before—"

"Holy cow." Zolta releases a long exhale. "Lizetta, if you have a silver cord, like I think you do, there is a big reason why you didn't stay locked in your body." She taps a finger to her lips and starts pacing. "The interesting thing about astral travel is that you are boundless. If she's really traveling—" Zolta halts. "Oh! It is so obvious! Of course! You need to—"

Harold appears in the corner, stopping Zolta dead in her tracks. She sees him? How can she see him and not see me? "Seriously, God, a manual! Would it have been so hard to give me a manual?"

"Why are you stopping?" Griffin asks. "What does Lizzie need to do?"

"She just …"

Harold wags a finger. *"Tisk, tisk, tisk."*

Zolta's look of deep thought snaps away. She tosses her hands up, making her turn cartoon-like again. "We're done!" Her strides whip toward the door to shove the boys out.

"No way!" Jensen protests. "You're on to something. Is it money you want? Believe me, whatever it is, I'll make sure you get it. We need to know what's—"

"I'm sorry," chimes out of her. "All I can tell you is that time is of the essence." Harold's torso enlarges. Wings slice through his jacket and flare up. Zolta seems to shrink. She looks to us and mutters so quietly that I have to strain to hear her. "There is a huge difference between traveling and dying. Dying sends you to the next plane. Traveling is nearly boundless, but you are confined to this plane." Like a lightning strike, her hands shoot out, her eyes flare, her teeth grit, and her voice grows harsh. "Leave! I command you to leave!"

Jensen again starts to protest. Zolta reaches into a drawer and pulls out a gun. Griffin's hands fly up in surrender. "Look," Jensen says, "all we want is—" Zolta fires a warning shot into a vase, spraying water and glass across the room. The guys flee, but I'm not budging.

Zolta turn sheepish in the presence of Harold. "Ernesta," he warns. "If they, or this girl, show up again, you ignore them. Got it?"

Rapidly, she nods. "Yes. I understand. Absolutely."

Harold puts me in my place as well. "Take what you've been given and be on your way. If she tells you anything else, ignore her!"

The sound of Peaches starting up seeps through the windows. It is soon drowned out by Bertha's roar. If I don't hurry, I will miss my ride, but Harold has pushed my buttons. "You make it sound like she's given me the keys to the kingdom." Bertha's tires squeal as Jensen's lead foot send her ripping out of the driveway.

Harold grabs me by the ear. I'm being schooled, yet the

lesson is lost on me. If anything, this has shown that there must be something I can do, or Harold wouldn't have gotten so bent. There is some kind of reason why all of this is happening. Harold must be hoping I don't figure it out; else his booty may be on the line.

Or maybe he wants me to get it, which is why he didn't force me out of here sooner!

Yeah! He could have stopped me from making it here. He could have kept me from communicating with anyone in the first place. My guardian angel is an ally.

"Just remember, in due time, everything changes. You really should listen to a mother's wisdom." Harold throws me out the door with the force of flying piano parts. Fear slams my eyes shut. When I open them, I'm at the hospital, clutching my flipping stomach and standing next to my mom, who sits in a chair, knitting. Well, doesn't that bruise my banana? Either I can travel on my own or Harold has angelic super strength.

All this time I've been walking or riding in cars. Does this mean my body simply needs to be told where to go? Okay, I want to be in the hallway.

Nothing happens.

Maybe I need force. I try to mentally throw myself forward.

Again nothing happens.

I tune out the world, and then focus on where I want to be. A slight movement is detected, and I've progressed to the doorway. I have super powers! This is awesome!

The familiar sound of Jensen's boots meandering down the hall grabs my attention. How did he get here so quickly? Granted, it is a short drive, but he got here way too fast for someone driving safely, or even dangerously.

I speak as he steps into me. "Jensen, you have got to be more careful!"

He halts and mutters, "Thank God that you're still here. Don't leave my side if you can help it, okay?" He proceeds into the room, kisses Mom on the head, and takes a seat.

What were Harold's parting words? *"Just remember, in due time, everything changes. You really should listen to a mother's wisdom."* What the heck does all that mean, and what does it have to do with astral travel? I take a seat next to Mom and listen intently while trying to remember everything she has ever told me.

26

Sunday, July 30

Lizetta

The moonlight that seeps through the window and shines upon Jensen and Etta as they sleep fills me with the warmth of being kissed by angels.

There must be answers in what I've been told. Shaking me by the shoulders was the first thing Harold said that stuck with me. What exactly did Zolta say when he flared his wings? Fudge bunnies! She was just about to tell me what I needed to do.

It may be foolish, but I have hope for this situation. While I am not convinced that my body will ever pop up and walk away, somehow I have found faith that this is happening for all the right reasons. The hope I hold is on an eternal scale. I'm witnessing too much not to see that this experience must have purpose, and I have faith that someday I will take joy in learning what that purpose was.

Jensen's cell phone rings. The sudden noise makes him and Etta bolt to attention. I touch his arm. "I'm still here."

JENSEN

My racing heart reminds me of when I over-tuned Bertha's engine. Warmth hits my arm. Lizetta is telling me she is still here and not to worry. My muscles unclench.

Etta recognizes AC/DC's "Hell's Bells" as Laura's ringtone and tucks her head back down. She's so fed up with the situation that Laura is now only worth Etta's bark if she is a direct threat. After pressing the ignore button, the phone is tossed back onto the nightstand. Two in the morning is way too early to deal with her drama.

I snuggle into the pillow. The second I'm comfortable, Laura sends the bells chiming again. Etta glares as I reach for the phone. She doesn't bother with the courtesy of growling. "Yes, I know. I'm an idiot. I did promise to help her, you know?"

Crap. Does Lizetta know what's going on? Does she know how conflicted I've been? I'm damned with guilt no matter what I do next, so I tell her that I need to hold true to my word. "Honey, it's a long story, but I promised to help a friend."

I don't even get a greeting in before Laura slurs her words out. "You remember that time we all went to Los Angeles to meet with that guy?"

Yeah, that was the first time I woke up and didn't remember where I was, or how I got there. This is gonna be a doozy.

"Remember how we each had one of those bottles with the tinsey winsey gold flakes in it because we all thought you were going to be super, filthy rich within like ... a week? After that hangover, I thought I was never going to touch anything cinnamomom ... cinnamomony again. But you know what? These bottles are soooo tasty!"

"Laura, we had an agreement. You're supposed to call *before* drinking."

"Yeah ... Well ... Larry has a bunch of guys here. They booted your replacement's replacement of the eighth replacement and are auditioning a new loser to replace next week. We got to talking and ..."

I envision her head nodding as her words trail off. Etta raises her eyes, and I swear to God she's giving me a don't-you-dare-help-her look. She's way smarter than I'll ever be. "Where are you now?"

Laura's voice perks up. "Home." Then I hear a swig and a swallow. "You should so totally come rescue me."

Yeah, there's no way I'm falling for it. If she's talking about my replacement, Larry pressured her into the call. Not only that, but "We had an agreement, and you broke it."

God, what is Lizetta making of all this? If she's aware of what's been going on, she's probably just sticking around until she finds a way to make franks and beans with my dude parts.

Laura's voice becomes strained. "You said you would do everything you could to help me."

There's no way I'm getting back to sleep. I pop up on the defense because the guilt is already seeping in. "Yes, I did say that, but you chose to drink before calling, which means you don't actually want help."

A smack blares through the phone. My educated guess says it's a bottle she's thrown in desperation, hitting a wall and denting it. "It's your fault that I screwed up! They started talking about how you bailed on them, just like you abandoned me. Then they brought up all the good times we've had, and all I could think was how much I miss you. But it also pissed me off. So I kept drinking. This is *your* fault, Jensen! My being drunk is *all your fault!* You bailed out on me when I thought you loved me!"

No, those guys aren't hurt. Laura has probably yapped enough for Larry to play her from a new angle. I stand by my promises, and normally our pact would send me over to be her knight in shining armor. But even if she did catch on to Larry's intention, if I happened to get jealous enough to reclaim my dignity, she could see how her victory was still inevitable. She really blew it, though. I would have kept up my end of the deal, if she had stayed clean and then claimed everyone else was out of hand. She's usually not so dumb as to screw up like this. "Larry got to you, didn't he?"

She stammers, but it's not from alcohol. Her voice is filled with desperation. "This—This is *your fault!* You need to help me!"

She forgets that I know her, too. "Laura, every day we make choices. Your bad one of allowing Larry to motivate your actions is *your* fault. If you can't accept that, I can't help you anymore." With a new sense of resolve, I lie back down.

There's no way I'm going to her now.

She plays the crying card. That's such a cruel way for me to think, especially since the emotion behind the tears makes me think they are real, but the days of caving to Laura's pain are gone. She's had her chance. My sobriety depends on me looking at it that way.

"Good night, Laura. You need to stand up to people on your own." I toss the phone onto the nightstand. I should turn it off, but I'm more concerned about knowing if something happens to Lizetta, than I am about ignoring another call from Laura. I swear Etta is smiling in approval. I pet her head before curling back into the bed. "God, Lizetta, you must really hate me right now. How do I even begin to explain?"

Laura

"You fucking bastard!" I scream at the phone. "How dare you hang up! What about me?"

He can't run away like this! I fucking need him to get Larry to leave me alone or at least give me enough stuff to help me suffer through this shitty existence. I keep talking, hoping that by some cosmic miracle Jensen will hear. "Please, it's not the same as before. It used to be fun to think I was upsetting you by being with other guys. Then you left, and I banged everyone in exchange for anything they would give me, just to ease my sorrow. Now they don't even ask. I'm passed around like … Hell, at least whores get paid."

JENSEN

My phone starts going crazy with calls from Laura again. It's a three round cycle of call and ignore. Eventually it beeps with a text message. *"Please help. It's ugly here."*

"Lizetta, you have to know what's going on. Do you understand that I need to help a friend who isn't strong enough to help herself? You're an understanding person.

How do I work through this without getting dragged down?"

The silence is so thick it's deafening. I turn to Etta, looking for a sign. All I see is a dog that's trying to sleep. If I know Lizetta, she is purposely holding her silence and letting me make this decision on my own. She's probably coaxing Etta to stay out of it as well. "Please, Lizetta. Can't you tell me anything?"

Nothing.

Nothing but silence and guilt.

Is Laura really so dumb as to fall for Larry's tricks again? Maybe she really is in trouble.

No. She's fine.

The image I had months ago, when I told Mom I left Laura behind like an abandoned soldier, haunts me. She's been through enough bad stuff. I'll do this to right my wrong. Then the score is even.

Etta doesn't bark as my feet hit the floor. Still, I know what she's thinking, and it changes nothing.

Bertha roars as I turnover her engine. My hand hits the gearshift, and a new kind of guilt smacks me.

I made promises to Lizetta too. One was to stay clean. While I have been challenged in that department, so far I have made it.

I touch my hand to the passenger seat, right where her heart would be if she were here. "You are with me, letting me make my own mistakes, aren't you?" My hand buzzes, and her radiating disappointment kicks me in the gut. No matter what, I will let someone down tonight.

Self-preservation is more important than being a savior. I shut off Bertha and head straight back to bed. "I'm sorry, honey. Thank you for respecting that I needed to make that decision myself. I promise that I will never let Laura into my life again. I have never broken a promise to you, and I will not start now. Laura is on her own."

Lizetta

Jensen spends nearly half an hour flopping back and forth in bed. Finally he smiles and tells himself, "I'm free. There is no way I can turn back now. That part of my life is truly over but …"

Jensen rolls over, as if looking at me. "Forgive me, Lizetta. There is one last thing I need to do before I can fulfill that promise. I'll do it this one time, and you can hear every word of it."

He faces upward. "Dear God, please bless Laura with whatever it is she needs to recover, but I am sorry, it can't come from me. Then, please let me know that she has made it. As much as I will hold true to my promise, I can't see myself ever escaping the guilt of hurting her." He releases a gratifying sigh. "Now I can let go of the urge to help. She's stronger now."

He rolls into his usual position and drifts off to sleep. I believe he will follow through on his promise, but guilt tore at him before. How will it be now that he knows how much worse Laura has become? *Lord, it's been such a fiery trail for Jensen and his faith. Please let him come to peace with this situation.*

A throat clears, and I find Harold standing in the corner. "Jensen will be fine," he assures. "Come with me." Since there are no signs of his normal, goofball self, I'm apprehensive over his invitation. Was that it? Jensen is done with Laura and now I move on? "Oh no! You are not taking me away!"

With gentle movements that imply peace, Harold closes his eyes. The smile of someone who understands the ways of the universe crosses his face. "It's not time for that yet. You can return to Jensen whenever you like. Let me show you what prayers do." His hand extends in a gesture of trust. Then he twists his hand so his pinky is extended. "You'll be back soon. I pinky swear."

Seriously? I can't say that I trust him, but in light of my revelations that he is an ally, and feeling deep in my soul that things are happening for the greater good, I sucker into it. Our pinkies lock, and my heart soars as the power of love flows through the touch. I swallow back the emotions of accepting that I am in the presence of a true angel. The peace he fills me with must be a taste of Heaven. Why hasn't he always shown me this? "Close your eyes," he says. "Now, focus on that text Laura sent."

The *whoosh* of wings breezes against my back, sending my hair twisting in its wind. My stomach turns woozy, and the dank smell of pot, alcohol, and rotting food hits my nose. Harold is nowhere in sight when I find myself standing in the threshold between a kitchen and a living room. Empty take-out boxes overflow in the garbage can, and crusty utensils are piled in the sink. The recycling can overflows with what must be as many hard liquor bottles as a bar would discard in a week. Some guy is passed out on the sofa.

White powder, a credit card, and a rolled up twenty-dollar bill are on the coffee table. I've never seen that stuff in person, but I don't need to be a genius to know it's not baking soda. Why would Harold send me here?

In the corner, Laura sits while staring at her phone. Black mascara and eyeliner run down her cheeks and are smeared across her face. Her finger is still on the send button from her last text to Jensen, *"Please help. It's ugly here."*

She sent it at least half an hour ago. How she still waits in hope of a reply tugs at my soul. This poor woman. Her heartbreak isn't from being jilted by an ex-boyfriend; it's from being spat on by life.

The crash of symbols comes from another room. It's accompanied by thumps and laughter. Was someone pushed into a drum kit?

The crack of a fist against a jaw follows, and applause erupts. "Cheers!" is yelled, and bottles clank.

With tender care, Laura touches a finger to her lips and

kisses it, then places the kiss on the screen. "Goodbye," she whispers, before walking away and leaving the phone behind. Now, the lines of coke on the coffee table hold her attention. Softly she concedes, "If he won't help me, no one will." She drops to her knees, grabs a rolled up bill and snorts up a line before switching to the other nostril and taking up a second one. Her hollow eyes that reflect a heart of broken dreams stare at the remaining five. I don't know anything about coke, or how much it takes for someone to OD, but she has got to stop.

Laura rubs her nose, and a trail of blood coats her hand. Her laugh is a nervous one.

From the room filled with drunken laughter, a man says, "Yeah, she's totally worthless. You'd think she could at least get a horn dog to drop his pants. Guess she only wants Daddy now."

Her eyes stay on the lines of death as she states, "The beginning is the end. Or is the end just the beginning?" Then she whispers, "Somebody please stop me." Her head drops and she brings the bill back to her nose.

My chest turns heavy for this horrible person who introduced me to a life-long battle with my body image and who nearly crossed Jensen over to the point of no return. How many others has she hurt? When I was a kid, every day I fantasized that she would move far away. Guilt plagued me for weeks after I dreamt of attending her funeral. Now she is about to leave this world in an act of weakness. Part of me wants to scream at her—to ask how she likes the desperation of knowing she needs to end the pain brought on by someone else's actions. She has to make the voices that tell her that she is worthless shut up. I had to do it. Jensen did, too. For both of us it was her voice—a voice that we will struggle to silence all of our lives because we let it get to us. But we are, and will stay, stronger than it.

She can be stronger too. Everyone has the strength to conquer the useless words of the hateful. I touch her shoulders, hoping she can feel love, and that it will be enough to guide her. "Please, Laura. Please stop. Don't let others control you. You are stronger than this."

Her motions slow, yet she continues on.

"Laura, think of Jensen. He will always blame himself, and this is not his fault."

With the bill in her nose, she plugs the other nostril.

"Laura! Stop!" I try to shake her, but all I can do is vibrate my hands and scream in her ear, "Laura, stop! Stop!" She rattles her head and shoulders and then freezes cold. Her eyes stay on the coke while growing bold. Like a flash, she heads for her bedroom and locks herself inside. She falls onto the bed and buries her head under a pillow. "It's okay," she says. "I'm safe. I just won't open the door." I reach out again and offer her words of hope, but instead of her finding the comfort I hope to give, she screams, "Go away! Everyone, go away and leave me alone!"

Harold appears at the head of her bed. He brushes her hair aside and gives Laura's forehead a kiss. Her body takes on a hint of Heaven's glow, and her breathing calms. "She needs more than this, but this experience will stay with her. See what Jensen's prayer has done? Each of us has the power to bring love to the world. Love transcends all, even death. So by extension, Laura will always carry this love."

I used to think prayers were merely messages to God. This experience has brought me a new level of enlightenment. Prayers do not reflect a one-to-one relationship. Jensen prayed for Laura, and that persuaded Harold to take me to her. For that, she will live to see another day. Messages to God are love letters to the universe that transcend all boundaries.

Please, God, give Laura strength and show her mercy. Help her find what she needs to escape her world and find your glory on earth.

I used to envy her. I wanted to have her looks, her popularity, and her self-esteem. Now I'd rather be dead than even step into her shoes.

JENSEN

This time, we have all accepted that the doctors are right.

I felt Lizetta next to me when I woke and wished her good morning. It almost seemed normal. Then my arm flinched. Often when I sense Lizetta near, I have moments where my body experiences a hum of energy. This morning, the energy was a fizz that faded into nothing. Before I could reach for the phone, Jimmy's call came. Even now, here beside Lizetta's body, I can barely sense her.

How do you bargain with God? What can you possibly promise that He doesn't already have? That you'll do better? That you will bring more joy into the world? That you'll spread His word? If you believe in God, these are all things that you should be doing anyway, so to make that kind of promise now means you either haven't been doing your job or were never a believer in the first place.

It's too late for prayers. Soon it will even be too late for goodbyes.

Where the hell is Mom? We don't have much longer.

Griffin paces with Judy as she shakes the stress off of her hands. Jimmy sits in a corner with his guitar case leaning against his leg. He taps it frantically. We need to rewind the clock a bit—back to before two big blood pressure drops happened—when Jimmy was here playing for Lizetta, before the machines went crazy—back to when I still felt miracles were possible.

Paul enters with his cell phone still in his hand. His eyes are evasive, meaning the news is bad. It's all the more reason not to let go of Lizetta's hand.

Everyone makes a beeline over. Paul's hand on my shoulder offers no comfort. "The attorney said, in California marriages are considered too personal in nature to fall under the rights of someone with Power Of Attorney. I'm sorry, son. For what it is worth, I know I speak for everyone when I say that in our eyes, you upheld your promise to marry her long ago."

The air leaves my lungs, and the last of my hope flees with it. One of the biggest promises of my life is now broken and shattered.

Mom finally arrives. Paul looks to her and shakes his head, conveying the bad news. She sets her purse on a chair and heads over with that look of sympathy that only a mom can have.

I won't stand for this. There is no room left on any of our plates of tragedy for a serving of broken promises that are topped with remorse. Having a piece of paper that says you are married may have its perks, but some get those through marrying in vain, like for money, convenience, or to keep people in the country. The lucky ones are those who get that piece of paper when they marry for the right reason. But the ones who get what marriage is really about are those who exchange vows even though it's not legal. Paperwork is for the now; vows are eternal.

Lizetta

He was going to marry me anyway. Mom was going to sign the documents on my behalf. It was a dream too good to be true. I'm heartbroken. Why does a law-making stranger have more of a say in my right to marry Jensen than the person I trust with the power to end my life and handle my final affairs does?

"Everyone, gather around," Jensen announces. "We have something very important that we want you all to witness, legal or not."

A river of hope coats my eyes. Oh, please, Jensen. Yes. I want this so badly.

Jensen pulls Etta's collar, along with a picture of her, from his pocket. He asks Griffin to hold them. He then kisses my engagement ring, and I add my apparitional hand to the grip, so that our three left hands are joined. My chest tightens as the man I will love for all of eternity shows the world one of the many reasons why I feel the way I do.

My tears build before his first word forms. "There isn't a doubt in my mind that Lizetta can hear me. I made a promise, and I am going to keep it." His tone of resolve breaks as the true sentiment of the moment takes over. "Lizetta, I take you to be my wife. To love, honor, and cherish for all of my days here on earth and for all that follow. No matter where you are, I will somehow be by your side, like I know you will be by mine. Please stay here, and continue to grace our lives with your beauty, but if you can't—" His voice shudders. The words are locked in by emotion, but love forces them out. "I promise to uphold your memory, to lift you up, to show you honor and dignity in any way that I can." The tears land on my sheets, covering me in a blanket of dreams half fulfilled. "I love you, now and always."

I'm in awe—floored by the level of love in this room that shows in bittersweet smiles and tight holds on loved ones. Mom is secure with Paul. Etta is here in spirit under Griffin's care. What really gets me though is how Jimmy not only has an arm around Arlene, but also how she and Griffin hold hands, having never been introduced. My family is giving me one last gift in showing they will stick together after I am gone. There is really only one thing left of importance. *Lord, if I truly have to leave now, then please, at least let Jensen somehow know how I feel.*

My heart races and breaks at the same time, as I make my vow to Jensen while having to accept he won't hear it. "Jensen, the day I met you, I became real. My heart may have been open, but my soul was closed. Then you showed me the light. Through that I grew and became whole. I take you to be my husband. To love, honor, and cherish for all of time. Someday, somehow, I will remain by your side, just as I know you will be by mine."

No kiss could seal this more than our hearts have. I step

into the space where Jensen stands, and finish the process that began long ago—joining our souls as one. "I will love and be with you, always."

JENSEN

My wife of three hours lies in her hospital bed while her life slips away. Does she know that in the eyes of everyone here we are married? I have to believe that she does, else my sanity may flee.

Just outside the room, Griffin and Mom are involved in deep conversation. Her concern is so indiscreet that I can't even head to the bathroom without her following in fear that I'm going to slip off and ingest something off limits. I don't blame her. Hell, I'm freaked out about what lies ahead for me, too.

What will become of my relationships with these people? They accepted me into their family long ago, and while they have accepted my marriage to Lizetta, will my welcome last or will I become a painful reminder of what they have lost?

I plop down next to Jimmy in our usual seats by Lizetta and take her hand. He looks at me, and although his shoulders don't move, I know he is shrugging in resignation to waiting for the worst. I slump back in the chair to stare at the ceiling. "Band names. We need to settle on one."

"You still want to do it? No matter what?" It's nice to hear hope in someone's voice again.

"No matter what, brother." I put out my hand, and he low fives it before mirroring my slouch.

"Okay. Let's do this. No screwing around this time."

Lizetta

Pain tears at my lower back, and my shoulders are tight even though I have none of those things. The cord that tethers me here has faded and thinned, going from silver fettuccine to glimmering angel hair.

Jensen and Jimmy brainstorm band names, and some of my fears about moving on release. My heart aches when I touch their shoulders, knowing they will make so many great things happen, and that I will miss every one of them. "Don't let my leaving end your kinship." Their conversation halts. How they swallow in unison is a sign of hope for their brotherhood that I accept with gratitude.

"You get that?" Jimmy asks.

Jensen nods and they stare at each other a moment before resuming talk of the future.

Mom sits with Paul. I can't look into the red orbs of my mother's pain. The decisions she has faced have been devastating. With a touch to her shoulder I tell her I love her. She curls into Paul's arms, sobbing. "Mothers are not supposed to bury their children. This can't be happening. I'm supposed to get to spoil the dickens out of my grand babies. What kind of god lets life work out this way?"

I want to give her words of wisdom—to comfort her in this awful time, to let her know it's not God's fault, and that in an odd way I brought this upon myself—but all I can do is say, "It's all right, Mom. God's going to take care of us all. I love you."

My touch to Paul's shoulder is accompanied by a simply stated, yet complex, message. "Thank you, Second Dad. I love you." Paul has always given me pearls of wisdom, and I have nothing to give back other than a whole lot of love to the man who saved a little girl from growing up a distraught, traumatized wreck after losing her father to a disease. Paul taught me how to trust. Without him, I never would have accepted Jensen. I may not have even accepted myself. A tidal wave of love flows out of my heart and through my touch to convey how grateful I am that Paul came into my life.

Outside the room, Griffin and Arlene are locked in conversation. "I tell you," Griffin whispers, "we are missing something critical."

"Something has been bothering me since Lizetta and I met," Arlene says. "She triggered the tip of a memory that I haven't been able to form. Is there anything you've left out?"

Griffin taps his lips. "Psychic ... Read the cards ... Pull an extra card for clarification ... No, that's all. Believe me, we were hanging on every word that woman said."

"Something isn't right here," Arlene muses.

"What was it Lizzie said that got you all tweaked out?"

"That's the thing. When I heard the seriousness in her voice, a memory flashed, but I couldn't grasp it. It had something to do with the patches in the painting."

"Are you talking about the patches of different colored grass?" Griffin asks.

"Yeah, do you remember something?"

"Not really." Suddenly he grips her arm. "Do you think the two different types of grass have something to do with the two influences? If Lizzie was the first, who is the second?"

Arlene's hand flies to her mouth, and my heart jumps in hope. "While I was painting, Dad went on about everything being one cohesive unit. Did the psychic say anything about two being one?"

Hope fades. None of that sounds familiar. I don't remember a single thing that Zolta or Harold said that could lead me to believe that.

Griffin shakes his head. "Nada. All I know is Lizzie was so freaked, that when we hauled ourselves out of there, it was like she had two left feet. When she tripped over the leg of the table and knocked a bunch of cards onto the floor, she just about lost it." Griffin smacks Arlene's arm. "Sitting straight up on the top, there was one card that you could not help but notice. If it had a voice, it would pierce your eardrums. It was some game show thing with freaky creatures around it."

Arlene reminds me of a teenager as she gasps, nearly breaking her whisper. "The Wheel of Fortune?"

"Yeah, that's it!"

She grips Griffin's arm, and I'm giddy with hope again. "Upside down or right side up?"

Confusion blankets Griffin's face. "Up so she could see it. How else would she know what card it was?"

"No!" Arlene smacks his arm. These two are peas in a pod. "Was the card's number at the top or at the bottom for her?"

Excitement tickles my veins when Harold appears in the corner and winks. "Listen to a mother's wisdom," he reminds me, and then disappears.

"I saw it dead on, so it was upside down for Lizzie."

"That's what I couldn't remember! They're not patches, they are spokes in the wheel of the Four Ages of Man, but in reverse of the way it normally turns. Griffin, you and I are messengers! Go distract Jensen."

Griffin casually approaches Jensen, asking how Etta is handling everything. Meanwhile, Arlene leans into my ear. "Lizetta, the dream is about phases. The answer lies in the past. Whatever you find there will change your soul forever."

Phases? Reverse spokes? What does … And suddenly it hits. The painting feels like it is moving left, or rather, counter clockwise. Time is the key. We want more of it because we think of it as something that is limited, but that only applies to our bodies. To our souls, time is boundless. Harold flicked me out of Zolta's house and into this room. A moment later Jensen walked in. He and Bertha peeled out of the parking lot in frustration, which means he would have been driving fast. But when he walked into the hospital, he was moving slowly. If he had been racing Bertha, he would have been charged with adrenaline. When Jensen gets angry, he takes time to calm himself. Since I was thrown into the future, I didn't see how that was possible.

Then there was early this morning, when Harold brought me to Laura. I thought it had been over half and hour since she sent that text; yet her finger was still on the phone.

A stagnant beep permeates the room. Nurses flood in.

"What's going on?" Jensen asks, his voice racing with fear.

His plea is ignored while a nurse mutters something about cardiac arrest. Someone rattles off vitals and a pit crew with a crash cart rolls in with the precision of this being an expected event. The doctor enters and looks to Mom. "You still want us to act?"

Mom hesitates. She can't back down now! I need more time. I turn to Griffin and rattle him, because he gets that some kind of puzzle is being put together and it creates a picture bigger than us all. "Don't let them stop, Griffin! Don't let them stop!"

"Yes!" Griffin yells. He turns to Mom. "Judy, please, go with my gut on this!"

"Yes," Mom tells the doctor.

Another person tells my family to leave as the doctor commands, "Let's go. Everybody, clear."

"This can't be happening," Jensen utters. "Engagements are supposed to be the beginning, not the end. Lizetta, I'm so sorry."

There must be a way to stay, or Harold wouldn't have been paying me the visits he has.

Jensen is right. What we had was supposed to be the beginning. That reminds me of Laura last night. What was it she said? The beginning is the end. It seems so fitting, but then—

I keep hearing about time.

The nurse tells Jensen he really shouldn't watch, but he refuses to go. "No. Marriage means promising to be with someone until the very end, and that's what I promised when I did the thing that robbed her of her life. I should have waited to propose. I should've—"

"Dammit, Jensen! Stop blaming yourself! And stop talking so much. I can't hear myself think!"

Laura commented about the end also being the beginning. Arlene talked of reverse time. Harold has sent me back and forth. Zolta said that I'm a traveler. Astral traveling is only bound to this plane, not to this time!

Arlene runs to Jensen. "Do not tell yourself that! You dared to live in a way that others only dream. Don't blame yourself for having the guts to live. You just keep grabbing life by the shoulders, and you keep shaking it. No matter what happens, keep shaking!"

The doctor places paddles on my chest and yells, "Clear!" Everybody steps back. The machine still wails that my heart has stopped. I try to close off my mind to the chaos and focus on where I was when the accident happened. I feel myself jerk forward. When I stop, I'm in the right space, but there's no crane in sight.

Crackers!

I focus more on that day—the weather, the position of the sun, the angle of the breeze, and the taste of hazelnut mocha that lingered in my mouth. A warp goes through me, and it reminds me of the wooziness I got when Harold threw me out of Zolta's shop. When I open my eyes, the crane is next to me. A block away, my healthy body rounds the corner.

I race up to myself and actually run through me. The old me is unfazed. I dash back through her. Still nothing happens. I spin and she keeps coming at me with the same grin while humming and clueless to everything else in the world. Meanwhile, the crane cranks upward.

"Listen to a mother's wisdom."

I try to grab her shoulders as she waltzes past. I can't grip, so I walk backward while keeping my hands in place and vibrating them, just like I did to Laura and much like Jensen's mother suggest he do. My old body stammers when I yell, "Lizetta! Stop!"

TEN DAYS AGO

Suddenly I feel odd. Like my body starts ... fizzing? Did I eat something bad? No, it's not an upset stomach but—

An electronic ring hits my ears. I slow down and try to place it. Weird.

With a shrug, I move on my way. Just a few blocks more

until—

There it is again. I need to slow down. Am I getting dizzy? Why do I feel so strange?

Creaking comes from above, drowning out the sounds of passing cars and clamoring people. It reminds me of someone lifting the lid on an old trunk in a horror movie.

"Stop!" someone yells. "Lady, you need to stop!"

A man runs in my direction. Is he yelling to me?

Boom!

Two shiny, black boards fly towards me. I cower. One hits me in the hip, the other in the arm that covers my face, and I fall back. My butt smacks onto the concrete, and a sharp pain shoots through my head as it hits the ground. Stars spark my vision before all goes black and a force yanks me upward and into the heavens.

Messages to God are love letters to the universe that transcend all boundaries.

27

Thursday, July 20

Sweat drips from my face as I race to the shade. The heat of the parched grass stings my feet. Pressure builds in my head as the distance narrows. Just a little more! I can make it!

Finally, I reach Nirvana. Grass cools my steps and rises between my toes. A breeze blows away the heat. I twirl and fall to the ground, spreading my arms like the wings of an angel who is claiming the land as my own. A sense of peace fills my heart, knowing it is here I will stay.

A haze of gray and blue coats my vision. Light trickles in. To my left, a machine beeps with every throb of my head.

In the distance there is scampering and chatter. A lady comes into view. "Hey, there you are," she says. Her smile breaks through the fog, bringing comfort. I hear beeping. I smell antiseptic. I'm back in my body, and in a bed. I'm in a hospital! Did I make it?

If I made it, why don't I recognize this nurse? Shouldn't this be like Dorothy coming out of Oz?

She alerts the Nurse's Station that I'm awake and requests they send in the doctor. Something is said about being in an Emergency Room. That's why I don't recognize her! When I didn't awake before, I was in Critical Care.

My hand gets a reassuring squeeze.

A squeeze! I felt a squeeze! And she smiled when I returned it!

"You gave us quite a scare. How are you feeling?"

"Like God is trying to drive a nail into my skull. What happened?"

She chuckles. "Sorry, I shouldn't laugh, but if you can

look at this with a sense of humor, you'll be much better off. You got brained with a piano."

This is the lamest bedside manner, ever. Oh no. This woman is reminding me of that crazy redhead. Maybe I was in Oz.

"Well, it didn't quite go like that. A piano fell from a crane. You barely dodged it enough to not get flattened, but you still got conked. You're lucky. Had you been a few steps closer, you may not have made it."

A doctor steps in and goes about checking me over. He asks me to move my arms and legs, and then state my name and birthday. Did I actually transcend time and make it back? Is now real? If I was just stressing out over a dream, I'm going to be cheesed!

The nurse returns and gives me a salacious look. "You up to visitors? A young man just arrived. He's very anxious to see you."

Jensen! I send her off with a grateful, "Yes, please!"

Steps approach my doorway and a head pops in—a head of flaming red hair. Yep, I was in Oz.

"Hello!" Harold clears his throat and slips his hands into his pockets, turning sheepish.

"Harold, what in fiery heck happened?"

He stares as if surprised; yet a ghost of a grin slips through his pretense. "Harold? I'm sorry, ma'am. The name is Albert. I'm the one who yelled for you to stop. You need to thank your guardian angel that you're all right."

"Harold, a little truth please? Starting with why you hushed Zolta."

He tosses his hands up. "No one ever allows me to have any fun! Zolta was about to send you down the wrong road. If I hadn't intervened, all would have gone amok."

He totally was covering his own tushy!

"No, I was not covering my own tushy. I was covering yours."

Ugh! This mind reading makes me crazy!

"Sorry."

"So what was all that about? Is it over? What about the painting? Was it some kind of test? Now that I am back, do I need to worry about Laura stealing Jensen?" Panic hits. "Wait. When is this? I didn't do some crazy time warp again, did I? Tell me I didn't land in an alternate universe where he's married her!"

Harold shakes and dips his head, then peers his eyes up to God. He must think I am an idiot. "Relax. The piano smacked you down just over an hour ago. And no, you are not now, nor have you ever been, in some alternate universe. Your travels are over, but you still have more burdens to bear. All I'm allowed to tell you is that you give Jensen reason to stay on the straight narrow. You also bring him the inspiration to keep writing, even if he needed an ego boost from your brother to show him he was worthy of respect. If he doesn't have that creative outlet to help him express his inner emotions, he'll stray."

"Does that make Jimmy one of the two women? Oh no way! Jimmy's gay?"

Harold walks to the wall and smacks his head into it. "No! Jimmy is not gay!"

"But what about the second woman? The one who is going to claim victory over Jensen."

Harold doesn't just toss his hands back; it's more like he tosses back his whole body. "Do you remember when you watched that old woman die? The prayer you made showed your desire to follow through on what you need to do. You have become privy to so much. What are you going to do with your knowledge?"

What? This guy still doesn't make any sense.

With a quick scope of the room, he tells me on the hush, "Remember, it may be your dream, but it is also Jensen's painting. Jensen has learned from the events you experienced, whether he realizes their existence or not."

Harold looks to the hallway as footsteps race towards us. When he turns back, his pale skin goes dark, his flaming hair turns gray, and his eyes fade into chocolate brown. My mouth drops in awe as I realize why he has always looked so odd to me—those cheekbones, that jawline.

"My grandson still needs help with his demons, else they will forever haunt him. Tell Jensen that Eddie and I are proud of him. Any time either of you is determined to do the right thing, we have your backs, whether it's Eddie coaxing you into hitting the Escape key, a clown dropping hints, or us helping him push Bertha." Jensen runs through Harold as he fades into a memory, yet his guidance echoes on. "Remember your prayer to live a life of boundless compassion, then you can both fly."

Jensen heads straight to my bed. "Oh, thank God!" he says. He kisses my forehead and then draws my hand to his heart. "They told me you would be okay, but I couldn't believe it until I saw you with my own eyes. From the moment I heard of the accident, I've been a wreck." His eyes go to the IV stuck into my arm, and his voice turns faint. "I know I did the right thing in asking you to marry me, but I feel so responsible for what happened."

"First off, I only have a few bruised ribs, a cracked tail bone, and one noodle of a headache. As far as anything else goes, don't be silly. Why would you feel that way?" Don't tell me that even now he is on that trip about feeling responsible.

"Because, you were looking for stuff for the wedding. If I hadn't proposed so soon, you wouldn't have been in that spot. Do you think it was a sign that we should slow down?"

Is he absolutely nuts? I'm the one who got conked on the head. It's easy to forget that the experience I just had isn't the same as the one he did. "Are you crazy? Haven't you learned to take life by the horns and rattle it? Seriously, Jensen, what more needs to happen for you to get the message?"

His mouth forms a hole of silence. It's the perfect companion to his gaze of disbelief, as his eyelids become windshield wipers to clear away the dust from his view. "How did you know?"

"Huh?"

"I came home for lunch and dozed off on the sofa. I had the craziest dream. Mom was telling me that I needed to continue to grab life by the horns and shake it. I don't remember anything before that part. Just all of a sudden, there she was, yelling so loudly that it woke me. Not much later, Jimmy called and said you had been in an accident and we all needed to get over here."

"That's—That's really ... odd." Oh, this madness just got freakier. I want to tell him about my own experience, but I need to get my head together. "Hey, honey, can you get me some water?"

"Of course." He kisses my hand, and those doggone, puppy eyes make me thank God all the more that I am safely with him. "Anything else you need?"

Just a dose of reality. "Can I borrow your phone? I need to call Griffin about something I found for the wedding."

Jensen sizes me up through scrutinizing eyes. A smile slips across as he hands me his phone. "I should tell you that you need to rest, but for a woman who nearly got her head bashed in, you sure are thinking clearly. Glad to see it."

I fake dialing until Jensen is out the door, and then search for Laura's name. I'm not the least bit surprised when I see both her and Larry listed. Jensen rounds the corner into the room, and I throw the phone onto the bed.

"Couldn't reach him?" Jensen asks.

"It can wait. I'd rather talk to you." I also need to focus on a plan of action. If Laura really is a junkie who won't leave Jensen alone, what I experienced was no dream: it was a warning shot.

28

Saturday, July 22

Lizetta

I used to take advantage of any excuse to sit on the sofa and do nothing. Now that I'm stuck home for a week and don't have much of a choice, the thought of doing it for another minute bores me out of my skull. I'm so anxious to enjoy living again that I've even done my makeup and put on presentable clothing. The really bad part of it is, I've only been home a day. Being locked up for a few more may make me a little crazy.

Jensen and Paul come in from the bedroom. They've spent the morning moving my stuff over as was planned before a killer piano tried to play my funeral march. Paul sweetly gave me an earful about it. "I know you, Lizzie. Once that stuff is there, you'll be too busy unpacking to rest. You've got to listen to the doctor." All the while Jensen stood next to him with his arms crossed and head nodding. Meanwhile I batted my lashes. Eventually they both tossed up their hands and caved.

Jensen plops a kiss on my head. "Last round. Be right back." He then bends down to tell Etta, "Watch her!"

Paul points his finger at me like the rock star he is. "Stay on that sofa!"

I wait until the cars drive off before I get up. This way they won't hear Etta bark when she catches me in the act. I'm going to fix Jensen dinner. Since my accident, my knight hasn't left my side, which means he has been sitting around and eating takeout food while grumbling about all of the chemicals in it. He can't fool me though. He's been pounding down fries like he fears he will never have a chance to eat them again.

With the exception of the four beers that have taken up permanent residence, the fridge that normally looks like Jensen's personal farmer's market is surprisingly barren. Those beers bring me relief every time this door is opened. They also serve as a constant reminder of how fortune has smiled on me. If Jensen ever throws them out, I'll feel like I've lost a friend.

Shuffling to the front door is difficult, but when I sling my purse over my shoulder, fire shoots through my back. Etta doesn't say a word. Instead she just stares at me. It's her way of politely saying that I'm being foolish.

"Okay, sweetie. You and the sofa win this round." Her tail wags as she follows behind. Her stride breaks. Her tail stiffens and she suddenly makes for the door with a bark of dislike. A peer through the peephole shows why—even though my past experience as an undead spy had me knowing before I looked.

Seeing Laura brings up so many conflicting emotions. For years she caused me pain. If what happened wasn't a dream, she has it in her to be far more awful than I ever gave her credit for. It also means that she's in a terrible state. I've always hated her. Now I have reason to despise her, but that doesn't mean she doesn't deserve freedom from the horrible things around her.

With a quick adjustment of my blouse and a rake of my fingers through my hair, I face my nemesis. Though I knew what to expect, my gut turns when I see the once vibrant girl who now looks like a skeleton that has been dragged through muck. "I heard what hap—" Her painted-on grin crashes when she sees a woman. Then her eyebrows rise in the center. After she clears her vision with a few blinks, she steps back. "Lizetta?"

I pretend that seeing her is a happy surprise. "Laura? Hey! What brings you here?"

"What are *you* doing here?"

It's horrible of me, but this is going to bring me immense

joy. "You know my fiancé? I can't believe Jensen has never mentioned you." Was that too cruel? I don't want to be her doormat, but—

"Fiancé?"

My hand pops up to show the ring. As she looks at my hand, I look at hers. It grips the neck of a bottle through a paper bag. Hello, plastic bottle of tequila.

"What!" Her body droops at my news. "*You* are the girl he's engaged to? *You?*"

I can understand her surprise, but did she have to use that belittling emphasis? It's hard to remember that she's not a tramp—she's an abuse victim with an addiction and a world of other problems that make her desperate.

"You can't be serious! You're the girl who has him all up in knots and bettering himself?"

Her words bring back the pain from the years of verbal abuse I endured. Why is it so shocking that Jensen loves me? It may sound cold, but even a junkie that lives a life of horror has no right to belittle me, especially when she has no idea what this heart is capable of. How much other beauty does she miss each day because she lets herself be blind?

I smile to myself. It wasn't long ago that I was blind, and I am so grateful for the inner vision I have found.

"Unbelievable!" Laura turns to storm off. She is so emaciated that she almost disappears before taking a step. My thoughts don't come from jealousy or even the snarky desire to shove a sandwich down her throat; my heart aches for her. Her walk is awkward, almost limp-like. Her heels hit the ground like a newborn puppy that has a hard time discovering how his paws function. Unlike a puppy, her swagger is completely void of the pep that implies she's happy to be alive. I remember that feeling. I experienced it almost every day as I walked home from school, emotionally destroyed because I had spent the day being her victim.

No one should feel like she does—so used that you want to die. No wonder why Jensen is torn. It's impossible not to want to give her the help she needs, but if he tries to play savior, he may crumble.

Laura

Shit! I've still got nothing. All I can tell Larry is that Jensen left me for an obnoxious heifer that is too stupid to be mean to me! She should have fought me a million times over by now. Lord knows I've kicked her enough. What does it take to get her to fight back? Now that little wuss is engaged to my man. And happy! She just got out of the hospital and she looks fucking happy!

When was the last time I was happy?

I'll find an angle. I have to.

29

Saturday, July 29

Lizetta

Pulling my car into the driveway of Good Samaritan breathed new life into me. I didn't even bother to set my purse down. Instead, I came straight to the kennels in the back to visit my friends. Another level of relief hits when I see who is back here. "Hi, Sherlock." He doesn't remember me, because to him we have never met, but I sure remember him. "Hi, Smiddy. Hi, Frankenweenie." I then wave to the poodle that nipped at me on this very day in a different lifetime. I can't help but giggle when it pretends to ignore me.

Being surrounded by my furry friends is what makes me whole, but strolling through this place feels wrong. The single pieces of art hanging on the wall in each exam room are the only sources of emotional brightness. Would it be so wrong to dress it up a bit more? The sparsely padded chairs remind me of the ones my family slept in while watching over me. It is no wonder why it was hard for them to sleep.

On my desk, a beautiful bouquet of roses awaits. Ah, Jensen!

That can't be. We left for work at the same time.

Griffin's effeminate voice graces me from behind, causing me to jump. "Don't go getting your panties all wet over those."

"Jeepers, Griffin! Are you trying to put me back in the hospital?"

"Oh, no way! You have no idea what hell I went through while you were gone. Remind me to quit before you leave for that honeymoon of yours. I am *not* taking the load here by myself ever again." He leans onto the corner of his desk and crosses his arms, eyeing me as I stare at the roses. "I may have exquisite taste and have gone to a real florist instead of Safeway, but they are not all that fascinating. What's on your mind?"

"I was in the hospital way too long, and it gave me plenty of time to think."

"You were just there for a night. You make it sound like weeks."

Oh, yeah. It's hard to keep reality straight. "Hey, how much time have you spent in a hospital bed?"

He waves me on. "Continue."

"One of the things that crossed my mind was, why are hospitals always so drab? They dress up maternity wards because someone is coming into the world, but when you get anywhere else in there, it is like death all over the place. And there's never a comfortable spot to sit while you are freaking out over the health of the person you love. Why do we treat people that way? I swear, it is like hospitals try to kill you off as quickly as possible so they can shuttle the next person in."

Griffin's chin recedes. "Ooh, what got into you while you were out? I hear near-death experiences do weird things to people, but you just took an intense nap."

Oh, if only he knew. "I used to have big dreams. It wasn't being a veterinarian that was important, it was doing something with meaning. Everyone needs a helping hand from time to time. What about the flea-infested cat who was tossed in a dumpster and now will swipe the hand of anyone who tries to help it? What about dogs who were raised to fight? Are they really hopeless? I want to change all that." I rethink my words to fit my resolve. "No, I *will* change that. I will help abused animals who would else be discarded."

I expect bestie to flameout and get all weird on me about losing my mind, but his straightening back shows I've got his attention. "I know you want to. I also know why you haven't. Do you?"

Yeah, I do now. "I let someone convince me I was less of a person, and it started a downhill spiral of allowing myself to find excuse after excuse to not work for what I wanted. When I learned that I couldn't be a vet, I wallowed. What I should've done was revamp my goals. But it's not too late. Jensen will be in school for a few more years while working. I can do it, too."

"How is this business going to survive? You expect someone to hand you money for saving an animal they picked up off of the street?" He says it sarcastically, but he may be right.

"Some people have pets with issues. They can pay us. We'll find a way to rehabilitate the rest. It just means studying up on non-profit businesses and charitable donations." Doubt washes over his eyes. I cut him off before he can naysay. "Hey, the idea may need work, but I'm telling you, the answer is in there somewhere. I'm doing this! You with me?"

Griffin's expression softens. He takes my hand, and I realize my appreciation for the touch of another will never be the same. "Hey, bestie, don't go getting so riled up. We've always had our hearts in the right places when it has come to taking care of these animals. If you're going to take a plunge, I'm there with you." He looks to the Lord for strength over what he is about to tell me. "I'll even go back to school, but you are doing the business part. You leave the behavioral part to me. I've seen you with poodles. Have mercy! There is one, itsy bitsy problem though. Where are we going to get enough seed money to persuade a bank to help us? Neither one of us has the last name, Rockefeller."

True, but I'm long past letting doubt intimidate me. That Lizetta was squashed by a keyboard. "You leave the money woes to me. Screw your brain in tight because we are going back to school!"

My little, yellow notepad with the generous wedding budget my parents gave us holds my attention. We could have an awesome party for a fraction of this amount. My parents also wouldn't have a qualm about me investing a chunk of this into my and Jensen's futures.

If we are really going to cut back, how much of the guest list do we need to trim? I don't need to invite everybody I know down to the mailman, just my immediate family and Griffin. "Hey," I roll over in bed to face Jensen, and a twinge of pain shoots across my back. I hate that I still have to take it easy. "How big of a wedding do you want?"

Jensen shrugs. "I don't have anybody to invite."

"No one?"

"Well, my mom, and then of course there are couple of people in my family that I should ask, but really, Mom is the only one I need there."

It is sad that a man as amazing as Jensen doesn't have a guest list that could fill a stadium. It is also a relief not to hear Laura mentioned. Then again, unless she's called him, he still has no idea that I know her. "So, we don't need to have an elaborate wedding?"

"Nope, I'm going along with whatever you want. If I had my way, we'd go to the park and let nature be our backdrop."

"Really? The park?"

"Actually, there is a spot where I planted a tree in memory of Granddad. If you and I, Mom, Paul, your mom, Jimmy, and Griffin drove over there, and then had dinner where we had our first date, I'd be content."

That settles it. No renting a big venue. No expensive caterer. No unwanted guests from our past. "Perfect! It's settled."

Jensen crosses his arms and sizes me up, just like Paul would do. It's awesome. "Wait a minute. What happened to the big dreams you had of the perfect day and a dress fit for royalty?"

"Oh, I am still getting my dress! I nearly died while trying to get it, so I am not going to miss out." Sweet Lord of all that will not change! A deadly neckline that plunges into beaded, French lace and is finished off with an epic train is mine!

"Yeah, but something weird is going on here."

I take his hands. Jensen is about to see the real me for the first time, because it's the first time I've seen it as well. "Every moment that I have with you is a dream come true. You have school to pay for, and I have visions for a future that I let myself think was unobtainable. It's not impossible, it's just not easy. This money can help us, and in doing that we will help others. You and I are a part of something greater than us. It is time we lived up to our full potentials and flew into a better life."

Jensen wraps his arms around me with caution, minding my bruised ribs. "I am so proud of you. Sometimes I get so wrapped up in the stress of life that I forget why I am going to school. It's not just to better me; it's to better the world. We can do better. Everyone can, they just need to find their way."

My notes get tossed aside. As I drift off to sleep, Harold's voice enters my head, "Close, but you're not there yet.

30

Sunday, July 30

Lizetta

Harold asked what I would do with the privileged knowledge I have acquired. I'm starting to understand just how much I absorbed, not only about others, but also about myself.

I thought my transformation started when Jensen brought Etta into Good Samaritan. When it actually happened was when I hit that Escape key, and I told the universe that it didn't have the right to dictate my future. Then Harold showed me that just because you stand up to the universe doesn't mean you shouldn't listen when it tries to guide you. The universe helps those who help themselves.

I hate that I never considered the girl who wronged me was hurting far worse. I also despise that her words, brought on by her own lack of self-respect, brought me down solely because I let them. Not only did I let her ruin my body image, I let her damage my spirit. I can blame others, and I can seek help, but in the end, it is up to each of us to choose what direction we spin the Wheel of Fortune.

Jensen has proven that spirits can be repaired. His was ripped to shreds with the loss of his brother, but he's taken the reins and changed his life. But sometimes we can't see what we need to do, or don't have the strength to act on it. Maybe it means we are weak, or maybe there are factors that others don't see. Someone has to help Laura, because so many have abused her that she needs to be shown she is worthy of life.

All this is a pep talk, because what I am doing is crazy, stupid, and somewhat self-abusive, but in the depths of my heart, I know it is right. Without boundless compassion, we are nothing, but what I am doing is also a gift to myself. It brings me closer to releasing a burden that I never should have carried.

With the arrangements made, I grab my yellow note pad and scratch a zero off the end of my dress budget. I could look at it bleakly, since I almost died for something I am not getting anyway. Instead, I accept that helping a fellow soul, even if it is one that on some levels I'll always despise, is far more important than spending a few hours in a ridiculously expensive dress. Maybe the accident was the only way to make me see that a dress can't bring anyone a life of happiness, but I can.

On a fresh sheet of paper from the pad that holds my dreams, I write a note to be mailed from another city. On this day in an alternate time, Jensen prayed for whatever Laura needed to recover. The love from the prayer is out there and calling me to act.

31

Tuesday, August 1

Laura

Larry bursts into my room—even though the door is shut and I could well be indecent. Of course a closed door won't stop him, but some days I like to think he is capable of showing a drop of respect. Stupid people like me never stop dreaming.

I don't get a good morning, or afternoon, or whatever time it is out of him. Not even a fuck off. An envelope is tossed onto the bed. He doesn't bother to put a little spin on it to make it interesting. Much like everything else around here, even his flick is boring.

It's got no return address. What a crappy job hand addressing junk mail would be.

The thing gets tossed. I plan for it to hit the floor. Instead it ricochets off of the wall and onto my pillow. Weird shit like that usually blows my mind, but when I am practically sober, it just freaks me out.

I hold the thing up to the beam of sunlight coming through the window. Whatever is inside looks handwritten, too. Sure. I'll bite, even though it is probably taken off of a printer and made to look real.

Dear Laura,
Please forgive the intrusion, but for a while now, I have watched you battle demons.

The fuck?

This is not an act of sympathy, it is a gift of caring. Arrangements

262

have been made for you at the Gann Rehabilitation Center. Thirteen weeks of meetings have been prepaid. All you need to do is call and ask for Dave. Please do not put him in an uncomfortable position by asking who arranged this. He won't tell you anyway. The moment you show up for the first meeting, I will be billed for the entire program, so please keep that in mind.

My throat starts closing in, and I blink to clear the water that is welling in my eyes. This is a joke, right? It's not funny, because I want it to be true so badly that I have to hold my breath to keep reading. I can't function and look at this at the same time.

Once you are done, there is a job waiting for you in Red Bluff. The salary isn't much, but it comes with a small apartment.

Whoever is playing this joke is winning, because they've got my eyes burning. I have to put the note down for a moment. Seeing it while knowing it is a joke is too cruel.

It would mean a huge move for you, but I am certain that, deep down inside, this is something you have been praying for.

I filth up my sheet while wiping away mascara-stained tears so I can see. This is so not funny!

Please don't let yourself down.

With Love,
The person whose life you changed

Praying for? Yes, every minute since Jensen bailed and basically called me out as being not worth his time. If this is real, he must be on some crazy guilt trip. That's the only way anyone would give a shit.

This isn't Jensen's handwriting. His looks like a chicken had a seizure. This is all circles and swirls. He must have made up with mommy and had her write it.

The envelope has a postmark from San Lorenzo. Who the crap lives there?

How dare someone fuck with me like this? This thing needs to be shredded and tossed.

The sound of the ripping paper hits my ears, and I freeze.

I can't tear this. I so want this to be true that I can't destroy it. I *need* this to be true. Someone showing they care is my only hope.

I Google the place into my phone. This has to be a hoax, and I won't be foolish enough to play into the hand of someone who is jerking me around.

The name comes up—repeatedly.

The place exists?

There are Yelp reviews from as far back as five years ago. Hell, they even have a Facebook page. The phone number on the note matches the one on the website. Still …

My jittery fingers can barely press the numbers on my phone. I down a swig of tequila as the other end rings, then another when the lady who answers says she's transferring me to Dave. If this is fake, I'm gonna lose my shit, but if it is real …

If it is real, I'm gonna drop my knees to the floor in shock that God doesn't just exists for others, He exists for me too.

I lose my ability to take in air as Dave confirms that all I need to do is show up. Somebody actually forked over a small fortune for thirteen weeks of appointments and group therapy. They couldn't afford accommodations, but there is a halfway house nearby. Dave assures I'll be safe there and will hold on to any belongings I'm afraid will get stolen. It sounds like he may actually care about me, too.

A weight floats off of my back and is replaced by an invisible blanket that wraps around me. I changed a life? When people say that, it's about something that was done for the better. I've been good to no one.

It must be Jensen, because giving him that heroin caused

him to shape up. Everyone else I know is passed out in the living room, and all I've done for them is—

Well, it's not worth saving me over.

The letter trembles in my hands as I grip it to my chest and cry so hard I am nearly screaming from the release of all of the fears I've had buried inside. Ten minutes ago I wanted to die, now I've found that there is one person out there who cares. Someone doesn't want me to rot in a gutter or to be used anymore. Dare I think that person must actually love me a little?

My knees hit the ground, and my head follows as I bow to whatever it is that is so powerful, it is making the impossible happen.

Thank you, God. Thank you for showing someone I am worth caring about. I absolutely promise I will not let either of you down.

32

Wednesday, August 2

Laura

Larry lies on the sofa, watching cartoons and nursing a fifth of Jack. I hang out in my room, standing near the threshold and shaking while awaiting opportunity. Finally, Larry heads off to pee, and I'm in action. The powder gets swirled into his bottle. Shaking it would form air bubbles. I can't risk him noticing anything different, and I certainly can't risk him waking.

The jingle of his buckle tells me he's just about done. I need to be out before he flushes. God knows he won't stop to wash his hands. I manage to make it back to my room before the bathroom door opens. I wait.

Finally, he passes out. I slip into the rafters in the garage and nab Larry's secret cash stash. There's a few grand in here. I must be hitting it mid-deal. There's gonna be hell to pay when someone doesn't get their score because Larry *misplaced* their funds.

With nothing but the clothes on my back and the cashed crammed into my boots, I walk under the cover of stars to the bus stop, then get lost in the shuffle of public transportation. I'm changing everything about me, including my name. Laura Muler just died.

Lizetta

The sky is a deep blue, partially obscured by clouds. Jensen and I lie curled under a tree as I rest in his arms. It gives me the same peace I used to find in my old dream. It is the peace of heaven on earth.

A girl with long, dark brown hair dashes toward us. Dark brown? That's perfect.

Laura runs past and into the distance without even nodding at our presence. Suddenly she stops, throws her arms to the sky, and smiles. "Come get me!" she screams to Heaven. A rainbow of light beams down and draws her up.

I wake just long enough to smile and nuzzle deeper into Jensen's arms. My dream came true, and so will Laura's. She is going to be just fine.

JENSEN

The sky is a deep blue, partially obscured by clouds. Lizetta and I lie curled under a tree as she rests in my arms. This is the way life is supposed to be for us—pleasant, peaceful, and free of troubles.

A figure with deep brown hair dashes past.

Laura? Her hair isn't brown, but wasn't that her?

My eyes follow as she runs into the distance. Suddenly she stops, throws her arms to the sky, and smiles. "Come get me!" she screams to Heaven. A rainbow of light beams down and draws her up.

I wake to find Lizetta tucked in my arms and a scent of change in the air. Something has happened. Oh God, did Laura die?

I kiss my angel on the forehead and head off to the kitchen for some water. The last I saw Laura, she looked like she was hitting bottom. I told her to go away before she even reached the top of the steps. I haven't heard a peep from her since. Did she finally get the hint or did—

How would I find out if she died? Would Larry call me? Would he even notice if she was dead on the sofa? Do I call? If she died, someone should show they care.

No. Stop right there.

If she is dead, there is nothing I can do. If she is alive, the last thing I need is to stir the pot.

But if she's dead, I killed her by rejecting her.

No, I am not her keeper. Laura put herself at risk. I am not responsible for her actions. I need to be free of her.

Back in bed, I tuck Lizetta into my arms. This is all I need to do right now, except …

It pains me to think that to fully be rid of Laura, I can't even pray for her. How can I find freedom yet not feel like I have forsaken her?

"Lord, please watch over the people of this earth. Keep them from harm, and guide them to make good decisions. When we fall, help us find salvation—no matter who we are or what we have done."

23

Sunday, May 27

JENSEN

I feel like a dork—a nervous, thrilled, dapper dork, but a dork nonetheless. Who wears a tuxedo to a park? Is it me, or is it unseasonably hot? I'm already melting, and I haven't even left my apartment.

I catch one last look in the bedroom mirror. Damn, that Bond guy's got nothing on me. Yeah, a tux in the park may be lame, but I look smoking.

Even if I looked like a damn fool, I wouldn't complain. This is the one indulgence Lizetta requested. She cast aside an extravagant reception space, live music, and elaborate flowers for an afternoon wedding in the park. However, she was adamant when it came to the attire. "I'll sacrifice a lot so I can get my business going, but it'll cheese my bacon if we look like hippies. Mom and I are going to crank out the greatest dress ever made, so there's no way in lollipops you guys are going to look like slouches!"

I just love her vibrant jargon!

With a spin, I check out my tails. Yeah, this totally works on me. A swipe and a toss land Bertha's keys in my hand and I start to head out.

Wait a minute. I'm not the one driving. Paul is picking me up. My keys get tossed onto the coffee table and my butt onto the sofa. "I'm forgetting something else. What is it I'm supposed to bring?" I loosen my collar that I swear is trying to suffocate me. "Man, heat stroke must be setting in."

Etta clears her throat. It's a face-palm moment. Idiot! I have got to relax. "Don't worry, Etta. I would never forget you." She cocks her head. I don't blame her. I would not believe me either. I've been a master at tripping over my feet all morning.

Etta changes her posture so that she is standing with her feet firmly centered; yet her ears stay down. Something is wrong, but she's not sure what. Her eyes go to the door, and then back to me. Her bark is a question that asks to explain whatever is coming up the stairs. It's probably my best man. My nearly forgetting Etta is exactly the reason why I'm not driving.

I am shocked to find a beautiful girl that locks my heart in my throat—a girl with silky, deep brown hair, sparkling eyes accented by a smidgen of makeup, and a trim, yet healthy, figure. Before me stands Laura Muler—not the infamous thorn in my side, but the beautiful person she is capable of being. My lids flicker in disbelief. I can't stop "Wow" from escaping my lips. The weight of the world flies off in discovering that she is alive and apparently well.

"I see you still can't resist looking at the beauty that is me. Are you really sure you want to get married today?"

What? How did she know? My eyes move past the beautiful body and onto the bag she grips. It's overflowing with white tissue and ribbon. "Here," she says, handing it to me. "Technically, it's a wedding present, but you and I both know it's really a thank you gift. And relax, I know your mind just went into the gutter, but this is something off of your registry."

"Thank you? For what?" Inviting her in would be the proper thing to do, but the last thing I need is Laura proving she is still her old self. With my luck, Lizetta will walk in. Instead of getting married today, I'll get buried.

Laura leans against the threshold, crossing her legs at the ankles and tilting her head in a cute way that reeks of trouble. The thing is, with her soft blue dress, that is of respectable length and covers all but the smallest amount of cleavage, she looks rather … dare I say, adorable?

"Come on, person whose life I changed. We both know what that means, and it's not as sweet as one would normally take it. I will always be grateful for what you did. It worked! It really worked. Of course, I'm sure you know that, as you probably get reports from my boss."

Laura has given me some puzzle pieces before but, "What are you talking about? And how do you know I am getting married today?"

She touches my cheek. "That's really cute. Don't ever change, okay? Tom left the wedding announcement on his desk. That's when I became certain that it was you who put me through rehab. After all the pain I caused Lizetta, how you got her to let Tom give me a job is a miracle of its own. Anyway, it's a long drive back to Red Bluff, and I don't want to be seen around here. No one knows where to find me, and it needs to stay that way."

She gives me a sweet kiss on the cheek, but in true Laura fashion it lingers. "I'll always love you," gets breathlessly whispered into my ear. She then leaves so quickly that I can't even catch the expression on her face.

I'm left standing like a schmuck. What the hell was that about? Paul has a brother named Tom in Red Bluff. If she's working for Tom, then someone in Lizetta's family is behind this.

What pain did she cause Lizetta? How do they know each other? *What* do they know about each other, and why has my future wife kept that little tidbit from me? I sure as hell am going to find out.

This whole thing reeks of Paul. Why wouldn't he tell me what he was doing? Didn't he know that I know her? Maybe he found out about the situation and wanted to ensure his daughter's rival disappeared. Did he think that Laura was a threat, or was he just continuing to star in his role as savior?

Paul pulls into the driveway and gets out of his car as Laura gets into hers. Eye contact is made, yet they go about their business like strangers. When Paul makes it up the steps, he watches Laura drive off. He's not wearing his tuxedo jacket or bow tie yet. Again, Paul is the sensible one. I'm so hot in this thing I'm about to melt all over the pavement. "Who is that little cutie?" he asks.

Now I'm in the shitty position of having to respect privacy. However, that's my ex-girlfriend and this is my future father-in-law. No one can fault me for asking. "How do you know her?"

Paul stares as if she is still there and he wouldn't mind watching a little more. "Her? Never seen her before in my life. A better question is, how does the man who is about to marry my daughter know her?"

"Really, Paul? I respect the whole confidentiality thing, but can you at least dodge a bit so I get a little of the picture?"

His putting his hand to my forehead reminds me of when I was a kid and Mom worried about my temperature. "Wedding jitters have gotten to you something bad. Take off that jacket and cool down. Don't you have a lick of sense in you?"

"She's my ex, and she works for your brother."

"Tom?"

"That's the only one I know of. Someone anonymously put her through rehab." Paul purses his lips together. "You ready to confess?"

I get a signature, double pat on the back. "You need to talk to Lizzie about that one."

"No kidding! How the hell does Lizetta—"

Now Paul's face is square in mine with his hands weighing down my shoulders. "You are about to marry a selfless woman. All those weight issues my daughter has, that girl who just left here is the source of them. For decades, she damn near ruined my daughter's self-esteem; yet when Lizzie found out all the reasons why, she sacrificed to help her and worked with Tom and me for a solution. Laura is why Lizzie never bought that fancy dress she was hell bent to get on the day of her accident. The rest you will need to talk to your wife about, if you choose to ask her. As far as I'm concerned, this conversation didn't happen. Got that? Lizzie not only helped that girl get her wings, she tossed her into the air and got her flying."

Lizetta had her heart set on that dress. Ever since her accident, she's wanted to do more for herself so she can help others. Something about that knock on the head changed my bride.

"Just remember," Paul says, "rehab is a personal and often private matter. It's not just that way for the people who experience it, it's that way for the sponsors, too."

Lizetta

First I was so freaked out about Griffin running late that I yelled at him over the phone, "Unless you have foregone the tux and are coming in a ball gown, there is no excuse for you to be late. Even then, you can whip on mascara and eyeliner faster than I can paint a nail." Now Jensen wants to see me before the wedding. My brain is frizzing because I am so freaked out. Like, this can't possibly be good.

Griffin and I pile into the Bel Air so Jimmy can take us to the park. My grip on Griffin's hand is so tight that it is making my own hand cramp. "Damn, Bra Buster, you have *got* to loosen up. You two wrote the simplest vows in the universe, and all you have to do is look luscious, spit out a couple words, get a kiss from your Sweetie Honey, and you are done, so just," his hands sweeps across the air like a glider to accentuate his point, "relax."

God, I hope he's right. Please let him be right. Why would Jensen want to meet early? He can't possibly want to call this off. Not after all we've been through.

We pull up, and Jensen's already in the parking lot, leaning against Paul's car and bouncing his foot on the pavement. I catch sight of his hand that holds a big, white bag that is overflowing with ribbon. Oh, thank God! It must be my wedding gift. But if I had to have it before the wedding, why not give it to me this morning, or God forbid, ease my mind by saying *why* he wanted to see me? "Men! I swear to God I will never understand them!"

"What did we do?" Jimmy and Griffin chime in unison as I pop out of the car and race toward Jensen.

JENSEN

Lizetta gets out of the car, and my heart does the stereotypical wedding thing by skidding to a stop. She looks stunning beyond words. My God, today I get to marry this woman and spend all of my tomorrows holding her. I'm so glad that I get to see her now, because if I waited until she made her entrance while looking this lovely, I would lose all ability to say my vows.

She throws what must be miles of train over her arm, grabs her dress at the sides and dashes toward me. Her veil flows in the breeze, yet her cascading golden hair barely moves. The sunlight radiates off of her every satin and lace-covered curve. She's so beautiful that breath is fleeting.

Like a lovesick fool, I dash to close the space between us.

Lizetta

Jensen's lips touch mine, and I'm both relieved and mortified. It's bad enough that he's seeing me in my dress before the wedding, but to kiss me before the vows start? Isn't there a curse that comes upon you if you do that? "What is so urgent that you have me stressed out before we get married?" Jensen closes his eyes, like he's trying to shut off something that could be trouble. Why did he kiss me if he's concerned about trouble?

"I don't know how to say this. I'm not upset, because what you did was amazing, but—Here." He holds out a bag. "It's a wedding present from Laura. Why didn't you tell me that you know her?"

Laura? Oh shizzles! "We—We went to school together."

"No, why didn't you tell me that you put my ex-girlfriend through rehab?"

My muscles squish into my bones. "Are you angry?"

Jensen sets down the bag and takes me by the hands. "Of course I'm not angry. What you did was beautiful. Who told you what was going on with her and who she was to me?"

My mouth goes dry, and I can't moisten it. He sees my discomfort.

"I'm sorry," he says. "I should have waited until later, but the moment I knew something was up, I had to find out more. Why would you do such a good deed for someone I'm so close to and keep it from me?"

Seriously? He's okay with this? "I didn't try to hide it intentionally." Nor would I. Harold taught me that prayers are love and once you send out love it lasts forever. Jensen prayed to learn when Laura was safe. My soul wasn't the only thing that transcended time.

"I know you didn't. That's the thing. If you wanted to hide it, you never would've gotten her a job working for Tom. Lizetta, what's going on?"

JENSEN

A crazy feeling flows through Lizetta's grip and into my soul. It's not the feeling of love and devotion I usually get when I look into those eyes. Instead, it is one that I have seen before, but not from her. In fact, I haven't seen a look like that since I was a teenager, so I know in all seriousness when she begins her story that the words she says are true.

"Your granddad says hi."

Lizetta's story is a wild one. Some would call it crazy, but to me it's fascinating. And I believe it. I believe absolutely every word.

Granddad always said that the powers of the universe are beyond comprehension. Now that I understand that I can't see all the universe can do, I have to wonder how many times those words rang true for me.

The music starts, and Paul and I stand in front of the tree I planted in memory of Granddad. Griffin stands just across the way. It seems odd that Paul isn't the one walking Lizetta down the aisle. I was torn about who should be Best Man until Jimmy said something that made perfect sense. "Paul is always the best man. No matter what he does or where he stands. You can't always count on your father, but you can always count on Paul." That made it a no-brainer. Then Jimmy followed it with, "Besides, it's going to irritate the hell out of my sister when we're strolling down that isle and I'm poking her in the ribs."

Lizetta's flowing gown reminds me of the cloak of an angel. A subtle smattering of rhinestones on her veil causes it to glimmer in the sun. I chuckle at her bouquet of white roses wrapped in teal ribbon. Of course, a die-hard Sharks fan would choose something teal over something blue. Then I realize the obvious. A peek at Jimmy, Paul, and Griffin all show that they have teal bow ties. Leave it to my girl!

Paul, Griffin, Judy, Mom and I gather around the minister as Jimmy walks Lizetta down a path of pink rose petals. When the time comes, we say the simplest of vows. "You and me, walking down the path of forever, together, no matter what tomorrow may bring. I will be with you, always." What greater thing can you say other than you will standby someone for eternity?

With the meeting of our lips, we take the song that we write together today, and put a finish on it so that all of our tomorrows can be filled with new medleys.

It is the responsibility of each person who can help himself to in turn help others. I may not have much power, but I can use what I have wisely.

Epilogue

DIVINE INTERVENTION
Friday, June 8

JENSEN

Lizetta's story haunts me. Even if you toss away the accident that was—and the accident that wasn't but was to her—how Lizetta put years of hurt aside so someone could live is admirable.

Addiction is personal. Getting help is personal. Paul is right in that there is a code of privacy among addicts and sponsors, but addicts know who their sponsors are. Laura needs to know, too.

I don't doubt that without Lizetta, Laura would have died. Not knowing that the person she may have hurt the most is the one who believed in her is not acceptable.

I also can't shake Laura's voice in my head that says words aimed at Lizetta. "I am so, so sorry. I was horrible. So horrible." It's a memory of something that didn't happen; yet somehow I know she means it.

Lizetta has grown, but her eyes still reflect the damage Laura has done, and Laura needs to face her past.

I place a call and hope my wife won't castrate me for it. The conversation starts with, "Laura, you need to know the truth so that you can do the right thing. Please, don't let me down."

FATE
Sunday, June 10

Laura

Lizetta Lansing is my flippin' savior. How the hell did that happen? First she takes my man, then she scrubs the grime away from my life and hands me a job and an apartment? Jensen has to be messing with me.

I pull up in front of the old farmhouse that Lizetta grew up in. It was foolish to make a flash appearance at Jensen's on his wedding day. There is no way I'd go back there again, just in case someone is keeping watch. Then again, has anyone even noticed I'm gone? Larry probably thinks I've been passed out in my room all this time.

Oh yeah. I ripped him off—big time. He's noticed. And he's pissed!

Music travels out of a barn that's got some ancient, blue car sitting in front of it. Is this a scene out of a Hallmark card? I mean, a barn? For God's sake, what century is this?

This is a terrible attitude for someone who has come to say thank you. For months I've said it to God, hoping that someday I could say it to the person responsible. Thing is, I've never had anyone to thank before, and it's freaking me out.

I step out of the car and ah … The signature wailing of Jensen's guitar hits me. Though it's a jagged pill to swallow, the smile of sweet memories crosses my face. That sound is the only part of my old life that I have missed.

Lizetta, her mom, a woman with tan skin and dark hair, and some buffed-out guy sit on the porch, rocking in chairs and sipping lemonade. I feel like I've landed on Mars. That lifestyle used to seem lame. Now it's one more thing to be jealous over. The whole situation is making me trembly.

I'm halfway up the driveway when Jensen sees me. I wave but keep heading for Lizetta. I need this over with, and

I don't think Jensen ever wants to see me again. After this, he'll get his wish.

And there is part of the reason why this is so difficult. This is the last time I will see the two people who want me to be happy—two people that also want nothing to do with me. I'm on the defensive because I know my presence really isn't wanted.

Lizetta's mom has a glass of lemonade ready for me. The familiar-looking, buffed guy kisses Lizetta on the head before he and the women take off inside. I came prepared with an opening line of asking Lizetta not to be angry and explaining how being a bitch wasn't my fault. However, the girl who should look like she wants to beat the shit out of me, smiles and says, "You look great."

I look great? What the hell do I say to that? I could handle it if she upsided me a few on the head, but to say I look great?

I am so not ready for this. How did I let Jensen set this up? How did Lizetta? She must have come unglued when he sprang this on her.

Laura blinks. She wasn't expecting a compliment.

"You don't have to sugar coat it. I know you want to let me have it." Laura's tone is one of regret. Although I believe her, I can't help but read through the words. I've learned a lot since I last knew this woman. Bullies always challenge their victims, whether they see it or not. They want you to run or to get emotional and freak out. Either of those fuels them. Never do they expect a simple rejection, so I smile and offer her a seat.

Laura withdraws, making her appear smaller. She gives a quick look to the barn where the guys keep playing, yet they've scarcely taken their eyes off of me. Laura's mouth slacks, and she raises a single eyebrow before she sits and stares at her hands. "I made fun of everything that you loved. I insulted animals because you cared about them. I stole a happy prom night from you. I called you ugly. Time and again, I robbed you of your self-esteem."

She is so repentant that her chin quivers. I'd like to feel triumphant, but I don't. Watching her now is almost as painful as when she attacked me.

"I watched it," she says. "I relished in it as you hid from me. Your clothes got baggier to hide your body. You would come into class late and with your head down. The harder I attacked, the more you cowered. I kicked you when you were down. I brought you to tears more times than I could count. When you ate something fattening, I mocked you. When you ate something low-calorie, I joked about it. You couldn't put a bite in your mouth, all because someone didn't want me to put one in mine."

She stops to gather herself. I am so torn. Part of me wants to yell at Jensen for setting this up. Part of me wants to tell Laura I forgive her because it is in my nature. But why should I forgive someone who caused me so much damage? Wasn't sending her to rehab enough? I may be a loving person, but this woman brought me years of pain. Then again, I really need to hear her side and know why I had to suffer.

"I need to stop hiding behind excuses," she continues. "Everyone knew your dad was no prince but ... My father is a perverse bastard." She then grabs a heavy dose of air to push down the emotion that is going to hit with her next sentence, no matter what she does. The desperation of wishing she had handled her hellish situation differently pours out. "And I let him turn me into one. I stooped to his level and did exactly what he did, but you wouldn't play along, even though you were in the same boat. Worst of all, you gave me chances, and—" Her breath shudders as she puts her head in her hands and the tears slither down. "If I had just reached out to you, if I had shown you something on those monkey bars to encourage you ..."

Laura bites the inside of her mouth, and I finish her

sentence in the way I know she intends but can't face. "Then you would have made a real friend who understood your pain."

A nerve has been hit, and the sobs start coming because we both know I meant it. "Instead, I stabbed you with my words, so I wouldn't hurt alone. If I could have just looked past my own pain …"

"You could have welcomed someone into your life that wanted you to be happy."

Laura diverts her eyes to the barn and then to the porch door before closing off her vision. She can't face me, but her words show she is trying to face who she was. "And maybe even a family that would have helped me escape before the unthinkable happened." Her sobs turn heavy as years of repressed pain crash down on her. She has probably faced them in therapy, but has she ever faced a victim? It has to be a different ball game.

I touch a hand to her knee and look to Jensen. The playing has stopped. If the sobbing were mine, there is not a doubt that those guys would be here next to me.

"Maybe I wouldn't have needed you to save me now, because you already would have. Instead, I hurt us both." She wipes away the tears and looks dead at me. "And I am so, so sorry for what I did. Truthfully though, I am more sorry that I wasn't strong enough to be like you. How can you even look at me now and not laugh, let alone have helped me?"

My eyes squeeze out hurt in memory of all of the other tears I shed. It's become impossible to hide the ghosts of my own suffering.

Her type of bullying was a mental battle. The use of verbal or physical force can make a bully think she has won, but I emotionally triumphed over her words. I may not be completely recovered from Laura's damage, but I won this battle long ago, because I found pride in who I am.

Still, a part of me wants to scream at her for all the nights I cried myself to sleep—for all of the nights I kept Griffin up because I was shattered—for the times I blew off parties because Laura might be there. Instead, I stand tall. "I helped you because through all of the horrible things you said, you helped me find compassion. I didn't want to be like you. I wanted to make the world better. That made me who I am today. When I realized how you hurt me and what I needed to overcome, I gave myself a second chance. I thought you deserved the same."

Her lips part in awe over my words. "I don't get it. We all knew you were going through hell with your dad, yet no one knew about me. You were strong, and I was jealous that you could face the same problems I hid from. I treated you like shit yet—" She shakes her head, and turns away while squeezing her eyes shut. She then seems to brave it up and finish facing her past. "I just hope that you will please find it in your heart to forgive me for what an insensitive ass I was, though you have already done more than anyone ever should. There was no reason for you, of all people, not to abandon me."

My stomach hardens. There it is. I have found my reason for forgiveness. The word abandon reminds me of Rufus. When I set him free in that park, he released all of his negativity and found new life. Even when he faced the unknown while dying in my arms, the chains of the sorrow he had felt just a few hours before were gone, and his new life had already begun. I want to be free like Rufus.

For the first time, I don't try to hide my emotions around Laura. The tears flow freely and with the happiness that we can both finally put this part of our lives away. "I forgive you, Laura. I know that you are truly sorry for the pain you caused and wish you could change the past for everyone's sake. For that, you have not only earned my respect, but also my love."

I hug her, and her fingers dig deeply into my back. The gesture gets returned. When we pull away, we both smile at each other, and our healing deepens.

With another hug and wishes for wonderful lives, we go

our separate ways. Now we are all free to fly.

More by Diane Rinella

THE ROCK AND ROLL FANTASY COLLECTION
Scary Modsters…and Creepy Freaks
It's A Marshmallow World
Queen Midas in Reverse
Voices Carry
Moonlight Serenade

THE FORBIDDEN FLOWER SERIES
Love's Forbidden Flower
Time's Forbidden Flower

About the Author

Enjoying San Francisco as a backdrop, the ghosts in USA Today Bestselling Author Diane Rinella's one hundred fifty-year-old Victorian home augment the chorus in her head. With insomnia as their catalyst, these voices have become multifarious characters that haunt her well into the sun's crowning hours, refusing to let go until they have manipulated her into succumbing to their whims. Her experiences as an actress, business owner, artisan cake designer, software project manager, Internet radio disc jockey, vintage rock n' roll journalist/fan girl, and lover of dark and quirky personalities influence her idiosyncratic writing.

You can visit her website at www.dianerinellaauthor.com and on Facebook at https://www.facebook.com/DianeRinellaAuthor/